AKEDAH: THE BINDING

Also by Bishop & Fuller

Blind Walls

Galahad's Fool

Realists

Co-creation: Fifty Years in the Making

Mythic Plays: from Inanna to Frankenstein

Rash Acts: 35 Snapshots for the Stage

Frankenstein (DVD)

The Tempest (DVD)

King Lear (DVD)

Descent of the Goddess Inanna (DVD)

Available at www.DamnedFool.com

Conrad Bishop & Elizabeth Fuller

AKEDAH: THE BINDING

— a novel —

WordWorkers Press
Sebastopol CA

Akedah: the Binding
© 2020 Conrad Bishop & Elizabeth Fuller

Printed in the United States of America.

For information:
eye@independenteye.org

For purchases:
www.damnedfool.com

ISBN: 978-0-9997287-4-1
Library of Congress Control Number: 2019919111
Book design by F. Ackerman

The Parable of the Old Man and the Young

So Abram rose, and clave the wood, and went,
And took the fire with him, and a knife.
And as they sojourned both of them together,
Isaac the first-born spake and said, My Father,
Behold the preparations, fire and iron,
But where the lamb for this burnt-offering?
Then Abram bound the youth with belts and straps,
and builded parapets and trenches there,
And stretchèd forth the knife to slay his son.
When lo! an angel called him out of heaven,
Saying, Lay not thy hand upon the lad,
Neither do anything to him. Behold,
A ram, caught in a thicket by its horns;
Offer the Ram of Pride instead of him.

But the old man would not so, but slew his son,
And half the seed of Europe, one by one.

—Wilfred Owen—

—1—

Stubblefield

Who do men say that I am? And whom say ye that I am?
Just kidding. I had a friend said that if there's a God he must be insane. Jimmy Kremper it was—we called him Jimmy Crapper and thought we were being clever—who had this thing about God. Not a belief in God but he couldn't help bringing God into a conversation even just talking football. *You think you're God* he said to me once. I told him God doesn't think he's God: he just sits there being God. Jimmy wasn't your heavy thinker but he was probably right that the almighty Geezer was nuts.

Though if he was talking about the Jehovah who wrote the Bible with all the typos and begats and genocides then clearly the dude liked to fuck with people's heads. That's me in spades. It always looks like I've got a master plan though in fact I don't have a clue. I'm just floating up here in my 23rd floor office suite behind a cedar desk the size of a battleship looking out magic casements on fairy seas forlorn: the vistas of Las Vegas.

To make it clear from the outset: I am not God. But I might be the closest thing to it that you'll find in America's imperial toilet bowl. My name is Stubblefield. Friends call me Stubbs but I'm not aware that I have any friends.

The ways Our Heavenly Father gets your bowels in a knot are legion. The phone rings and there's nobody on the line but He's there. The email from the orphaned Nigerian princess begs to give you a million bucks and sure you know it's a scam but He's there. You meet a bum on the street and hand him a buck and he says gimme more and you do it because that Sonofabitch is there. You don't have the balls to say no and I say *the balls* irrespective of gender. The question goes very deep but I'll stop with the God stuff lest God gets too bigheaded.

But I'm not the leading man of this little foxtrot: I'm only the guy who asks if you'd like to dance. The hero is Vernon McGurren, pronounced *Ma-gurn*, he always had to explain. I might give the impression that I look down on this dude from a height approaching infinity but in fact I have a warm feeling for those of his ilk—the myriad chumps who think themselves middle-class but in fact form the excess population. I myself emerged from the vast mass of losers up to the luxury suite of the 23rd floor so I had great empathy with Vern. Though I never let empathy interfere with my whims.

You might wonder how I know all this stuff about Vernon McGurren. Some of it he told me and the rest I just heard in his heartbeat. I do listen closely to heartbeats. Heartbeats can be monetized.

Sometimes a notion pops into the head that seems lunatic but by then it's been done and no turning back. That's likely how God created the human race (God again, sorry). And which would be the only excuse for Vernon McGurren to be born of woman. Of course they all told him he was special and if he studied hard and brushed his teeth he'd get rich and grow a big penis and drive a Lexus. By second grade he knew that was total horseshit though only Daddy said *horseshit* as long as Daddy was on the premises which wasn't long and that was fine with Vernon who didn't like the belt strap. He did like that Daddy promised to let him shoot the big shotgun but then Daddy took it with him when he disappeared. That's what you do if you're Daddy.

When the man his mom called the bastard split they moved to Omaha—Mom and little Vernon—to live with his mom's mom

Gramma Pitzer who raised geraniums and smelled like bacon grease. Once Vern's mom told him he'd been born in Hibbing Minnesota where the famous Bob Dylan grew up so Vernon could be famous too. He might be an airplane pilot because he was always looking up in the sky. In fact he was looking for flying saucers because his cousin Benny told him they kidnapped people and did stuff to you that was even worse than what the queers did though he didn't know who were the queers or what they did but it must be pretty awful.

From seventh grade on Vernon called himself Vern as might be expected. And once he got out of Central High having nearly flunked senior English he did in fact join the Air Force which was better than night shift at the Quik-Stop where his friend Henry landed. His main imperative of course was getting laid. He'd had a couple of girls as clumsy as himself in the ways of the flesh but he couldn't see how he might be attractive except maybe his curly hair though he practiced looking handsome in the mirror. In seventh grade Charlene had told him he looked like a weasel and that stuck for years. But he felt that a snazzy uniform might bring them panting. If Bob Dylan came from Hibbing Minnesota then maybe if he flew F-16s he might get famous like Bob Dylan although he'd never heard of Bob Dylan flying anything. Vern thought in Moebius squiggles.

He got stationed in Minot North Dakota. Forget the F-16s: he tested colorblind. So he worked in Supplies piloting a forklift to stack toothpaste and dental floss and toilet paper—critical ordnance to win whatever war. They said he'd learn valuable skills but he'd never seen a whole lot of doctors or lawyers or bankers driving forklifts.

Still at Minot you had the Minutemen missiles and the B-52s— more megatonnage than anywhere on the face of the Earth. Blacks at the air base too and you had to work with them. At Central High there'd been lots of blacks. Vern had nothing against the blacks except they talked too loud and acted so special. Either they were glaring at you or laughing like little kids. Not to blame them for that—in this life you needed some laughs.

But after a while on the base they weren't so bad. They were a lot like him. They even kidded around with him and that felt good. *We lead the world in the absorbency of our toilet paper!* Sergeant Wilson joked. Sergeant Wilson was black and had a big booming voice but he was pretty funny and he treated Vern okay. Sign over the gate to the base: *Only the Best Come North.* Nice to think that.

And his fourth week in Minot he met Gayla. She was pushing a dolly of cans to refill the Coke machine. Suddenly he felt thirsty. He came up to her as she swung open the front of the machine and she took his buck and handed him a Coke. He said something dumb about lady deliverymen and she turned to look at him. Deep brown eyes. Black hair slicked in a bun. Light coffee skin—maybe part black but that was okay. She must be older. She must be hot. Vern was hopeless at chatting up girls but he managed a few goofy blurts.

—Nothing like a Coke on a cold day.

—You think?

—I'm joking.

He drank his Coke and watched her wheel the dolly away. Blue coveralls. Wide hips. He saw possibilities and on breaks hung around the Coke machine.

Two days later at the Duck Bar in Minot they ran into each other and fell into talking over the din. Gayla Krelle had a boyfriend on a bomber crew which was why she'd come to Minot but she wasn't happy about it.

—He flies here, flies there, and I'm stuck in fucking Minot.

—Guess you never know.

—But you learn.

—So where'd you come from?

—Omaha.

Amazing. They were both from Omaha and she'd gone to North High which always beat Central in basketball. That was all the excuse they needed after a week or so of sniffing each other to get down to the business of ruffling Gayla's bed. A startling revelation to Vern: some women really liked it. She had a faint funny sour-milk smell but it worked its way into him. She had thought to ditch Bomber Boy and move back to Omaha but decided to stay a while. Their little frisk lasted a year and a half. He was pretty happy for a while.

Then he met Merna. She worked at the hospital carting bedpans and mopping up stuff that sick people spewed. And here came
battered-up Vernon on a stretcher. He had quarreled with Gayla and
gone out to a bar and picked a fight with a guy he couldn't have beat
if he'd packed an Uzi. Merna took one look at him—

—Omigod, what happened to you?

—Bar fight.

—Well, you better just fight cripples.

It was three days till they let him out. Lots of chit-chat whenever
she found a minute to stop into his room. They went through bits
of life-story pretty fast. Merna's dad was career Navy stationed in
Norfolk Virginia but bouncing around the world. She'd hated her
mom until Mom was killed in a car crash and after that she loved her.
Her dad shipped her out to live with an aunt in Minot.

And lo in those hurried minutes between bedpans it was love.
Vern was dumbstruck. She wasn't sexy like Gayla. She was round-
faced and mouse-blonde and corn-fed and blunt. A couple years
older than him but she had a funny giggle or sometimes guffaw and
she always made him laugh.

—You got a sense of humor, Merna, like what's her name on TV?

—Well, spend all day with bedpans you better be able to laugh.

Laughter was something new for Vern McGurren. Almost as
good as fondling breasts. He wasn't much in the brain department
or a big home run hitter in bed so he never knew what she saw in
him. She said she liked his curly brown hair and something about
his chipmunk cheekbones and smile—

—And you don't have tattoos or missing an ear or too fat to live.
You'll do fine.

He knew he was no great catch but it didn't seem to matter. He
only knew that Merna saw him and saw right through him and liked
whatever she saw. There was always that tight little clench around her
mouth but as long as they could laugh they'd be okay. So he thought.

Vernon had told her about Gayla and said they'd split up which
by his genius for self-deception he considered to be not a total lie
given the fact that when he was fucking Merna he wasn't fucking

Gayla. Gayla had a hunch that he was catting around and finally caught on to his juggling act. Quarrels and promises and ramshackle lies but then Merna said she was pregnant. That decided it. She asked Vern to marry her and he did. Gayla called him an asshole but moved back to Omaha without a whole lot of fuss.

The genius of the human mind is a marvel to me. I've always had a knack for looking through walls or poking my finger into souls to read Braille off the pimples. I could see characters moving in rooms and hear the thoughts they coughed up like phlegm. Deceit may demand an Olympic-level agility but it's grounded in deep belief of your own impossible lies.

Pregnancy seemed to sharpen Merna's sense of humor. The first trimester—the best part mostly I'm told—she was always joking.

—A marriage made in heaven. Or at least in Minot.

And then in the twelfth week she miscarried. Suddenly no more laughs. The names she'd been sifting were dead. She was turned inside out. Vern had never really cared about having kids but he didn't want the laughing to stop.

It helped that God showed up. Until Vern met Merna he'd never been to church except a couple of times with Gramma Pitzer. The only reason his mother believed in God was to have someone to blame for her pathetic life. But Merna was raised Lutheran and whether or not she believed in God she believed in going to church. It was just one of those things that normal women did like shaving their armpits. Vern was resistant at first.

—I don't need to sit there and listen to that crap.

—It can't hurt you, honey.

—It's total crap.

—Well, do it for me.

And so after losing the pregnancy they started to go to church. And he found that most of the time he liked it as long as they talked about Jesus and God and stayed off calling him guilty for being alive.

Every week it was one quiet hour for the two of them washed in the bath of the Hammond organ and words that sounded deep and didn't mean a thing. One quiet hour when he didn't have to think.

Nearly two years they went on dog-paddling but at least not sinking. When his enlistment was up they moved to Omaha. His mom was there and even though he believed he'd closed the door on the Gayla business she might be there too. He tried learning computers. The future was in computers they said and he got the schooling paid through veterans' benefits. But the school was a string of dingy rooms on the third floor of a building in North Omaha where he'd get off the bus and see black faces staring at him in less than a joking mood. And the crap they taught was ten years out of date. Not that Vern had much of a head for computers. He'd sit at the monitor working through an assignment and wind up looking at tits.

Then Gayla again. He'd imagined meeting her on the street—those wide hips and dark dreamy eyes—but finally looked in the phone book and there she was. At that point he was drinking a lot and to him it seemed like she must want to be found or she wouldn't be in the phone book. It took three days before he finally made the call. Like inviting Kristi to the senior prom.

—Hi. This is Vern.

—Oh. Hi.

—I'm in Omaha now. Could I see you?

—I guess. Sure. Why not?

He was jubilant that she'd missed him or said she did. He would tell Merna he was going over to see his mom but spend most of his time in regions unknown. Until Gayla got pregnant.

—I'm pregnant, Vern.

—Oh shit, how did that happen?

—Well you were there at the time.

These women kept getting pregnant even when told not to. Vern scrounged up money for an abortion but Gayla took the money and moved to Denver to stay with her sister. Which was the last he heard from her until he heard more. Life went on with Merna, but at a later date things happened in Denver.

Then the boat business. He had met a guy whose cousin had a speedboat franchise in Fremont Nebraska and was looking to sell out. Good business he said. No competition.

—Sounds crazy selling speedboats to farmers, but it's like shooting fish in a barrel.

—So why does he want to sell?

—Cause he married into money.

So Vern borrowed some bucks from his mom plus a cheesy loan and went into business putting farmers into speedboats. They moved to Fremont about forty-odd miles from Omaha and Merna got a job at the Hormel plant while Vern started shooting fish in the barrel. Turned out there wasn't one damned fish.

So all this stuff makes you wonder. Does Vernon McGurren have the makings of an action hero? Why would he merit five minutes of my attention assuming I've got a luxury suite on the 23rd floor? Why fuck with his head? I was never that child prodigy who pulled legs off beetles or set cats on fire though I do like practical jokes. I can say only that I thought it might be the right time for Vernon and me to meet. By accident of course.

—2—

Vernon

Right from the start I fell for my own dumb ideas. Anything to keep up my hopes. Air Force: aspire to fly F-16s and wind up stacking toilet rolls. And then I would come up with some brilliant scheme, bet my shirt, and watch it all crumble to dust. Dust to dust, they say, but for me it was dust to start with. Some vision would run in my head like the first line of a song when you can't remember the next. If they want to torture the terrorists, they should just play the same song twenty-four hours a day, just the first line, and watch them start clawing the walls. Life does that to you anyway.

It was my Army buddy Clyde who gave me the nudge to go west. We were Air Force to be exact, but I always called them my Army buddies so people wouldn't ask, *Oh, what did you fly?* I wasn't about to brag that I flew a forklift.

Buddies you could always depend on for dumb advice, and I was a sucker for any flaky notion that pooped down on my head. That was Merna's joke. She had many occasions to use it, but it wasn't a load of laughs. We were in Omaha and then Fremont, and the speedboat thing went belly-up. Back to Omaha, tried selling cars, other stuff, but I was never a salesman except selling myself on crap. Next years—how many years, chrissake, slogging through oatmeal, sixteen, seventeen years, it goes by in one fart. And then the capper. I didn't know Galya had a son. Until he showed up one day at the door. I'd given her money to have an abortion, not to have a son.

And then my buddy Clyde said there were tons of jobs in California. Old Mrs. Baggett from church, with the pimply nose, warned me—

—Well, California, that's one step away from Hell.

—So, Hell and Omaha, how do you tell the difference?

It was a joke but she puckered up. I'm not the best jokester. Still, California seemed like a good idea, so we moved to Denver.

—We better sneak up slow on California.

That was my joke, but there was another reason for Denver: Gayla Krelle. We pull these great con jobs on ourselves, amazing I couldn't see it. I guess that's why we elect crooks to public office: we want a guy in there who understands us.

Denver, it came to a head. All my life I've tried to forget Denver, tell myself no, it wasn't really me, I was just the star in some pathetic movie that nobody wanted to watch. Got it on again with Gayla, just couldn't let it go. Maybe pretending I was in my twenties again. I blamed her for encouraging me, or at least not telling me to get lost.

And then the capper. I didn't know Galya had a son. Until he showed up one day at the door. I'd given her money to have an abortion, not to have a son.

So I tried telling myself I hadn't humped the lady I humped. I hadn't sat on the park bench staring at the 9mm. I hadn't taken that twenty out of the till at Radio Shack—the only time in my life I'd ever done something as stupid as that, but maybe I hadn't done it. I hadn't torn out Merna's heart and flipped it into the trash. No way could she ever forgive me for what I hadn't done.

But in fact I did all that, and I knew it in my gut. Like my dad's belt, it left welts that were slow to fade, One minute I was the sacred child of God, next minute a scribble on the men's room wall. I watched TV a lot.

And suddenly I was forty-four. How did I manage that? Before, it all seemed pretend, then I took one look in the mirror and saw,

Oh shit, my life is over half done, I'm halfway dead. It was hard to tell one month from another. I slipped on a banana peel and fell into my forties hard.

Merna laughed when I said that, right in the midst of a fight. At that point in time we could fight but still laugh. Less so later. That's been a pattern: we lose the laughter, then get it back.

The jobs. Sometimes they just vanished out from under me. *We're downsizing, we'll give you a call.* A couple of times it was the drinking, even though I never came to work drunk, just tired out, strung out, hung over. I could have done that without the drink.

—You're drinking like a fish, Vern.

—Hey, no, more like a duck.

And she'd do her best to laugh, but neither of us thought it was funny. Sometimes at work I'd get instructions screwed up, where my mind would work it around so I thought I was doing what they said, but I was off on some weird detour they'd never thought of. To Merna I'd lay out the logic behind my screw-up, and she'd pretend to shake me by the ear like a little kid.

—If you weren't so smart you wouldn't be so stupid.

And we'd both try to laugh it off. I remembered my mom used to say that lots of folks take up the space where you could better plant a turnip. In fact most people don't know how dumb they are, but I did, so maybe that proved I had brains. My third-grade teacher Miss Young thought I was pretty smart, but in fourth grade Mrs. Schumaris offered a second opinion. Sometimes my brain ran around like chickens.

And I wondered how women so different as Gayla Krelle and Merna would be attracted to me. Maybe the curly hair, green eyes, and puffy cheeks that go pointy like a fox. Maybe women like guys who look sneaky so they think he might make a million bucks. Or maybe I looked harmless after they saw what else was out there, all the studs with the bulldog jaw and whisker stubble and the dead-fish eyes of my dad. I'd try to fake it, but most of the time I figured that anybody attracted to me was seriously mistaken. Some day, I thought, I'd prove myself. I was still waiting for the day.

After I lost the job at Radio Shack, I actually put three bullets in my 9mm that I jokingly called *Daddy's amigo* and sat on a bench by the lake in City Park watching the ducks for half an hour before I unloaded it. There was something about the ducks.

But then, when I was really down for the count, God was standing there waiting. First Saturday of November the whole thing exploded with Merna, after the kid I paid to get rid of showed up at the door, and she was packing up to leave. I didn't have one more excuse left in me. Like the dry heaves: I'd try to come up with words and nothing was there. She was in the bedroom packing, swearing, crying, and then she came to the door.

—You want to go with me to church? Tomorrow?

—What church?

—Whatever.

We hadn't hardly been to church in Omaha, only twice in Fremont, never in Denver. In Minot I didn't mind going. The music gave me some peace of mind, and then we'd stop in at Tony's for a beer as a chaser. What she had in mind I had no idea, but anything was better than having her walk out the door. We were too far from any Lutheran church and the car had been repossessed, so the closest thing was something called the Church of God.

—Sounds like a bunch of Holy Rollers.

—It's a church, Vern. I mean God is God, whether it's Walmart or Sears.

She would say these funny things at the strangest times. So we walked the six blocks to the Church of God. It was a white frame building, very simple, just a cross in the front and not much of a pulpit, more like a podium, and about forty people in folding chairs. They were friendly, and it turned out they didn't throw fits but just sang the usual stuff, and some old guy from the congregation read Scripture, some *Love thy neighbor* stuff, which was okay, I could use some of that right then. Other people got up and did the invocation or asked for prayers for their cousin's arthritis. You'd think the preacher would do all that, but the way they did it made it seem more real. Like somebody really believed it.

Then up came Reverend Bud. It turned out his name was Robert Delaney, but he'd always been called Bud—

—Starting right at my mama's nipple.

He said that once, which surprised me, coming from a preacher. He was wearing a pullover and a green sport jacket, and I thought what kind of hippie shit is this? But first thing when he got to the podium, he looked directly at me and Merna.

—Hey, thanks for coming, and welcome to the Church of God.

That got my attention, and from there he started talking and I could never remember what it was he said or how long he said it. I only felt being spoken to like a brother or the way I imagined it must be for your brother to tell you things. He didn't talk much about Jesus, but he talked the way Jesus must have talked. Deep in the gut you had a need for the words and so he just spoke them, words I needed to hear, and I felt scared that I'd never be the same.

Afterwards we didn't stop for a beer, we just went home and made love. We talked and we talked and told each other things, and the talking was sweeter even than making love. Finally she spoke the words, almost too softly to hear—

—Let's give it another try.

From then on we went to the Church of God, and things got much better. I could never exactly believe in Jesus, God, miracles, all that, but you saw it there, felt it in the friendliness, the cheer, and from deep inside you could hear the promise. After all this crazy roller coaster ride, we were still together. I even started to pray.

But every time I think about the hellish thing in Denver, I have to stop and tell myself, *Hey, remember Zach.* Zach was born in Denver. What a surprise. After we'd run the gauntlet, welts and scars and bruises, then God gave us the gift. Or I guess the two of us did it, but God turned the music up. Merna was forty-two. Right after supper she told me she was pregnant, and she laughed. That was so good to hear. I never knew that I wanted a son till all of a sudden I had one.

It was right at that time I began to have second sight.

Not exactly what I prayed for. I would've lots rather had a new car or a steady job, but there it was. Once I had seen a magazine article in the dentist's office, *What about Second Sight?* and I thought, well, so what about it? But the phrase stuck. Then right at the time of the birth came the first tiny blips. Maybe it came from seeing my son. First time I saw him, Merna nursing him, he looked so much like me, I thought, *Hey, great, I get a new start in life.* It's only later you realize, *No, he's himself.*

Second sight, it was like when the TVs were little screens, and I'd stay up for the midnight horror show, so it all shrank down to a peephole through the dark. I would catch a glimpse, a shimmer like shapes in fog, but with hard sharp edges. Shapes I couldn't make out, but like ripply puddles or old men's eyes or my mother's hands. Like the way a child sees giant mouths or fingers that fumble around. Glimmers too quick to make out, but they'd burn as if God stuck a finger into my head. It happened three times before I told Merna.

—You better go to the doctor, hon, get your blood sugar checked. You eat too much sugary stuff you'll get diabetes.

—I eat what you put on the table.

—You'd eat the tabletop if I let you.

She was joking, but I knew she was scared.

About that time we rented a movie where people had to stay in the sunlight because the dark would devour them. But in sunlight they'd cast a shadow, and the shadow would slither up their legs like a vine and start to suck, and pretty soon they were nothing but husks. Merna stopped watching it, but for me it seemed to carry a message. I couldn't tell what.

And around then, I dreamed I was in church where the priest had robes like a Catholic, but feathers too. Feathers out of his head, and a mask like a Halloween skull. There was a bunch of tourists, and the guide was talking some language with lots of clicks like a bug. The sun went back of a cloud and my shadow disappeared, so nobody could see me standing there. I woke in a sweat. On TV I'd seen a woman who hallucinated Indians, flamingos, snakes in broad daylight. She thought it must be the Devil, but they found a tumor the size of a grapefruit inside her head. I couldn't tell Merna the dreams or she'd nag me to go to the doctor.

I would have these flashes every couple of weeks, like I was being told something I needed to know, like maybe go see the doctor. So she got me to the doctor, who said to stop smoking. I did cut back and the flashes came less often, but when they came they were sharp as a deer in the headlights, staring straight at me.

A couple of times I talked to Reverend Bud, the only person I'd ever known I could talk to like that, like a brother. Not that brothers in the Bible had the best track record, but we have this sense of what's meant by brotherhood. I knew just the way he looked at me that the answers would have to come out of me. *Think of everything as a test,* he said, *from a teacher who really likes you.* That didn't really help. I just wondered when I'd stop flunking it.

The thing in Denver with Gayla Krelle, all that happened from feeling sorry for myself, calling myself a loser, wanting to grab that extra little piece of the pie that I knew I didn't deserve. I guess the Devil exploits that vulnerability, if you believe in the Devil, or God, one or the other—how do you tell the difference? No, *exploits* is too strong a word. Reverend Bud got it right—

—My friends, God is love. But you know, God can't help slamming you a pie in the face if you're really asking for it.

I never believed in Hell or Hellfire except what you do to yourself. You're so damned hungry, so you keep pulling the same shit you've pulled all your life, over and over, till you start to scream and never stop, and that's eternal damnation. In my opinion at least.

I just wanted to make a living. I wanted the love of my wife and my son, and their respect. I wanted some laughs and a future and to live where the paint wasn't peeling or linoleum cold on the feet. I wanted the flashes and blurs to come clear. They say count your blessings. I kept trying.

And here I am fifty-five. Chico, California. One kid. Part-time at Walmart.

—3—

Stubblefield

At that point I met Vernon and Vernon met me. Lots of ways that could happen. I might have squawked at him out of a burning bush. I might have knocked him off his donkey. I might have slithered up his leg and hissed *Eat the fucking apple*. But more likely he was in a Chico dive late afternoon where a tired blonde who looked like she'd had a hard day's night was tending bar. Down the counter a shapeless old couple sagged over their stools. Music pounded out oblivion. The barroom had little wads of dollar bills stuck to the ceiling by the hundreds. A cheerful touch though clearly fake. Drunk enough and you'd think they were real. Even drunker you'd think they'd fall in your lap.

Vern might have just imagined that some guy who seemed a bit out of place in his blue polyester suit sat on the next stool over and started to chat but in fact it was Vern who began the conversation.

—So what brings you to Chico?

—Business. What brings you?

—Wish I knew.

—Good enough reason.

I don't remember what I told him my business was. Maybe import/export. Maybe exploring shale deposits for fracking. Maybe pulling strings with the county for a new Indian casino. But the probable truth was that I just sprouted up on the bar stool right out of his fantasy. One TV behind the bar was tuned to ESPN where a dude was prancing around like a Nazi goose pumping his fist after scoring a touchdown. The other TV had a howling punk jerking off his guitar with a sea of lassies writhing and creaming. Images of studsmanship. If you're watching that stuff and the next stool is empty it's either going to fill with a hooker's butt or with some shark in a shiny suit talking crap about Indian casinos.

So we chatted. He watched those guys pumping their fists and flaunting their dicks to the wet squealing females and he heard what he wanted to hear. It all flowed from there and whatever I said to him was just frosting on the meatballs. He told me more about his life than I ever wanted to know and gave a little shrug at the end of each sad decade. But I already knew the gist of it. After all I more or less made him up and called him Vernon. Or somebody did—maybe his mommy and daddy in some distracted moment.

Made him up? In the sense that we raise a hog in order to eat it. No disservice to the hog which wouldn't exist if we didn't give it free room and board. And in turn those pork chops define us as they round our bellies and clog our arteries. If I were sitting on the bar stool all by myself in Chico or Macon or Pewaukee and didn't take shape as some dimwit's last best hope I might just bubble up and pop. Maybe we just made up each other

—Well, tell you what, Vern, we should check out the possibilities.

—Like what?

—Just options. Potentials. Druthers.

In every heart there's all the stuff that dwelt in Vern McGurren. Learn that and you'll make big bucks and be headlined hot shit and even get elected to save America from Americans. The world might not be the worse for it though for sure it won't be the better.

—I don't like email, Vern. I'd rather talk to people.

—Or these tweets that they do.

—Fuck tweets. Lemme hear a guy's voice so I can tell if he's full of crap.

—It's more real.

As if people hadn't been talking shit for thousands of years before tweets but we both agreed that the human voice was the unquenchable fount of truth. I gave him my cell number on the back of my card and he scribbled his on a coaster. After a while he asked me what I'd had in mind.

—Like you were saying about possibilities?

—Well, let me ask you, Vern. What would you like the possibilities to be?

—Well, I don't know, I just thought maybe—

—See, this is the problem so many guys have. They wait to be told. They hope somebody's got the answer and says what they want to hear, only that never happens in a million years. All the politicians: *What the American people want is blah blah blah.* Say you just want a decent life the next line is *Sorry bub.*

—I guess.

Vern was a guy who kept himself zippered up tight. He was not an open fly. He looked up at the TV to see if the answer was there but the dude had just thrown an intercepted pass. He glanced at the withered old couple down at the end of the bar: in the image of God created He them.

—No, but well, a better job, something with a future, something—

—I hear you. I hear you. I do.

—But I mean the little guys, small businesses, they don't offer anything secure, they're just hanging on, and the big huge outfits, they don't give a damn. You're just another flea on the dog.

—Well there's gotta be organization, Vern.

—Organization, okay, but—

He floundered for words to curse out the corporate bastards but checked himself thinking maybe that I was one of those corporate bastards that he didn't want to offend. He fumbled through the pocket change in his head. I took pity—

—Because that's how things get done that are bigger than building a doghouse. Difference is, is the company made out of humans or numbers some MBA pulls out of his bunghole. Sounds to me you're looking for a place that invests in people. That looks very carefully at the guys they might invest in and makes a full commitment.

—Right, I mean—

—We agree.

Vern never looked me in the eye. He tried to. Little squirrelly glances and then he'd shift to the TV or the old zombies on their stools or his own puffy-pointy face in the mirror back of the bar. The twitch of a hungry coyote. He took another rabbit sip of his beer. He sipped delicately as if his illusions might vanish at the bottom of the mug. I checked my cell phone to make him think that I needed to. Basic business principle: never let the other guy think that you've got the time for him. It gives your words that value-added edge and contradicts the effect of a cheap suit. I favor cheap suits to put guys at ease. Not impressive to the *chicas* but I wasn't hunting pussy.

—You got kids, Vern?

—Son. Zach. Sixteen. No, seventeen. Great kid.

He said it as if he was taking his vitamins and took another sip to wash it down. He hoped it was true.

—Seventeen. Great.

There was a long silence between us. They say that between the electrons of an atom there's almost infinite distance. And the whole universe might get lost in the gaps between the quarks of the human soul. (I said that once to a very intelligent lady named Marylu and scored big.) I checked my watch and got up abruptly and offered Vern a quick handshake with a five-dollar tip for the bar girl and left my Glenfiddich unsipped. Impressive details all.

Next day he called me. Or I must have called him: a guy with broken knees doesn't take the first step. We chatted the way guys chat when they're sniffing each other's butts. We talked about my three divorces and the great kids I never had. He told me about his wife and son. He sounded like a mouse in the Superdome spooked by its thunderous squeak.

—Well, could we talk? I mean an appointment, like?

—Certainly could. Only problem being that I'm in Las Vegas right now.

—Las Vegas.

—Late flight charter.

In fact I wasn't. I was in Wichita but Las Vegas packs a wallop. Some novelist wrote about Satan setting up his empire in Las Vegas and the book sold millions of copies. Satan has lots of fans out there and Las Vegas was the place to stick him. Vern was impressed. He was a simple soul. If there were more like him the world would be a better place for simple souls if not for the psychopaths who run stuff. Under my bald contempt for folks like Vernon I've always held a respect. It's not true that sociopaths have no feelings. I'm deeply moved by suffering. I love it.

At this point even a simple soul should have got his guard up. Should he not question this Las Vegas honcho pulling strings in Chico? Recruiting talent on bar stools? Should he not try to fathom my scam? But those guys pumping their fists and plunking their magic twangers were just too much. No arguing with hunger. Hunger makes the world go round. Dial it down a point and the economy throws a shit fit. Babies know they need that breast but from there on they watch the ads. If ad men could target babies directly the little crappers would scream for seven nipples and silicone boobs and a pacifier with a Twitter feed and diapers by Pierre Cardin. Man shall not live by tit alone.

And I might have questioned my own motives which were so unreadable as to be unspeakable. What did I see in a loser like Vernon? Why pull a profitless scam? Granted the sucker's credit card debt descends to the seventh generation but I would surely not be around to collect.

For me the answer was simple: it's what I do. It never occurred to Vern was that there might not be a scam or any rational goal. An act of God they call it. A joke. One glitch on the Weather Channel and the morning drizzle blows up to a twister that flings the squealing school bus over the edge. Just a passing whim of that Joker in the Sky. And is it really a con if the con man delivers his promise?

—So tell you what, Vern, let's sleep on it. I'll get back. Maybe not tomorrow, I've got a thing in Houston, but meantime let's let this realm of the possible possibilities settle in and see what bobs to the top.

—Great. Yeh, fine. Great.

—So, *hasta luego.*

—Right.

We went back and forth for three weeks and I could hear the strain in his voice when he hit my voicemail and left his little whine. If I ever felt sorry for anyone on the planet it was for good old Vern. All he wanted in life was a decent salary and the respect of his wife and son. Was that too much to ask? Sure it was. Read the news. Jesus said forgive them seventy times seven but he set no limit on the service charges.

I had been brusque the last time we talked so I knew he'd be brooding ashes to ashes and dust to dust. I waited three days to call him back and I could tell he was set to break out in shingles.

—So how's it going, Vern?

—Fine. Fine.

—Hey, sorry I cut it short last time. Things are hopping here.

—No problem. No sweat.

—Well, in fact I sweat a lot, but that's just the name of the game.

—You can say that again.

—I have said so many times.

He squeezed out a chuckle. I gave it a beat to settle. I was inside his head and so dark in there I had to squint. There was always that moment where it could go so many ways. What worked for one guy didn't work for another. For a stooge who was into conspiracies I might talk about the Jews inventing AIDS or lesbians cutting off babies' pricks but that wouldn't work for Vern. He knew his hidden oppressor. It wasn't the Rothschilds or the Illuminati: it was the assistant floor manager at the Walmart. And for him the fewer words the better because in fact he had a poetic ear: from the overtones and reverb he wove depths of meaning way deeper than the facts. Like Columbus he didn't have a clue that he was in America and what that meant. Give him the ball and he'd run with it—even his own matched pair. It was enough for me to say five words—

—It looks like a go.

And you could hear his breath like a drowning man surfacing to gasp the whole sky into his lungs. I let it set there. Give his imagination time to make the movie.

—So that means . . .

—Here's what it is, Vern, and it's really up to you. It's your choice, totally yours.

—Okay.

—The way it works: I guide my team. I consider myself the coach. I'm not out on the field getting my head split open—been there, done that—but I'm guiding the team. Who carries the ball and who blocks the kick and who makes it in the clutch. So when we're acquiring players it's how they fit. You follow me?

—Sure. I mean I think so.

—Good. So I'm thinking, which is totally up to you, is this—

—Okay—

—Come to Las Vegas. Now let me be perfectly clear. I'm not talking job interview. That's not the issue. We're looking at how you fit. Talk to guys, play around, check it out. I'm not saying what. What we do, we start with the general and hone it down to exact.

I philosophized for a while about teamwork and trust and other virtues that are dead as dogshit. My brain wandered back to the duck pool at the carnival midway where you paid a quarter to pick up a plastic duck and see what prize you won. You never knew what number was under its little yellow ass but that number would yield some wondrous piece of crap. That number ruled. Vern was picking up his plastic duck.

—So what say you?

Another long silence that matched the reign of the pharaohs and then he fumbled around the way I expected him to fumble around.

—So I guess . . . what I'm trying to understand is . . . I mean you don't really know much about . . . I mean this is . . . strange.

—It is, Vernon, yes it is. So this is the first hurdle, so to speak: do you trust my judgment or do you question it? Questioning is a virtue up to a point, but past that point things quickly fall apart. You follow?

—Yeh. Okay. Las Vegas?

—Las Vegas, as I think I said. Or you can try Kansas City if you really prefer it, but I happen to be in Las Vegas right now.

—No, I mean yes, I mean— I guess there are cheap flights, I mean they want people to come there so it's probably cheaper than if—

—It's a little more complicated, Vernon. Not complicated, but just some vital specifics. You've got a car?

—Ninety-nine Chevy, new tires, it's doing pretty well although the transmission sounds funny—

—That's your mode of conveyance. You follow? St. Paul made his trips on a horse, the Virgin Mary rode a donkey, and monks hiked hundreds of miles on their knees, so it's not that weird. It's the difference between a trip and a pilgrimage. Not in the religious sense, but just that this is a journey of significance where you read the road signs and you count the roadkill and you stop for a Coke. When Moses got word to conquer the Promised Land, he didn't book a flight with his travel agent.

—Yeh, well, I guess— I'll have to check at work—

—Well sure, cause there's a major future in stocking the shelves at Walmart. Don't want to risk that gold mine.

I was pretty blunt but I had to be. I got it across that this was his destiny and if he backed out now then it might be *Sorry bub*. He thought about that for a minute.

—Yeh, okay, well, I guess I could.

—Great. That's great. Hey, bring along your son.

4

Zach

So picture this kid, call him Zach. He's seventeen, tall and skinny, narrow bony face, glasses, curly hair like his dad—looks okay in a flaky kind of way. He has to do a book report for Miss Plankett's senior English. Dad asked if they still did book reports in school and the wise-ass offspring said sure, it's the best way to make kids hate books. In fact the kid reads a lot when he's not indulging in self-abuse, but for reports he just looks up some book on Wikipedia, rewrites the blurb, and adds snark. Why waste time reading it? He'll probably just try to kill himself again if Rebecca dumps him. This time he'll do it more expeditiously.

No, third-person-present is no refuge, and Miss Plankett calls it pretentious. Call me Zach.

This particular book I actually read. I was curious, not sure why. It's an oral report, so I'm in my teensy room in the trailer, facing a sour green wall, slouched over the scruffy desk we got at a second-hand place with three floors of dead people's junk. In class I'll just mutter it, but here I record myself in Garageband so I can fiddle around, zombify my voice, add drums and reverb and samples from an old Godzilla movie. It comes out pretty special. But right now I'd better practice.

—So my oral report is The Historical Abraham and the author is David Rosenberg. And what it's about is, was there really an Abraham? Or he starts out Abram. Which is important because he founded the Jews and Christians but the Muslims believe in him too cause they're descended from his first son Ishmael instead of his real son Isaac.

Is that phrasing stupid enough? I can't help getting all A's, but in class I do my best to sound like a troglodyte. I try to fit in. Though I do want to impress Miss Plankett.

—And the most interesting part is when God tells Abraham to kill his son Isaac and he's going to do it except then God tells him not to and he kills a sheep instead. Which Christians think is a symbol of Jesus, but is Jesus the son or the sheep, and does the sheep get resurrected?

I'd better leave out the Jesus part. Rebecca's Catholic, and anyway it sounds smart-ass. Smart-ass is sexy if you're dark-skinned with greasy hair like Arturo, my best friend, way more acidulous than I—I like that word. If you're flunking every subject like him—which I kind of wish I was—then it's cool to be smart-ass. He's bonking Millie Stivers.

—Which proves he loves God so he gets rich and fathers all the Jews. And the way it relates to us I guess is it's about having faith. Or maybe we just do stuff because we're told to do it. Nobody asked Isaac how he felt with the knife at his neck.

I play it back. I hate the sound of my voice: high, tense, whiny. I try it again pitched low. No better. I should just mumble like Wesley does, which makes him sound mysterious. The mystery being, was he born without a brain or did he just forget to water it? Stop with the cleverness, Zach: you're the only one who thinks you're funny. Though I get a smirk from Artie now and then. I run it back.

—Jews and Christians but the Muslims believe in him too cause they're descended from his first son Ishmael instead of his real son Isaac. And the most interesting part is when God tells Abraham to kill his son Isaac and he's going to do it—

I click it off and stare at the screen. Then crash it goes black, like the film where they slip on the wet spot and skid into the future. My dad said something like that once. He scares me. I'm too much like him. He thinks I don't hear him, but I listen with naked ears. (Miss Plankett would question that image.) The future: it creeps me out.

But that might be the short story I have to do. *A story you have a stake in,* Miss Plankett said, and she gave me an extra week. An update of Abraham, the *Akedah,* the binding, with the accent on the *Ak.* Start with this kid still battling the ravages of puberty, and of course he thinks he's the only human on Earth and everyone else is there to cook him dinner and buy him an iPhone. Be honest, Zach, that's you. And the family gobbles manna in the silence of their trailer and Dad gets their second-hand camel ready for the trip. Mom watches them ride off, her hand raised in benediction, as they disappear into the mythic dimension. But this is Chico High School, and the only mythic dimension here is Millie Stivers' bosom.

It's one of those days when there's nothing in my brain but dandruff. And then, hey, hold on! I've got time for the book report and short story and the history test, all of it. We're off to Las Vegas. By the time I get back and it all comes due, I might not even be conscious.

Mom calls me to breakfast, and next minute I'm sitting with Dad at the table. She refills his coffee cup while I trace a line of egg yolk on my plate with a tine of my fork. The letter Z. Mom looks at me.

—What are you doing, Zach?

—Studying.

She frowns. These days she frowns a lot. She goes to the counter and puts a small sack in a larger paper sack and rolls the top.

—All right, I packed lunches, boiled eggs, peanut butter sandwiches, you can see what's there. Then some chicken for supper, potatoes. At least start out with stuff that's not grease.

—The boy likes grease.

—Vern—

—Hey, I'm joking.

Dad strains to bring sunlight into the morning. Mom doesn't help with the heavy lift, so Dad takes shelter under his eyelids.

—Well, I just hope you get something besides fast food. They have all these cows on drugs now. I read about stuff, half the time I don't know if what I put on the table is full of drugs or—

—Gifts from God. Merna, you know we appreciate—

—More toast? Zach? Vern?

—I think we're fine.

She swipes crumbs from the counter with a sponge, trying to put the brakes on, then flattens her hands to the Formica and stands there. We stare at the back of her blouse. Dull rose. She likes rose.

—I'm sorry, Vern, you know how I feel about this—

—I know.

—It's like a fist—

—Yeh, you said—

—And I'm trying to be positive, supportive, and you're trying—

—I'm trying to make us a life.

Mom writes on the grocery list stuck to the door of the fridge. The cartoon she taped there is gone: a lady standing at the sink and saying, *Some day my prince will come.* Funny, I guess, but I aspired to be the only one in the family with problems, not her. I guess all three of us want to be an only child.

She looks older than she ought to. I could see it even before I got to the age where you can't stand your parents. Which is a couple of years before you're oblivious to their existence. I know she had a miscarriage a long time ago, and trouble with Dad and then trouble with me, and the moves the moves the moves. You can see it all in her eyes. She'd gone blonde, then brunette, then back to mouse color, and now that the gray is starting in she's tried that shade of black that she must know looks fake. Maybe she'll let it go gray so Dad will have to look at the gray. I think she wants to punish us both. If she doesn't, she ought to.

Once in a while she laughs. She's got this big funny laugh when she lets it go. I always loved to hear her laugh. A couple of times, from some silly thing, she'd fall into a laughing jag that went on and on. She hasn't done that for a while, but I hear it in my head.

There's love there, I think, or at least the memory of it. *Male and female created He them*, is the story. Then He stuck them in a garden, totally clueless, naked to the gnats, and sentenced them to death for chomping a Golden Delicious. I said that once after church and of course Dad got freaked. After that, they didn't make me go to church. They didn't want me gathering evidence.

Mom scrapes out the skillet and looks for a place to set it. She makes a grim little chuckle—

—This kitchen . . .

Someplace we lived when I was little, the kitchen was big. I'd wrap around Daddy's leg and he'd drag me across the tile and I'd sing *Alligator alligator*. It was real tile then. I remember Mom said once that a kitchen makes a home, but that wasn't a single-wide trailer. Mobile home, they call this, but it's more like a plastic shell for hermit crabs.

Mom looks around for more crumbs to swipe off. When she can't do it with a sponge she does it with words—

—Well so I'll ride to work with Rosella. Mexicans are okay, like everybody else, there's good and there's bad, only I've got to listen to her talk about her bowels. I know more about her bowels than I do about my own.

—I'm sorry.

—Get bowel trouble just listening to her.

—I'm sorry, Merna.

—I'm just worried.

—I know. I love you.

—I know.

They gargle up a driblet of laughter. They're trying really hard. Then Dad waves his fork like a prophet with a fork in his hand.

—*They sow not, neither do they spin.*

He squeezes out a grin. I can see, she can see, he can see that he has no idea what he means. He's just trying to keep things light.

—Dad?

—Hm?

—Who sows not?

—The lilies. I was joking. *Consider the lilies*—

—I'll do that.

I hate doing that to him. Like playing ping-pong with Artie who puts these funny twists to the ball, makes me look like a fool, and then slams it past like a bullet. Supposedly my friend. But I do it with words. And I keep thinking that Dad is so stupid, too stupid to live, and yet we're so much alike, even though my mind embraces a vastly more educated state of confusion.

—Well, that's okay for church, but I don't see a lot of damn lilies in this trailer court.

Mom sets a thermos by the sack on the table, then moves around the kitchen as if she's looking for something to swat. I wipe up the last smear of yolk with my finger and lick it.

—Mom?

—What? Don't use your finger for that.

—Sorry.

—You look like a monkey.

She can't help saying stuff like that or tasting the sourness. I keep fingering up yolk that isn't there. Mom sets the sack on the table and looks down at the fake wood-grain linoleum that somebody thought would make us happy. Nothing left to say, but neither Mom nor Dad can figure how to stop saying it. I'm about to applaud the comedy act but think better of it: we're driving hairpin turns. I want to scream so loud I'd shake mountains—we all do—but then we'd have to deal with the avalanche. Dad pipes up with what passes for jollity.

—Is that a new blouse?

—Sally's Thrift. You like it?

—Nice color for you.

—Thanks for noticing.

—I notice. I notice a lot. Every day.

Dad looks at his watch. Mom sees him looking at his watch, and he hopes she'll say, *Just go.* She wants to get us out the door. She wants us to be gone because she loves us. She wants us to come back different. No matter how, just different.

—Look, I don't need to go, if you really— I just thought this is one hell of an opportunity. What the pastor said in the sermon last week, said God puts it out there, you have to be ready—

—What sermon?

—Last week, the virgins with the lamps, wedding guests or—

—That wasn't last week, Vern. Last week was Abraham and Isaac and God saying, *Kill your son*, and that gave me the cold shivers.

—Don't kill me, Dad.

I pop into their eyes. They look at me. Dad does a little fiddling with his fingers like the air is too thick to breathe.

—It's an opportunity, hon, that's all it is. God helps him that helps himself, and this life you better help yourself to whatever you can. Reach across the table and grab it. Cause somebody said—

Dad doesn't hear what he's saying. He just needs to fill the air with subjects and predicates. Like me spelling my name in egg yolk.

—Guy on TV said what this country was all about was land. Like Moses where God says let's make a deal, but now—

—Vern, right now we don't need politics—

—But now, all I'm saying, it's not land, it's just real estate. I mean, coming out to California, it wasn't anything like we thought it was. Chico: pavement is pavement, traffic is traffic, shit is shit. Golden West, we might as well be in West Omaha.

—Might as well.

—But my point being, this is an opportunity.

Dad, he's not that stupid. He knows he's just running off at the mouth and Mom knows it too. How many walls does the rat bang its nose on before it scores the cheese? Dad gets caught in the bramble bush of words. Every word is a thistle.

I get up from the table and take my plate to the sink and wash it. I always procrastinate on the dishes, but I'm in a guilty phase. They watch me and wonder why is he doing that? What does that mean? Will he try it again? No, not this morning anyway.

—But it's no b.s., I don't think. I mean Zach looked him up on the Web, didn't you, Zach?

—Yes.

—You looked him up on the Web. Three hotels in Las Vegas, real estate, baseball team, casinos, cable TV, incredible, and this guy says come talk to me. He all but promised. *See where you fit*, is exactly what he said. Anyway it's better than living off twenty hours a week and—

—And my job.

—And your job, I was gonna say.

—So I packed your brown suit, but if you want your blue one that's okay, whatever.

—Brown's fine. Hon, could you just, like, relax a little?

—Well, I just wonder what's the deal with taking Zach along.

—Deal? No deal.

—Well so there's this business thing, this great opportunity, this big deal, but they don't usually say, *Oh be sure to bring your son.* Anyway not the big shots that I kiss their asses all my life.

—Mom, it's *Big shots whose asses I kiss all my life.*

—Don't get smart with me.

—Sorry.

I wanted to kick myself. Why can't I keep my mouth shut? She sounds so dumb sometimes, but she's smarter than I ever thought of being. *My son the comedian,* she said once, and that stung for days. It stings right now.

Dad glances at the clock above the stove. It's running slow again. Does that put us ahead of time or behind? I'd get up on a chair and set it, but then they'd wonder why is he doing that? Rehearsing to hang himself? Dad only knows that he needs to leave, that anything that wants to be said has been said. Once he told about the time his little sister cried till they did a funeral for their dead cat. She asked him to say something over the grave to make it okay. *Good cats go to heaven,* he said. Maybe right now he ought to say, *Good cats go to heaven.* He smiles at me, whatever that means.

—Okay, sure, I talk about opportunity. Your mom was remembering back in Nebraska, after the speedboat thing, I sold cars, used cars, and I wasn't the greatest salesman. This old farmer, Norwegian farmer, he was all set to buy, didn't need selling, just liked the color. So he takes out his checkbook and like a fool I tell him, *Here, I'll start it up.* And I couldn't get it started. Did myself out of a sale.

—Your dad came home draggedy-ass, told it to me like a joke.

—Well, you have to laugh or else you'd kill yourself.

—Ho ho.

From me. They look at me. I grimace the way they do on TV when some comedian farts. Mom always said that I have a gift for humor but it's pretty hard to take. Dad folds his hands.

—Could we—? I know it's pretty funny saying grace after breakfast, but we're not gonna be all together for a while so—

—Now I lay me down to sleep—

Dad glares at me. I bow my head, but I know Mom keeps looking at me. Dad prays as if he just jumped over the cliff and has to get it said before he splats on the rocks. Some day God might listen.

—Dear Lord, we thank Thee for everything and for this opportunity, which wouldn't be there I don't think if we hadn't got on the right track. Cause there's a lotta water under the bridge. Lotta water, but we're in this great country with a great future. They talk about the good old days like it's all in the past, but that's where this country went wrong, they start dredging up stuff, we did this, did that, but we gotta look to the future and the opportunity . . .

He blanks out. I see Mom staring at him. I shouldn't say anything, but I do.

—Amen.

—Enough of that, Zach.

Mom's protecting him, as if a turtle needs protection. She clears the rest of the stuff from the table and motions me to step aside so she can deal with the dishes. I wave my hand as if to say whatever. I give her a peck on the cheek, mumble something, start to move away, but she embraces me and holds on tight. I pat her on the back and wait till she lets go. I try not to look in her face. I wonder if I'll ever learn to love.

—So I guess you're off. So take care of yourself, cause you're still my little boy. It took us a lotta years before you came along, lotta hard knocks, but so just call and tell me what's going on. Have a good time. Take a lotta pictures. Your dad said you'd go through Yosemite, that's supposed to be nice.

I give her another peck and disengage, pick up the paper sack and thermos, go out the door to the car. The end of the trailer is peeling and needs a coat of paint. I think how stupid to try killing yourself with pills that turn out to be Mom's hormones. My parents aren't the only lame-brains in the family. And then I'm sitting there in the car hearing their words. Making it up, stringing it out, knowing it's all in my head but totally true. *Denver*, somebody says. Our DNA is all ears.

I saw the letter about the woman dying. From Lannie, his name is. I have a brother. I'd met him long ago but couldn't get clear who he was. I'm not the only begotten son. That might be where my short story starts. *Something you have a stake in*, Miss Plankett said. Every good story needs a long-lost brother. Call him some other name in the story, I guess.

Mom comes to Dad and they hug, look in each other's eyes where they haven't looked for a while. I'm seeing it. They say each other's names, or maybe they say their own. Which would work better?

So it's four p.m. on a Friday. I've turned in my story, and Miss Plankett asks me to come in after school to talk about it. I come into the classroom. She's sitting at her desk. I like Miss Plankett a lot, even though she hates mixed metaphors. She has the pages in front of her on her desk, *Hey Zach*, she says with a curious smile. Then Donna Plankett rises, comes around to me, takes my hand, and guides it under her tangerine sweater. Her blonde hair is loose to her shoulder, and her eyes are full.

That won't ever remotely happen, but the fantasy helps me get through most afternoons with minimal despair, and it fills an empty moment now. Our yearning keeps us alive.

—5—

Merna

I pictured Zach sitting out there in the car hearing us. Hearing through walls. Hearing the words spoken over the table, knowing it's all in his head but totally true. He could hear what we said even when we were silent. He heard how we breathe. Zach was too damned smart.

Vern was waiting to get kicked out. I turned off the faucet, stood staring at the floor tile—linoleum, not tile—and dried my hands on a towel till they were way past dry.

—Sorry, Vern. It's not easy to wipe the past, wash out the smell—

—Lotta earthquakes.

—My hands start shaking. Maybe that's age.

—It's worry. It's Zach—

—That's part of it, but—

—Zach being gone. But he's okay, hon, he's alive.

—I still dream where I come in and see him. Kneeled down, bent over, all white—

And Vern looked into my eyes. I only woke up an hour ago but he saw that my eyes were so damned tired. Start the day tired and finish tired. I knew he wanted to change that, see me fresh again. I needed to see him see that.

—I'm just on edge today. I'm sorry, Vern, I know that— More coffee? No, I'm nuts, I just filled your cup. I was having dreams, I can't remember what.

—You were crying in your sleep.

He said I was crying in my sleep. I didn't think I was crying in my sleep, but I'd have good reason to. Better change the subject.

—So, well, for clothes, I packed three days, but how long you're gonna be gone— I guess go to the laundromat if you need to.

—We're okay for clothes.

—You'd let'em rot and fall off if I know you.

—Whatever.

He tossed away my words like a candy wrapper. He cared but he didn't. Sometimes he made himself so small.

—You just say whatever. This whole business is whatever. Damned if I know what it is, but I guess I'm not supposed to know, so okay, whatever.

And I was sounding exactly like my mother, which made me mad, and the madder I got the more I sounded like my mother. The generations they passeth away but the sour milk stink of it never.

—I'm sorry, Vern. I start boiling up like when you boiled over the rice. That was—

—That was pretty funny—

—You said, *Oh, it swells up!*

We both gave a chuckle to clear out the phlegm. One thing we still had, those moments.

—So you've got the cell phone? And the charger?

—We're not going to Antarctica, hon.

—Well you might as well be. You take him outta school. It must be pretty important to take him outta school in the fall of his senior year and run off to God knows where.

—Las Vegas, dammit. Very simple. Las Vegas. We've been through this, Merna.

—I dunno.

—You keep saying I dunno I dunno—

—Well I dunno.

He sat down. He was set to pick up the stuff and go and now he sat back down. That's what I got for running my mouth: more talk. Why couldn't I let it go? I hung onto stuff like a pup hangs onto a tit. He sat down and there we went for another lap round the track.

—So Merna, look, I know there's a history here, where I'm taking off on the road, there's a history and it's not something I'm proud of, I've said that, I've told you—

—Denver.

—Denver? Is that what you're thinking? Denver?

—You said it, I didn't.

—I don't know where the hell that's coming from. Okay, I deserve it, but that was a lotta years ago, and I mean I'm standing in front of Jesus Christ right now and you gotta give me some credit for that. I wouldn't be taking Zach along if I'm gonna be playing around—

—I never said that.

—Whatever.

I let the *whatever* dangle there. *Dingleberry on the cat's ass,* my dad used to say. I turned to the sink, started the dishes, tried to get *opportunity* out of my mind, and the first thing he said—

—It's an opportunity. That's all it is, an opportunity to consider.

—Opportunity . . .

—Opportunity. Or maybe it's not, maybe it's all b.s.

Zach was out in the car waiting for this clown show to end, and I felt like he heard every word. Not his fault, but I couldn't stand him knowing. Or if he knew. I felt like screaming but suddenly saw I was using soap on the cast iron skillet, and that stopped me dead. I rinsed off, came back to the table, sat down, trying to sound like the loving wife.

—So never mind. I'm just crazy, okay? So it's gonna be hot, but the food should last today. There's no blue ice in the freezer, it was out and I didn't get it back in—

—Plus which the lady is dead.

—Who?

—Year ago. Her son sent me the notice. I didn't talk to him, he just sent me a letter and said she was dead.

—Her son.

—My son. Okay, my son. I said it. If you need me to say it I said it.

—You never told me.

—I told you. You knew that.

—About the letter.

—No, I did.

—I knew about the son, but I didn't know the letter.

I saw the letter. His name was Lannie. Zach had a brother, half-brother, whatever. Vern did that. He told me, and I already knew because the son came to visit, long time ago, and Vern was honest about it. I don't know why it should hurt like it did.

—I'm sorry, Vern, I can't help it. I just get going, and I oughta be supportive, but something gets into me. I know you're trying.

—Trying to make it happen. Trying to make a life.

— Maybe I've just heard *opportunity* once too often.

—I'm not as much of a bastard as I sound like sometimes.

I dried my hands. He still had a need to talk, so at least I could listen. Okay, sit down, listen. Vern plugged on.

—The guy was being friendly. We talked about kids. He's got grown kids. Women talk about their kids, men do it too. He was being friendly, so I talked about Zach, he said bring him along, you'll have a great time, the Caesar's Palace magic acts, Broadway shows, the circus, fantastic. It started out, *Hi, how's it going?* and we talked. This was a casual conversation in a bar.

—What were you drinking?

—Nothing.

—In a bar?

—Club soda. One beer.

—One beer.

—That's what I said.

—And what's the name of this guy?

—Stubblefield.

—Stubblefield.

—Yeh. Darryl Stubblefield. Or Derek. Darren, Dixon. Some funny name.

I don't know why I couldn't let go of the bone. It was like some stupid cop show and I was grilling the suspect and couldn't shut my mouth. I wanted him to go and I was holding him there like a bloated tick.

—Well, you showed me his card, that's all I know, he's got a business card. Everybody's got a business card. Plumber's got a business card. I oughta get a business card if I figure out what's my business.

I knew how I looked. I felt my face making a funny twist, lips flat and tight, little sickles at each corner, meaning I was going to say something totally weird to end it. But I didn't. I couldn't let him walk out the door.

—I don't ask much, Vern, you know that. I just want to get to the point where Zach is on his own and the days of the month run out before the money does. And have you not kicking yourself for once in your life. Because for better or worse we're together. That's what we said.

Vern stared at the floor.

—That's right.

—And I meant it.

—Me too.

I felt like Zach was out there watching us act ridiculous. Vern stared at the floor tile, the linoleum, which needed mopping pretty bad. And I was thinking—why was I thinking it?—how Vern had so much trouble parking the car. He never got it in on a single shot, always backed and filled. Same as he did now. Funny me thinking it. Funny me thinking Zach saw it. Sometimes the kid was so smart I hated him.

—Well, be sure he drinks a lotta water, you too. You got the camera, take some snapshots. I'd like to see Yosemite sometime. And give me a call when you get to Las Vegas, or before. Every day if you can.

—So it's about six hundred miles. Go down the I-5 past Sacramento, then through Yosemite. And Death Valley, Las Vegas, and then we'll see. So I'll call you, we'll keep in touch. And snapshots, sure. He said Tuesday, Wednesday for sure, he's a busy guy, or could be Friday, who knows? But I'm doing the best I can.

—Keep an eye on him, I mean Zach. Take care of him. Just watch out for him, for godsake.

—I need you to trust me.

—I do.

Zach was all that mattered to me in my cramped little world. Of course I loved Vernon. A wife loves her husband, that's the whole point, not to mention my cast iron skillet and memories of my crazy mom. But however much the hate would well up, Zach was stuck in my soul.

Vern and I risked a kiss, a peck anyway, then he picked up the rest of the stuff and went out. I went to the door to wave as they backed out, then to the sink to finish the dishes. I'd have the whole time to myself, a week, maybe more, the time after work at least. I should go out to a movie or play, I liked plays, there must be some plays, or go to a bar, get plastered, hey, why not? But that's wasn't you, Merna, nothing like you. You're the type that stays home and worries the worry lines into your face, so just get started on that.

Still, I guess we were doing okay. More than most.

—6—

Vernon

She waved as I backed out. We never had it easy, but we did okay. Whatever would happen would happen. I drove three blocks down Epply Street and stopped at the stoplight, a FedEx truck in front of us, and there it was again. Second sight.

In flashes and flickers. Like the future, but as if I'd already lived it. A sheep or a goat. Grandpa raised pigs before he got too old, and Grandma had her chickens, which Grandpa hated, wouldn't ever eat chicken, but they never raised sheep or goats. Caught in a tangle of manzanitas or brambles—

—Light's green, Dad.

Some idiot honked, and I lurched through the intersection. A jerk in the thistles, then a dazzle of sun, and I was behind the steering wheel. I should have turned left, but I didn't notice. It felt like Zach was looking at me funny. Off to a merry start.

—Okay, Zach, you can tell your mom is kind of upset, For a start she doesn't want to live the rest of her life in a trailer park. I mean call it Homewood Estates and call it a mobile home, but it's still a trailer park. When I was a kid the people who lived in trailer parks we called trailer trash. I didn't know that meant us.

—Where you going, Dad?

—Freeway.

—You missed the turn.

I mumbled *Shit* but I don't think he heard. I didn't want that kind of language in our house. I tried to focus. There were things on my mind, but they talk about fart and chew gum. I swerved into the Safeway lot to get myself turned around, but an old lady was backing out and I had to stop. Halfway out she saw me and hit her brakes, but she was too far out for me to get around, so I sat there. The car behind me beeped. The old lady lurched back a foot and stopped again. The driver behind leaned on his horn. Some idiot kid, I thought. Old ladies and kids, the world is full of old ladies and kids. She lurched backward another inch and sat there. She wore some kind of hat that looked like a bird's nest on her head. I wanted to kill her.

I took a breath, and this fat blobby sow with a cart full of bags and kids walked right in front of me like the Queen of Sheba. If the cart tipped over, I thought, the kids would scatter like roaches—but no, that was just the way I grew up. I worked with blacks on the base and we got along. The kid behind me started to pull around, but a car came the other direction and everything jammed. I reversed, backed up to the cross lane and managed to turn out the way I came in. I hoped the old bird-nest lady died of a stroke. Not literally.

Traffic was heavy, so I had to wait till a hole opened up and I gunned it into the right-hand lane.

—Dad?

I was going the same direction as before.

—This must be some kinda test, huh, Zach? Test of character?

No problem, just take a right at the light, go around the block and back the other way. We were on Esplanade, which intersected West East Avenue, and that would work. I never could get used to something called *West East*. Hadn't anybody ever asked the point of it? We drove in silence. I flashed Zach a smile. Gayla Krelle always said she liked my smile. Whenever I smiled I thought of Gayla Krelle, though I didn't want to. Some things you can't avoid.

—So I picked up some travel stuff, Zach. It's in the glove compartment if you want to look. Las Vegas means *the meadows,* it says.

The Spanish discovered it in seventeen, eighteen something. This was before the casinos, I guess.

—No kidding.

—I was joking. No, but I was reading that thing. They called it *jornada de muerte*. Journey of death.

—Who called it Las Vegas then? Norwegians?

Whenever I started talking to him, my so-called IQ went down by a hundred points and I sprouted donkey ears. That's what he saw, anyway, and that's what I felt. The kid was always one step ahead. You'd try to pin him down but it was like the old Pin the Tail on the Donkey game and the donkey would always move his butt when you tried to pin the tail.

—Seems like you're feeling okay. Got the sense of humor fired up.

A man in a brown sport jacket was riding a bicycle alongside us. I let him go ahead through the intersection and then took a right to a street where we could probably double back.

—Was that your history teacher?

—Mr. Bingham.

—He rides a bike? Kinda funny for a teacher to ride a bike.

—Around the classroom too.

—What?

—I'm joking, Dad.

I took a right on Weber Street, which would take us back to the freeway entrance. I needed to concentrate, get the damned sheep out of my head. Nobody gets lost in Chico, California.

Here was the God-given chance. My son was sitting beside me, thousands of miles. This was the chance to reach out, to talk, to know each other. When he was little he called me Daddy. That felt so good, but you never know what you really have when you have it. Then came the teenage years and we all go crazy then. I wasn't Daddy any more, I was this pathetic boob sitting there taking up space. A cartoon, like where they draw the President with big ears and a droopy nose. But now we were here, together, a pilgrimage, and it felt like a gift from God. I was with my son. Even if nothing came of it in Vegas, I felt more certain than ever that this was a gift from God.

—Look, Zach, I wanted to say— Your mother and I— She's just in kind of a state, and what she was saying, Denver, that must have been kind of confusing because that was before you were born, and that was a very rough time, so I didn't want you to worry—

—What about Denver?

—When she mentioned Denver.

—When?

Then I realized that Zach was already out the door. He hadn't heard it, and now that I'd brought it up it was lying there between us like a dried-up turd. I flashed on the fat lady at the sideshow when I was nine or ten, and I thought they must inflate her like a balloon to get like that. I was looking for a street to cut over and seeing the fat lady, although what she had to do with anything . . .

—Well, never mind. Denver was a time when we had some trouble, but we got through it and now we're here.

—Dad, I could drive some. There's not a lot of traffic.

—No, this is my treat. I mean I'd be happy to switch off with you driving, you're fine to drive, but your mom gets upset. Plus it's hard for me to get used to you behind the wheel.

—Whatever.

—Look, I know you didn't want to come, so I'm sorry, okay? You got your life, you got your girlfriend, school paper, but I didn't bring it up, I was just talking to this guy, said I had a son, he said bring him along. And I could have said you're in school, but I didn't want to start things off on the wrong foot, because this is a real opportunity, and sometimes you don't ask questions, you just go on faith. That's what built this country was faith—

—Okay.

—And you pick up from your mom that I've gone off on wild goose chases. Speedboats, used cars, then coming out here for the real estate boom, and put all this trust in friends—

—Okay.

—Friends. Jesus said love your enemies, which is damned good advice instead of trusting your friends. So maybe it's a wild goose chase, just all a wild goose chase, but Sergeant Wilson said, he was funny, he said, Well, wild geese know where they're going. All heading in one direction honking like taxicabs—

—Dad?

—What!

I was almost shouting. I do that. I start ranting and raving like Mom did, can't even hear what I say till it's all emptied out. I was only trying to talk to my son. My son sitting there asking—

—Where are we going right now?

And I'd forgotten to look for a turn. Weber Street had veered away from Esplanade and we were going some crazy direction and my words squawking out like Grandma's chickens, just cackle and cackle till I got it all said and I never do. I grunted under my breath. I guess it sounded like cursing. It wasn't a curse, but Zach snickered.

Nothing more got said. In twenty minutes we were back where we should have turned to start with, and then I was on Highway 99 going south. The sheep was gone, the goat, the fat lady, Sergeant Wilson—only a kind of tingly zing in the air, kind of a flicker. We finally started the journey.

—Well, sorry.

—Huh?

—Sorry for the mix-up.

—No problem, Dad.

—Weatherman says we'll stay dry.

Some grade in school they did story time and read fairy tales. It was always a little kid going out to seek his fortune. And then he'd meet an old beggar and give him his sandwich and get some kind of magic dingus, and then he'd kill the dragon and get rich. But now I thought, no, it's not when you meet the dragon: the challenge is at the start, just getting out the door, getting out of the Safeway lot. Once you jump off the cliff, it's gravity takes you the rest of the way.

If I said that to Zach he'd think I was nuts, but I had to say something besides, *I'm sorry I'm sorry I'm sorry.*

—Sometimes I'm thinking I should have stayed in the military. Whole question of right and wrong, it comes down to who told you to do it. I would have saved a lot of mistakes, cause I was young and not thinking about a higher power, just thinking the profit margin on power boats or the wiggle in some woman's butt. And I was never a salesman. The real salesmen, they make you think, *Hey, I just love doing you a favor, giving you this deal.* If the customer senses you're needy, you're dead. But in the military you don't have to sell nothing, you just do what you're told. It's not all about killing, there's more to it than that, but even killing people is easier than selling'em a boat.

—Buy this or die.

—What?

—I'm joking, Dad.

—I'm trying to converse.

Nothing was said for a while, and then I saw we were running on empty. Shell station off there, high priced but we needed gas. Great start, I thought. I filled up, pulled back onto the highway. I could feel Zach's stare.

—What happened in Denver, Dad?

—Look, I better concentrate on the road. I've made too many screw-ups already.

—Well, give me a clue.

—Just drop it.

I tried to think if it was shorter to take the I-5, and then the whole craziness of this trip hit me. I couldn't speak five words to my son that weren't total bullshit, so how would this Las Vegas honcho not see through me the second I walked in the door? How did I even know it wasn't his big joke?

Maybe Zach had seen the letter from Denver about the woman being dead. We got so few letters I never checked any more and Merna just opened the bills. He could have read it then sealed it up. It was just after Zach had broken up with that little Jewish girl—no, that was Luann somebody, this one was Jewish—and they thought his surliness came from that. Maybe the whole thing distracted him the way desperate housewives watched the daytime soaps to see women whose lives were worse than theirs. Why had he asked about Denver? Well, tell your son the truth, dammit, he's old enough to know.

—Denver, well okay, you're old enough to know.

Spin out the whole thing, flush it, be honest. He already thinks you're a screw-up, so you can't make it any worse. What's that sign? Road construction. Okay, go ahead and say it. It's all in the past, you can't make it worse. I opened my mouth without knowing what crap would come out.

—Denver, okay. We had some trouble. I was kinda nuts, and I was drinking some, not being the best husband, I guess, I— So we had some trouble and almost broke up for a while and then— Then we got back together. That was it.

I glanced at Zach. He gave me an *are-you-kidding?* look and stared at the road ahead.

—Look, Zach, there's no point in dredging up the gory details, but what's important is the future. You can't get stuck in the past, you look ahead. That's what this country's all about, it's—

He was thinking, *Sure, Dad.* He had this thirst, we all do, for honesty. We think it'll be like a big long glug of cold beer when you're really sweating, and if two people, married couple or father and son or even just buddies, could say what's true, what they've done, how they feel, what they're so damned ashamed of, what they really want in the world— But you can't. Not in a million years. You just dance around it, eyes tight shut.

Zach was stone silent. Where were we? Yuba City, or maybe we weren't there yet. Freeways all go from nowhere to nowhere. The sky was overcast. It must be near Halloween. I hadn't paid any attention to Halloween for years. They don't trick or treat in the trailer park, or at least they don't come to us. And now here I was taking my son out on trick or treat.

No, it was way past Halloween. This was November. Time flies. Focus on driving. Okay, so follow 99 South and all decisions come later. We passed through a cut in a ridge that looked like saw teeth and drove past a town that just stretched on. Towns used to have edges. They'd talk about the edge of town—people lived on the edge of town, you drove out to the edge of town—but now they just stretch on. Shopping malls, fast food, warehouses, car lots, office strips where the blinds are down, what they're doing in there—

My mind was playing blind man's buff. That's life: getting spun in all directions and then grope around while everyone's laughing and dodging out of the way. I had to stop thinking. Roads were coming into the freeway, not a freeway yet, you could turn off and stop for— I was doing it again. My brain was squawking like chickens. *Say something, talk, find words—*

—Look. Orchards. What are they, I wonder?

—Trees.

—We should look up what they grow here. You could google it. We ought to know stuff like that.

—Okay.

—Did you see that sign back there, little town, there was a sign for tuxedo rentals? Who'd wear a tux in a town like that? And two car-washes. You wouldn't think there'd be enough cars to keep it going.

—Maybe they wash horses too. Keep'em shiny.

I laughed. Sometimes Zach came up with funny stuff when it wasn't choked out by the brambles. But it never felt like his jokes made him happy. You didn't know whether to laugh or spit out the bitters. Something took hold and he clenched his teeth to stay sane. Or stay nuts so people would think he was sane. Maybe he picked it up from me.

Another shopping mall and more fields, then down to two lanes. When did that happen? Dry fields. How did they get so dry? It's all green and then death sets in. The only guys who survived in the Bible were the ones that got a special deal. It must have been Pastor Finch who asked it, weird for him: what was so special about Abraham? All these clueless tribes wandering in the desert, just looking to survive, and God picks this guy out of the hat. But he still had to pass the test.

A fruit stand was coming up. I always wanted to stop at fruit stands and never did. We went to Yellowstone once, and I'd said to Merna we should take our time and stop at things and really get the feel of the country, this great land. And then I drove hell for leather and came back two days early. That was the feel of this great land. You're either two days early or a lifetime late.

But we were finally on our way. It was going to be good, I kept telling myself. The little kid in the fairy tale, he gets out the door, he stumbles around, but he gets out of town and that's the hardest part. And he's got his sandwich ready to give away to the beggar. All I had to do now was follow the road. I could see hills in the distance. Mountains?

—Can you see if those are mountains? With snow on top? Or just clouds. Maybe just clouds.

The road would take us there, and my son beside me. *Our hearts shall rejoice*, it says. I don't remember where, but it's in the Bible. Or it better be.

—Dad?

—Huh?

—Did you ever take my brother on a trip?

—What brother?

—The one we never talk about.

That had to come up. I knew it had to. It's the nature of sons to google the sins of their fathers. I kept my mouth shut.

What I always forget is I love him. The sarcasm, the smarty-mouth jokes, it's the bumper cars at the carnival banging each other, jarring, bonking, and we swerve around to bang each other again, and I forget. I forget that first moment I saw him, that tiny creature sucking tittie that would try to grow up a man. Trying like I do. I'd dreamt I was talking and he was hearing me. I was being heard. *The love and respect of my wife and my son*—that's what I said I wanted and that's what this trip was about. If I could find the words.

Akedah means the binding, according to Pastor Finch. Binding the son to the rock. How did that fly into the head? I kept going off track. Somewhere I missed the trapeze and I'm falling and falling and falling.

—7—

Zach

The moment he opens the door and flips on the overhead light, Dad starts with the lamentations.

—Look at that. Can you believe this is what you pay seventy bucks for? It's a barracks. Seventy bucks to sleep in a bed. You feel like you'd better stay awake all night just to get your money's worth.

Motels for him were one of our grievous social ills. Spending bucks just to sleep seemed like paying to breathe air. There should be places to sack out, he once said, not expecting anyone to listen. Not for the homeless—you didn't want to nap where some bum had sluffed off his lice—but people should be able to sleep without paying through the nose. We usually did our best to not talk politics.

I follow him through the door with a paper sack and a six-pack of beer, then pull the door shut and set the sack on the floor.

—Four motels.

—What?

—I think there's gonna be four motels. This is number one.

—What are you talking about?

—I just said that for effect.

Most of what I say, I've noticed, I say for effect. I try to twist my grimace into the shape of a smile. Dad flips on a bedside lamp—maybe to use up some of the power he's paid for—then tosses his suitcase onto one of the double beds. He hears me mumble—

—Where do you want the six-pack?

—No fridge of course. Some places have little fridges, they used to have, but now they're all run by Hindus or Muslims, those kinds. By the sink, I guess. See that clerk at the Quik-Stop, old shriveled pig looking over at you when I'm buying the beer? Thinks I'm corrupting a minor. I felt like saying, *It's my son for chrissake!* None of her business.

The corruptible minor sets the six-pack by the bathroom sink and parks himself on a bed staring at the blank TV. One of those old fat monitors that weigh a ton.

—The clicker's there on the night table, Zach. Turn it on if you want. You need the bathroom first? We pay that much we better use it all we can.

Strange: we both say funny things, but we almost never laugh. I keep staring at the screen. Dad goes into the bathroom. When he comes out, his enigmatic son is still absorbed in watching nothing.

—Hey, it's a long day, Zach. We better eat what your mother packed, fried chicken, I guess, and a couple baked potatoes. And if you'd like a beer, well, it's a special occasion, that's okay, and then you oughta do your homework cause I promised your mom.

—Let me see how this turns out.

—What?

—Reality show, nothing happens. I'm joking.

I get up and start unpacking the paper sack: two tuppers of fried chicken and baked potatoes in foil wrap and raw carrots. Dad pulls two cans from the six-pack.

—Beer?

The underage kid ignores the offer but takes a chicken breast, drumstick, and cold potato onto a paper plate and then stands like a pillar of salt. The father pops a tab, picks out his food, and stands by the dresser eating. Both of us stand ready. This feels so weird. What am I doing here? *Bring along your son.* So I've been brought along, eating a drumstick.

—And then homework, okay? Your mom got all your assignments, which I never thought of, but she's always kept us afloat. She said you're not doing so good in history, so be sure to do your history.

—There isn't much, Dad. Just one week. God created the world a week ago.

—I'm serious.

—No, but I remember when I was little they said God created the world in a week, and I thought they meant last week.

I can tell he doesn't know how to react. It's not right to joke like that, but still he can't quite conceal that he thinks it's pretty funny.

—That's pretty good. I mean what goes through a kid's head.

—It was confusing, because I remembered my birthday was more than a week before, so how could I be born in Denver if Denver didn't exist?

—Well, I'm not to blame for everything.

Neither of us had any idea why he said that. I could only feel his pain and clench myself against it. I pretended not to hear it, but the silence between us shivered, like being shaken very gently the way Mom jiggled me to wake up when I overslept. I wonder if Dad felt the shiver.

—Want to check what's on TV?

Right, Dad: tell your kid to do his homework and then say check the TV. I hated when Dad said stupid stuff, but hated even more that he heard himself say it. I hated having empathy with torment. Now he opens his suitcase to unpack his toothbrush and shaving stuff. He should hang up his suit to keep it from getting wrinkled, but then he'd have to fold it, and he can't fold it as well as Mom did, so he shuts the suitcase. His voice goes all chirpy.

—Didn't you bring your suitcase in?

—My stuff's in the zipper thing.

—You don't need a change of clothes?

I don't return the ball, just keep watching the blankness of reality. Dad sips his beer, resisting the urge to chug it.

—Well, I wish we'd got farther. I thought we'd be clear the other side of Yosemite by now, but starting late and then that jog around

Sacramento, and Chico before that, I don't know how we got screwed up so much. These maps you can't trust any more, and the signs, you follow the signs you're worse off than if you just closed your eyes tight shut and stepped on the gas.

—You turned on I-80 was the problem.

—Well, or I could have gone straight down the I-5 or the 99, either one, and then cut over, but it's all a big tangle, they just spend your tax dollars on roads to nowhere. We could have been clear the other side of Yosemite.

Dad takes his shaving stuff into the bathroom. I pick up the remote, gird up my courage, and click it. The TV belches and flashes on.

Click click click click click click. Little cartoon animals are speaking Spanish. A guy throws a ball through a hoop. Wendy's is putting a special cheese on its burger. The weatherman jokes about rain. Women should talk to their doctor about something that's hard to pronounce. A plumber wins $2,000. A funnyman tries to fix a squirt flower but squirts himself. Tonya sits with shadows across her face and a dark figure says *Hi Tonya* and she says *I know you.*

I sit watching the cadavers—a world overrun by hyperactive designer zombies who laugh like car alarms and grin like razor blades. End of the show and they wave goodbye come back tomorrow and let us pretend we love you. I click it off.

—Well Dad, anyway we're here.

—What?

—I said we're here.

—Hold on.

He appears at the bathroom door.

—What'd you say?

—We're here.

—You want to check the TV?

He comes to the nightstand and picks up the remote and starts his own channel-surfing: news weather cartoons cartoons basketball car chases explosions baseball talking heads soccer a crooner a screamer a monster the shopping channel *America's Got Talent*—

—Pathetic.

He mutes the sound and continues surfing the images that dance and blossom and die to frenzied mute applause.

—Same stuff, I guess.

—Well, Dad, see: they run the same show over and over and we forget we saw it, but it gives us a sense of security, like the world will never change. It'll stay as stupid as it always was.

He clicks it off. He's going to say it: *You've got your mother's smart mouth. She's got a heart of gold but her words can cut like a whip. There are comics who do that and people laugh. Maybe you'll be a comic. Comics have a dark side, but they make lots of money.* Dad's said it more than once and he's about to say it again . . . but he doesn't. There's a lot that he doesn't say.

He's watching his son take a couple of carrot sticks from the sack and another piece of chicken. He's about to say something about carrot sticks but we can't drive a thousand miles talking about carrot sticks. *We're father and son*, he'd say, and by now it's too late.

—Well, but TV, I guess the positive side is we all see the same stuff so we've all got something in common. There's kind of a, whatta you call it, culture? world view? I guess the downside is it's pretty stupid. They all sound like they're talking to five-year-olds. *In the news tonight, boys and girls*, or *What the Broncos need if they're gonna win is to score more points.*

—You sound like me, Dad. You call me cynical.

—But there's the history channel, we never look at that, you might look at that for the history.

—Boom boom.

—What?

—Boom boom bam wham boomity bam. That's history. I already know it. We're the greatest country and we won all the wars except the ones we lost and that's why we're number one.

—I don't like that kinda talk, you know that.

—Sorry.

—Course, history— I mean when I was in school there was less.

—Not so many Crusades, I guess.

—That's funny.

—So laugh. Or titter, giggle, guffaw, whatever.

—Well, they teach George Washington, Napoleon, that stuff. But I'd start thinking if the general stepped in a pile of horse manure. With all those horses, they must have. That's the kind of thing ran through my head. I could never concentrate.

—That's history.

In our talk between father and son, at least we agree on the horse manure. He pops the other beer, then sits on his bed, takes a bite of his stuffed potato. He looks at it more closely. Bacon bits.

—She put bacon in here.

He puts it down and picks up his chicken drumstick. *Bacon bits.* Mom probably thought he'd like it. They try. They try so hard it hurts. I'd like to think I would do better, but if I ever got into Rebecca's pants, would we attain a mystic communion or would I just complain about bacon bits?

Dad looks around. This whole time he's never looked at the room, just opened the door and spouted complaints about Hindus and Muslims and how much it cost. Now he sees it. Brown curtains and knotty pine walls. Reading lights on the bedside stands as if he wanted to read. Table tent on the writing desk with an ad for a drooling burger.

We have the same eyes. We're so different and so alike. What I hate in him I hate in me. Would that qualify as empathy? What do you call it if you hate their pain but you hate feeling it?

But the drive down from Chico with sun through the trees was a great way to start the day. And the wind making waves in the heavy grass and hills like the haunches of lions or big bumpy dogs just lying there spotted with green and catching the sun. No buildings for miles and miles. We both saw it. We have the same eyes.

—It was a pretty nice drive. Morning sun.

—Yes, Dad, it was. Very much so. Right on.

—I can't say a thing without you starting to—

—No, I agree, it was beautiful. Yes. Morning sun is great in the morning.

I take a bite of my baked potato and Dad looks up from his drumstick and sees I don't mind the bacon bits. I get up and take two books from the backpack I left at the door, then pull the single chair to the desk and open a book and stare.

—Only you better finish your dinner.

I get up to fetch my paper plate from the nightstand. Back at the desk I flip through the pages to find my place. History never goes up to the present day, which means there's no evidence that we still exist.

—So we're in the Middle Ages now. Kinda murky in here.

There is silence in Heaven for the space of a minute or two. Dad takes a swig of his beer and laughs.

—My uncle called his heart the old banger.

—Is that gonna be on the test?

—Dunno why I thought of that. Just had a flash.

He clicks on the TV again. Some political thing. To Dad, they just want to get your vote, and he doesn't vote. He switches channels. It blares more goofiness.

—You want me to do my history?

—I'll shut up.

—I wasn't saying shut up, Dad, I was asking.

He clicks it off and stares at a water stain on the ceiling, the shape of an angel or maybe a dragon. Some lady had seen the face of Jesus in her pizza, got her name in the paper for that. Jesus with mushrooms and pepperoni, no knowing if she ate it. I crunch a carrot stick and flip my pages.

—Funny your history teacher's riding a bike.

—People ride bikes.

—In a suit?

—Sport jacket.

—What kind of stuff does he talk about?

—Reality.

—I didn't know they taught that.

—You're cynical, Dad.

Dad's as gloomy as I am, but he's scared to encourage it in his son. He sits on the edge of the bed trying to sip his beer in moderation.

He studies the TV remote in his hand as if deciphering code, then puts it down and looks around for something.

—I better make a call. He said call any time even if it's late. I'd call your mother too, only she's probably in bed by now. But tomorrow's another day.

—That seems kind of obvious. We'd be surprised if it wasn't.

He jerks around to look at me. Just an off-hand joke, but I can taste his spurt of bile. I know that he hates his spasms of anger. His voice goes nearly too flat to hear.

—It's not so obvious, dammit. It means look to the future. You don't have to be stuck in the past and all the stupid bullshit. It means start fresh.

—Then why am I doing history?

No reply to that. Dad finds the cell phone under the paper sack and sits on the bed again. He chugs his last swallow of beer and stares at the phone, then gets up to get another can and sees me watching him.

—Sure you don't want to split one?

—Don't let me stop you, Dad.

He pops a can and holds it out to me, but I pat my history book with all due piety.

—Sorry, but we're studying Prohibition.

In fact I'd like some beer but I can't play the game. Dad stands a moment, not sure if he's being mocked, then sits on the bed and takes a swig. I can't restrain a dry chuckle.

—We're not really. I just said that. In actual fact we're launching the Crusades. *Actual fact.* People say that but what other kind is there?

—Maybe you'll be on the Late Show some day.

Dad is clearly tired of the jokes. So am I. He starts to punch the cell phone then waggles it and puts it down on the nightstand.

—No, call him in the morning. We're all past working hours.

He stands up and starts to take off his shirt humming something from *Sergeant Pepper*. I remember his telling me how his older cousin Johnny turned him on to the Beatles. He liked the bounciness and the songs that didn't make any sense, although Johnny said they had hidden meanings. He'd asked what were the hidden meanings, but Johnny wouldn't say. There were always hidden meanings and people who said they knew, but they'd never say. Dad seemed always to wonder if there really were, and how do you get on the inside track?

—So, Zach, I think I'm gonna sign off. Start about seven o'clock? Up early, say six? Hey, look at that. We each got a bed of our own, double beds, that's luxury.

I close my history book and shut off the desk lamp. We both strip down to underwear and pull back the bedclothes. He fumbles with his travel alarm to set the time, takes a final swig, then sets his third beer can on the nightstand and kneels down by his bed.

—My knees feel funny. I need to stop now and then to walk around the car. You want to join me? I mean to pray? Not saying you have to.

He's not saying I have to. Which means, *No problem, Zach, if you want to stab me to the heart. I'm used to it.*

He folds his hands and bows his head. His mind is blank but he has to pretend to talk to God. He sounds fake when he tries to pray out loud, but he does his best to squeeze it out. I stand watching him.

—Dear Lord, we thank you for your blessings and this great opportunity, which we hope is gonna work out. And if it doesn't . . .

He trails off. Across the room, I kneel down by my bed, fold my hands, keep my eyes on my dad. He catches my stare, then bows his head again and gropes for words.

—But the drive down here and over across, we got lost but those hills were so beautiful, like lions, and the climb up the mountains, little roads winding back around, and tomorrow we'll see Yosemite, all God's creation, and on into the future, whatever happens . . .

—Whatever happens.

The father looks up at his son. Is the kid praying or mocking? But I catch it in his eyes: at least this kid is alive. No matter how much smarty-mouth snark at least I'm alive. Amazing what you can see in the eyes. But he sees me grinning a little grin and his anger comes up like vomit.

—I don't know where you get this *brother* stuff, Zach, goddammit.

—You talking to me or to God?

—There's no brother, and that whole Denver thing— I'm not some kind of stupid asshole. If you've got a stupid asshole for a dad, what does that make you?

—In the name of Christ Jesus, amen.

—You want to go home? We both say this is all stupid, go home? I've made plenty mistakes and maybe this is one more. We forget the whole fucking thing, we go home.

He's ridiculous, on his knees yelling, and he knows it, and I'm a heartless prick for making him do it, and I know it too. He starts to get up.

—No, Dad. I like being here. Being together.

He gets up and crawls into bed without a word. After a while I pull myself up and crawl into the other bed and turn out the light.

—Night, Dad.

—Night.

We settle. Low hum from the heating vent and the broom-whisks of passing traffic. He's trying to fade into the dark where he can't be seen. He draws a deep breath.

—Tell you one thing, Zach. I don't believe that stuff about Original Sin. We make it up as we go along. We do it all to ourselves.

He has no idea why he said that but it sounds like something his son would like his father to say. We're bound together like Siamese twins. The original ones I read about, Chang and Eng with a wad of gristle between them. They shared a liver, married, had a ton of kids, which gave me heavy fantasies. Dad and I didn't go that far, but I feel the gristle between us.

I ought to be dumb. They say the most loving kids are the mentally challenged—kids with Downs or something. They just cuddle up. Otherwise, we want to hate our dads but be proud of them. To be free but have breakfast every day. To say the meanest things and still be loved. My dad tries to feel thankful, tries to thank God that he's got a son, but I've always known in my gut that he never wanted kids.

Never.

—8—

Vernon

I woke ten minutes before what I'd set the alarm, reached to shut it off, then turned over and went back to sleep. Blurry mouth murmuring, grinning—someone was in my head. The time we got burgled, they only took the TV and a pin of Merna's that she had from her mom, but we felt the presence for weeks. They were still in the rooms. You could feel the blur.

—Dad? You awake? Dad?

My eyes opened into the sun. I grabbed at the dream, but it slipped out the door like Merna's cat, streaking out into traffic. Dreams and cats, squashed flat.

—Huh?

—You wanted to leave at seven. It's way past seven.

—Damned alarm . . .

—You turned it off.

—When?

—It's eight-thirty.

—Why didn't you wake me up?

—You were asleep.

Weird logic. He wasn't the genius he thought he was. I pulled myself up, reached for my clothes, shoved my foot into an inside-out pants leg, took a deep breath, straightened out the pants. Zach was already dressed and staring at the blank TV. I stumbled to the bathroom, somebody still in my head that I couldn't see, but pissing did the trick. It was me that was pissing, the one and only.

When I came out, Zach had neatened the covers on both beds. Like covering tracks in that story where they're pursued by wolves, but how to outrun the smell? My mind was scuttering like Grandma's chickens. Dreams dug in like ticks, and if you pulled you'd leave the head. I rubbed my face to clear my brain.

Nothing left to pack. Zach had already stowed the food from the night before and left the suitcase open for my kit. I fetched it from the bathroom, then realized I hadn't shaved, but packed it anyway. I said we better get breakfast, a place I saw, greasy spoon.

—*One greasy spoon, please, and coffee.*

—You're starting up early today.

But I didn't know if he said it. I might have just thought it. Lots of times he said funny stuff, but I couldn't ever laugh. It was like chigger bites, like his elbow was jabbing. Someone in my head: the mouth was a blur.

Start off the day like that, there's no place to go but up. I remembered seeing a rundown diner back a block or so, like in the movie once about a bus that stopped at a diner, and lots of characters and a sweet young waitress with a face like a valentine. We walked over there, across a couple of parking lots, and it turned out to be some franchise place called Buddy's. There wasn't any Buddy, just a signboard with a cartoon Buddy, a smile and a big fat ass. Nothing like the movie.

More knotty pine wallboard with tinsel draped over the tops of the windows and little splurges of plastic poinsettias on the sills. A naked Christmas tree in the corner they must be getting set to trim. A couple of farmers in one corner at the back, hunched like fireplugs over their ham and eggs—ratty little guy in a railroad hat and a burly red-faced lump in a baseball cap. And the waitress was no valentine—saggy chops and built like a bag of potatoes, name tag, *Hi, I'm Frieda!* But at least she was friendly.

—What'll it be, gentlemen?

We ordered. She wrote a while on her pad like she was taking a spelling quiz. And she was a talker.

—You all on vacation? Yosemite?

—Nope, business. Las Vegas. My son here's along for the ride.

—Las Vegas, my sister goes there. She and her husband, they like to play the, whatcha call it, blackjack? I think they always lose. They don't say, but they always come back kinda grim. I'll settle for Yosemite.

—Well, we're just driving through. Heading on to Las Vegas.

—Driving through? Well, you know Tioga Pass is closed.

—What's that?

—Tioga Pass. East on the 120.

—What, you can't get into a national park?

—No problem getting in, you just can't get out the other side. I mean it's snowed the last two days. 120 is closed, 104, Highway 4, you'd have to make a horseshoe up and across 88, then see if Monitor Pass is open. If it's not then you take a little diagonal up to Minden, hit the 395. You might need chains, though.

—Chains? Hell, I haven't had chains since Denver.

—Well, you might be okay. Tune 1620 on the radio, they'll tell you. And you said coffee?

I nodded. The waitress walked off and I could tell she felt her arthritis set in. I remembered when Merna was on her feet all day and liked it when I rubbed her calves. All these things were coming back, the way they say your whole life flashes. Zach said he didn't wake me up because I was asleep, or maybe he didn't say it. Try to work that one out. Now he was fiddling with the salt shaker.

—Hey, don't fiddle with that.

A young couple, thirties maybe, professionals they looked like, came in and sat in a booth. The guy was joking and she was smiling at him. She looked like she maybe loved him, even though he had this thin little chin beard and already going bald. He must be into computers, or advertising maybe. That'd be a good job, just sit there and think of slogans all day. Probably from San Francisco, probably made good money. They'd stay in a fancy hotel in Yosemite, if there was a fancy hotel, and hike around, and they wouldn't care if it snowed, they'd nuzzle each other in bed—

My brain was working funny again. Why was the cook wearing a stocking cap? I could see him through the service window: old black guy in a bright green stocking cap. Black guys in green stocking caps cooking pancakes, c'mon. But he looked busy. He wasn't lounging around. It's a stereotype that all black guys lounge around. I know that much at least. I can't be accused of that.

How long did it take to do pancakes? Zach was still fiddling with the shaker, tapping it on the table. He shouldn't be doing that, but I couldn't think of a reason to tell him why not. I gave a chuckle, startled myself. He looked up.

—No, I was remembering— Nothing, just way back, I'm having funny— I'm not woke up yet.

—So Dad, couldn't we go around Yosemite to the south?

— But why that ever came to mind— On the news I remember it said, back when they hit the World Trade Towers—

—Cause Death Valley is to the south, so there's no point in going north if—

—No, listen. On the news they said, before the airplanes hit, they said that all the passengers said a prayer, even some of the terrorists joined'em, said a prayer. And that was on the news, I distinctly remember, and I thought, hey wow, that's weird but it's inspirational that even— But then I didn't hear it any more. And then I thought, hold on, okay, how does anyone know that? If they're all dead, so who'd be alive to tell it? It's crap, it's total— They just say what they think you want to hear. I mean this was actually on the news.

I heard myself talking, but the words were from somebody else. Something inside. The same blurry mouth. I didn't remember hearing that on the news, but how else could it be in my head?

—You don't have to entertain me, Dad. I already committed suicide.

—Dammit, you know this could be a pretty great trip depending on your attitude.

—I won't do it again.

—What?

—Kill myself.

—That's not something to joke about!

I spoke louder than I wanted to, but this damned kid— I said it more quietly.

—That's not something to joke about.

—Sorry.

—I'm trying to talk to you.

—Don't let me stop you, Dad.

He was trying to get to me. Just to prove he was smart? I watched the computer guy and his wife, who were holding hands. Or maybe she wasn't his wife. Maybe it was like Denver, where Gayla Krelle wanted to go out to restaurants, which was natural, but I felt creepy every time, that someone might see us. Not that I was big news in Denver, but like that guy, what if I knew him? What if he felt so goddamned ashamed of what he was doing? I couldn't look.

The waitress brought us two platters of pancakes and bacon, served with a smile. People loom up and fill holes in the air.

—Oop, sorry, I'll get your coffee. We're shorthanded today.

She hobbled away. How many miles did she walk every day? Zach stared at his stack, then opened his butter pats and spread them with great precision. I buttered my pancakes and poured on more maple syrup than I wanted, but the syrup caught glittery sunlight. I saw shapes like raccoons in the glitter. Raccoons had paws with fingers—they looked like fingers almost—and the waitress came with our coffee. I wondered if that was her name. Lots of women were changing their names, but probably not to *Frieda*.

—Here you are. Creamer's there, sugar if you want. So you better come back and take some time in Yosemite, hike up to the falls. I wish I got over there more. It's hard when you're so close, you think, well, I'll do it one of these days, and then you never do.

—Well, we'll take a rain check. Have to get to Las Vegas.

—Well, that's a ways. My sister and her husband, they always fly, find some special deal, but then they come back broke—

Zach had his mouth full of pancake, but you could tell he just had to say something smart—

—No, we've got a big business deal. Military hardware.

—Zach—

—Clothes pins. They shoot rubber bands.

Dead silence over the face of the pancakes. I tried to hold onto a thread.

—He's joking. I told him how we used to do that in school.

I chuckled, gestured with my fork. Zach grinned a happy clown grin with eyebrows high. The waitress nodded, put the check on the table without much of a smile.

—Well, I guess we gotta support the military, with all the suicide bombers—

—Yeh, well, I was in the Air Force.

—What did you fly?

—Different stuff.

I glanced at Zach, but he was into his pancakes.

—You can pay at the register there.

She hobbled away a little faster than before. Zach finished his pancakes in great mouthfuls. He knew what his limits were with his mom, but with me he had to see how far he could go. I left the rest of my breakfast, picked up the check.

—Dad, you better finish, you're a growing boy.

I stood up too fast. Bright fog. Zach was saying something about going south. I went to pay the check. A little skinny cashier, pinched-in face, Filipino maybe, rang it up, while I watched the yuppie types pecking away at their mushroom omelets and smiling smiling smiling. A sign at the register—*Howdy, Y'all!*—and a donation jar for Rollie "Buck" Lewis, but you couldn't tell what was so wrong with Rollie that made him worth your dollar. Zach was waiting at the door. The fake poinsettias glittered to make sure you knew they were fake. It still felt like a dream.

We walked back across the parking lot. A big semi was parked across half a dozen spaces, chugging out exhaust. On the side it said WALMART, and I thought of going up and joking with the driver,

Hey, bro, we both work for the same dudes, but I thought better. He
might not like to have his nose rubbed in it. Do unto others, they say,
or don't do, depending. Then we were back in the room.

—I better make that call.

—Whatever.

I picked up the cell phone, poked it, then poked off. No reason
why, except I was still off balance. Only one beer last night. Or the
same one several times.

—Too early to call.

We loaded out stuff to the car, and I walked up to the office
and left the key. When I got back, Zach was sitting in the driver's
seat. I stood there, looked down at the concrete, waited. Finally he
shrugged, opened the door, got out, went around to the passenger
side. We got in, belted up. I fumbled and found the sun glasses, put
them on. I wasn't seeing the mouth.

I thought to say, *Hey, Zach, thanks, but—* But I didn't. Lots of
things I thought to say and didn't. You learn from experience. Open
up, say that you're driving through Yosemite, and some wrinkled
old biddie tells you you can't. And Merna could count all the times I
came home with promises, plans, and total lies. *This is gonna change
things, honey, I promise. This is one hundred percent guaranteed.* I
couldn't stand the sound of my own voice croaking out promises
like a country music song. But I believed what I heard myself say. I
believed my own bullshit, which took some doing, though I'm not
the only guy in the world with a talent for that.

I started the car, pulled out to skirt around the iced-up clog of
Yosemite. We drove back west out of Groveland on the 120—same
curving road, but brighter, sharper in the morning sun—and Chinese
Camp, which was historical, supposedly, but basically just a bunch of
old broken-down shacks. Then we hit the 49 North. Zach had said
something about heading south, but I'd already checked the directions for north, and on the map it seemed like we'd still be driving
through green stuff around Yosemite, unless they shut off the scenery
right at the edge of the park. We could still do snapshots for Merna.
She was back there praying for us, I knew. I put my trust in that.

One thing I remembered from Reverend Bud: things that start out bad don't have to stay that way. Safeway parking jam and missing the turns, Yosemite, plastic poinsettias, all the flailings and fumbles— that didn't mean you'd flunked the test. You just had to keep the vision. Hold to the course. Decide to go north, so dammit, go north.

At Jackson we hit the 88 and turned east. Locked for hours behind a steering wheel, you start to wonder. You're in the driver's seat, you're in control, but the road is taking you where it wants to go. Turn this way, that way, but you're still on a track that was laid out long ago.

Long ago. It was all set in motion way before you were even a kid. Trace it back. *Your dad took off*, your mom said, *You're the man of the house now, Vernon*, and you really believed it. Being five years old, you had no way of knowing. She had to get the furnace fixed, and you knew you ought to do it instead of her, you were the man of the house, but you didn't know how. Some day you'd be grown up, you'd have to get the furnace fixed, and in kindergarten they only taught you to finger-paint. Nowadays Merna took care of that stuff. And I never figured what it meant to have white spots under the fingernails.

Somebody said how the moving finger writes. I think we read that in school. Although what it meant—

Not a lot of scenery, just trees. We drove through flatland, then rolling hills, then descended into the mountains. *Descended*: the stretch of the road went lower and lower, with rock walls looming up, and the lower you went the higher the walls. I thought I should tell Zach to take snapshots out the window, but I was too far deep in my head. *You're the man of the house now.* You're left with that commandment all your life, knowing you'll never measure up. You're not a bum. You can work, you can slave, you can bang your head on the wall. You spend your life paying your dues, but they never let you into the club.

My buddy Clyde came to mind. He told about a guy he knew who had a German shepherd, this place in the hills. One time the dog barked at a squirrel, heard his own bark echo back and thought it was some damn dog barking at him, so he barked back at his echo which barked back at him, and it never stopped. After two days the guy had to have him put down. I think Clyde made it up, but it had the ring of truth.

The 88 got us across the northern stretch. Monitor Pass was closed, so we took the diagonal to Minden, hit the 395 and headed southeast. It was only then it occurred to me what Zach was trying to tell me: we could have gone around Yosemite to the south.

I saw the blurry mouth again.

—9—

Stubblefield

Vern heard some black guy on TV talk about *white privilege*. That seemed to him like a great idea: he definitely wanted some of that. Would you need to fill out a form? Could you do it online? How long would it take?

But why torment myself with Vernon McGurren when five minutes of talking with him was like eating hair? Vern never took a breath that wasn't stale air. You wanted to smash his face just to let in a breeze. My motive? So many options. I might be a sociopath sodomized as an infant by a jolly uncle. I might be an ex-Marine haunted by having never killed a soul. I might be a metaphor like Melville's white whale whose power was in its mystery. I might be the herpes virus. I might be only a ring tone.

And indeed I might be the Lord God of Hosts who's lost prestige and needs to prove he still has what it takes. Let's face the question directly. Am I God? And if I am do I exist? Though the better question might be: who creates God? I'd say the consumer. If you're in the market for a god just pick one out of the catalog and he's shipped next-day-delivery. Squeeze any guy hard enough and a god pops out.

But I bear scant resemblance to a higher power. I'm hedged in by my business card. I'm five-eight, one seventy-five, with sandy hair going bald and a roundish face the texture of processed ham. I piss five or six times a day in modest amounts as we all hope to do till the plumbing fails. Right now I scan my office and it looks solid. Cedar desk, upholstered leather chair, a view from the twenty-third floor to the skyline and mountains. Two butt-ugly de Koonings over the liquor cabinet. I'm surrounded by objective evidence that I'm no fake. I do exist no matter how much I regret it.

All I have in common with God is a lack of motive. Some kid opens fire on his classmates and people squeal *Why oh why?* But when Job gets squashed and asks for an explanation then God gets highly offended: *Who are you to question the whirlwind?* Fact is the old bastard had not a clue why he did it except to prove that he could. Or that he was hooked on human despair: it got him high. That's what's meant by a higher power.

If Vern had a pot to piss in he'd be the perfect mark for a scam. Except that the grifter's classic ploy—engaging the mark's own greed with the prospect of something for nothing—would be problematic with Vern. He could never imagine getting something for nothing: his expectation was flat zilch nothing ever.

Yet his thirst extended way beyond money. A honeybee stings and rips out its wee yellow gut for the greater good of the hive. With Vern it wasn't he wanted something he didn't deserve. He just wanted that extra edge. What guy who pays his rent and most of his taxes doesn't deserve a little advantage? Course if we all got that extra edge then it wouldn't be extra any more and we'd just get plopped in the pot with all the other stewed roosters.

Vern heard a still small voice inside him that wasn't him. The little voice knew all that his heart desired and like God that little rascal had a voracious need to torture his chosen people. To make'em really feel it. I was so far inside the dude I could hear his gut rumble and think it was me. I could feel his yearning: that itch that starts in the hard-up groin when you get your first woodie but twenty years later it's an itch in your hard-up bank account.

I was the victim of Vern McGurren. I was addicted. I was locked in a cell inside him thinking *What the fuck!* No more pleasant for him: imagine someone squeezing your heart and hissing *There is a me inside you.* So deep that I could say his prayers before he said them. I could write his will. I could wipe his ass and check for blood. I was almost him.

I waited and he called. Two rings, a buzz, connect. He likely heard my voice distant, tinny, like Bugs Bunny almost.

—Yes?

—Hi, yeh, Mr. Stubblefield, Vern McGurren. You asked me to call, I hope it's not too early, but you said anytime. So this is—

—Anytime.

—Right, so you asked me to let you know when we're coming in, so I don't know, we're just this side of Yosemite, but we have to take a loop up around because there's snow, I guess, in the mountains, so maybe tomorrow or day after tomorrow. We'll be starting up early, but it's probably another day—

—You're where?

—Yosemite.

—Yosemite. Fine.

—Fine, yeh. But so we might make it by the end of tomorrow, or—

—So that's what you'll do.

—So you asked me to keep you posted—

—Right, Vern, so I'm posted. I'm off to DC on the redeye for a hearing at the FCC where some commissioners are trying to think for themselves. And then back to Vegas, so next day say about two in the afternoon, call my personal secretary, Wendall, extension 242. Meantime, keep the faith.

—Two o'clock?

—I need to repeat myself?

—Sorry.

—You bring your son?

—Oh yeh, he's here, he's taking some time outta school, I mean this is a big deal for him. But he's doing his homework, although I think kids learn a lot more from—

The line went dead. It would take him a moment to realize that I'd hung up. He thinks he's God, Vern would say, but no point getting pissed at God. He'd give Zach a smile and point to the phone.

—Good stuff.

—Awesome.

Notice how these people all start to sound like me? Like the Bible where they all sound like Shakespeare with *thees* and *thous* and *wherefores*. But that's the nature of a virus: it spreads.

—10—

Zach

So we take the 88 up over the top of Yosemite. The southern route would have been shorter, but Dad gets mixed up, maybe thinks, well, stay on the top of the map so we don't get hit by falling rocks. He's weird today, just blanking out. Or saying a dozen times how it's good we saved thirty bucks by not going through the park.

—I didn't know you had to pay to see national parks. I never paid to see Yellowstone. I don't think I did, but you think of all the money the government throws away—

He'd start cursing the government but it's too early in the day, and I might make some smart-ass crack. But right now it's easy driving, gentle curves, rolling hills. The sun cuts through the pines, then it all thins out to scrub brush and reddish gravel blanketing the slopes. Past the hills you catch glimpses of misty gray mountains and layers of blue, greenish blue, cream. And we save thirty bucks.

Dad wants to talk. It's time for father and son to talk, but I can't bear the thought of it. The silence is an unscratched itch. He reaches over to poke on the radio, one blurt, then he pokes it off.

—We oughta talk. I mean we don't get much chance to talk and now there's time, I mean, for chrissake, I'm your father.

—See the road sign?

—What?

—Icy roads.

—I guess that's for when it's icy.

—Or else just to bug you.

—Not a lot of scenery. I guess you gotta get off the road to see stuff. Trees right up to the road.

—Well yes, Dad, they cut down the trees that were in the road cause they knew we were coming through.

We drive on. He wants to say that no scenery's worth thirty bucks and we'd see the same stuff in Yosemite, just trees and hills and curves in the road, but he's already said that two or three times. He keeps glancing over at me, hoping I'll start to talk, anything, even stuff he doesn't want to hear. I try to say something that won't make it worse, but it probably will.

—Okay, this was on the news. This airline, they're flying from New York to someplace, maybe Las Vegas, I dunno—

—Who?

—The airplane. People mostly fly in airplanes, Dad. No, seriously— So they start to take off, and this lady gets really paranoid, acrophobic, and she's about to scream, so the woman in the seat beside her says just breathe, breathe deep and calm down—

—This is on the news?

—So she's breathing, and they take off, but then in the seat behind they hear this guy saying on his cell phone, *Where's the bomb?* He's like, *I looked in the toilets, I can't find the bomb.* In this creepy accent.

—Hold on—

—And the lady really freaks out, so the other woman turns around to the guy and says, *You can't talk on a cell phone, they don't allow cell phones.* Which gets him very confused, and the Feds come in and shoot him.

—This is on the TV?

—Comedy Central.

—You trying to make fun of me or what?

Yes, Dad, I am. *Sorry, Dad,* I want to say. When I start talking I can never distinguish between acupuncture and a stab in the face.

It's like the tooth that hurts, but you can't help biting down to make it hurt more.

Slow driving, but the curves are peaceful. You can almost think it's the world as it should be. Granite slabs, lava rock up the slopes, blue hills, groves of conifers. I'd like to see redwoods circled around an old mama tree, but we don't get redwoods here. Somewhere to the south, for thirty bucks, there are peaks and domes and waterfalls that might make us happy some day if we had the time. I imagine a stir of wind in the grass, little kids running through it, playing in rain. Imagine they're out in the meadows, baptized by rain. Till it turns to hail and screams, and the kids run for cover till they're all struck down by the vengeful Lord God of Hosts—

I could put that in my story. I dreamt about Miss Plankett last night. I think she likes me when I'm insane, as long as I stick to the rules of punctuation.

—My own dad was just like me.

Dad's giving it another try. I see the gears grinding. From all that I've ever heard, he's nothing like his old man. He'd never think of hitting Mom, he'd never leave her, and he's always worked hard even if nothing came of it. His own father would've never put up with my smart mouth. Maybe Dad's so heavy into God because it's so familiar, that God acts exactly like his dad—*Do what I say or else! Do it or die!*—and out of the blue comes the whack of a hand. It's the teacher who sends the whole class down to be burned in the furnace because a couple of kids were passing notes. It's all such incredible bullshit and Dad knows it, I know that he knows it, but still he has to believe it because that's all he's got. I have a lot of feeling for Dad, even though I can't stand to look at him.

—I'd just as soon we didn't fight.

—Sorry, Dad.

—We oughta see some scenery pretty soon.

We drive on past a million trees that don't qualify as scenery. Dad punches on the radio, but all he gets is static and a couple of Jesus stations, and he's not ready to deal with Jesus this early in the day. We pass a little gas station with a couple of cars out front by a big blue

Pepsi truck, and Dad jokes about filling up on Pepsi. He sees I'm not listening or at least trying not to, so he flips on the radio again, then flips it off. I should start to count how many times he does that. He makes another try at talking.

—Maybe watch over there to the south, your side, might be some place you can see through the trees. This brochure, you could see Half Dome, big rock, maybe kind of a ways from here.

—Kinda maybe forty miles or so.

—Well, it's pretty big. Rock formation, I guess it's famous.

—Tissa-ack.

—What's that?

—The Indian name is Tissa-ack, something like that. I googled it.

—So that means something?

—Well, the story is, this woman and her husband, there's a lake, and she's so thirsty she runs ahead and drinks it all up, the whole lake. So her husband starts beating her up—

—This is some Indian crap?

I give up and look out the side window.

—Sorry. I didn't mean it that way. Go on.

—So he's beating her up, and she throws the baby at him. So the Great Spirit, Jehovah, Allah, Thor, whoever, gets pissed and turns them all into granite. Shazam.

—That was a comic book, where they said *Shazam*.

—So now you can see her face in the flat side of Half Dome.

He's quiet. Wanting to say something about Indian crap? Counting the thirty bucks? One of those spells of blanking out?

—My mom would've done that if Dad hadn't split. Might be better off. I could be a scenic wonder.

—But you can't see it from here.

I open the glove compartment and close it, just to see if it works. Or to make Dad think I'm as weird as he is. Not to worry, Dad, you're already turned to stone. Maybe not to stone. Stale bread.

Good thing I didn't say that. I'm learning self-control. He glances at me and then starts talking like his tongue is unraveling, like he doesn't know what he's saying till he hears the words spew out.

—Well, I think they make up a lot of that stuff. But nothing looks like what they show in the pictures. Nothing does. They do stuff to the photos and you're just seeing what you want to see. But I mean if you see something out there, take some snapshots. Your mom said take lots of snapshots, cause this is a pretty special trip. Pretty soon we're supposed to get to Mono Lake, so keep a watch for that.

Relief: he's back to being dumb old Dad. He's fine when he just sounds stupid, and I'm able to feel I transcend my lowly parentage. It's only when I see the hideous desperation—

And I stare out the side watching the brown and green and reddish-gray shapelessness whip past. The hill banks are steeper now, more red gravel, pines and scrub brush intermixed with manzanitas. We've been on the 88 for hours, no beginning, no end, just the slow sideways slippage of the sun. It's watching the dopey father and repellent son on the road to nowhere. What am I doing here? Why am I not faking my book report and doing my sports-page write-up on the cheerleading squad and getting water-boarded by Rebecca and staring at the neatly-packaged buttocks of Miss Plankett? There must be some deep motive for the father to bring along the son. *Bring along your son*, says the voice on the phone, and they hop the nearest camel to the mountaintop.

Dad tries to think of something to say to get us back on whatever track. Not easy for father and son to talk when there's so much to be said and never the words to say it. Mom should've stuffed the potatoes with vocabulary instead of bacon.

—Hey, better take some snapshots.

I scrooch around in the seat, reach down, fetch up Dad's iPhone, point through the windshield and take a couple of shots.

—Get anything?

—Trees.

—Good stuff.

I stash the phone in the glove compartment, where it's quick at hand if we spot a woolly mammoth.

—So your mother made some sandwiches for lunch. We should pull over pretty soon.

—What kinda sandwiches?

—I dunno, peanut butter maybe. She's big on peanut butter.

—Mind if we stop for something else?

—Like what?

—Burrito?

—You see a burrito stand? Chrissake, we're in the wilderness. The wildlife don't eat burritos.

—Bear-ritos.

Dad teeters on the edge of anger, then laughs.

—Okay, that's pretty good, Zach. Anyway . . .

Weird, thinking of peanut butter and burritos while circumventing Yosemite. All that wonderment. If we could drive in and never drive out. If we had hiking shoes and a map and time to see it. Eight hundred miles of trails, waterfall down the mountain slant, hike into the spray, climb like flies on the face of the mother. Zip line across the valley, they hook you up and you glide hundreds of feet over the tips of the trees, seeing for miles, all the scenery we'd ever want to see. If we had time. Which we don't.

—Well, check the map if you find it. I suppose we could take some side trips off the road, side roads, just to see what's there. Or look, right there, is that a historical marker? Something happened there, I guess. Only we're past it now.

—Zoom zoom.

—And the brochure, it said there were giant sequoias. In Yosemite, some grove, I mean. But there must be giant sequoias other places, too, if we could find a turn-off.

—So let's do.

—I mean if we had the time.

We drive on. Dad tries to think of more to say, but his brain is all one-way streets with the traffic coming at him. The idea of paying thirty bucks, even if he didn't pay thirty bucks, is as bad as having paid the thirty bucks. What a rip-off, he's thinking, what a—

Sacrifice. I could feel the word come into his head before he said it. It came out of totally nowhere and he had to say it and I had to listen. Dad doesn't know if I'd heard him or if he's actually spoken.

—Zach, you know, I know you're not big on religion, I mean we don't try to force it on you even though— But I was just wondering— You don't have to say, but— If like the kids your age, your generation, so to speak, think about the concept of sacrifice?

What? Sacrifice of thirty bucks? Sacrifice of giant sequoias? Loss of a week of Rebecca drawing me closer and pushing me back?

—You mean like in voodoo they kill a chicken?

—No, I mean, didn't you say your friend Sammy was going to join the Marines? Like that's making a sacrifice for your country?

— Well, Dad, I don't think he's thinking, *Hey, I'm gonna join the Marines and get killed.* Nobody thinks they're gonna get killed.

—That's not what I'm asking.

—What are you asking?

—I'm not talking about religion, cause there you put yourself in the hands of God, and whatever you get it's not from what you deserve, it's what the pastor calls, what does he call it, God's grace. You don't deserve it but you get it.

—Like you win the Lottery without buying a ticket.

—No, dammit, if you accept what's offered. He gives you the opportunity, but you've gotta reach out to take it. Like a camera, you've still gotta point it, and then maybe you get a snapshot.

—Smile, God.

—I'm trying to converse.

I start to make a joke, but then I hold back. Dad keeps trying to open the door to Jesus, but if I keep my mouth shut then Jesus gets tired of knocking and leaves.

—Once, it was pretty funny, Reverend Bud asked what's the difference between the Father, Son, and Holy Ghost, and three shots of whiskey? Answer being, *The promise.* As long as you don't stagger to the toilet and piss it away. He didn't say it like that.

—Interesting.

—But I guess I don't set the best example. Start off the morning sour, complain about this and that, the scenery, the thirty bucks. Something else Reverend Bud said: *it's not very polite to ask Jesus into your heart if he has to put up with the stink.*

Sometimes he couldn't get off the subject of Reverend Bud. Sometimes it felt as if he hated the guy.

—When I was a kid I got caught in a swarm of bees. It was like God come down on your head.

Sometimes he has a way with words. They come out of nowhere, like a sneeze. We have way too much in common. Words and pointy noses, and a sense of total futility. And hating a God that neither of us believes in.

No sign of a burrito, so Dad pulls over onto a gravel strip with a trash can, parks near it, which I guess feels more authorized. The bank slopes up to a low crest dotted with scrubby shrubs and a big flat rock. Beyond it, some bushes.

—I guess we can eat in the car.

—I'll hit the restroom.

I gesture toward the bushes maybe twenty yards away. He reaches over the seat to grab food while I get out of the car and walk up the slope to the bushes at the crest. I look back and see him unwrapping a sandwich. Now he's got me thinking about God. What if an angel came thundering down and ordered him, *Throw it out the window!* If God demanded he sacrifice his sandwich? Would that be a test of faith or what?

I go into the bushes and take a leak. I'm coming back down the slope and I stop. A tall skinny man is sitting on the rock. Reflector glasses, cowboy hat, black hair. He seems to be staring at me. He looks familiar. I wave hi.

—How's it going?

I think I say it out loud, but I'm not certain. If I say it again, he might hear. He sits there like a statue. Or dead and propped upright. I scramble down the slope to the car and get in the car and slam the door and push the button to lock it. I look back and he's gone.

Dad's not the only one who's nuts.

We're back on the road. The sandwiches are eaten, and we pass the water thermos to satisfy Mom. Silence between us, then Dad is asking how far to Mono Lake. No way to say, I tell him, since we don't know where we are. The hills are more gravelly now, more barren, so we must be getting somewhere. I'm wanting to say something funny about this highway being blue on the map though in fact it's just highway color, but I can't think how to phrase it. I wonder why I'm obsessed with being funny. Maybe like with Rebecca: draw the world closer and push it back.

Out my side window we pass a rock that looks like the skinny man, only without the hat, then it's gone. The sky goes cloudy and the shadows gray out. Coming over a rise, Dad makes a little snort.

—There it is. See there? Mono Lake. That's supposed to be beautiful.

—So is it?

—You can see just a little sliver.

It's a sliver of sheen against the overcast hills. Now the surface comes into view, a white sheet of steel, then it's lost again behind a hill. Around a curve and again we see its long stretch like a drowsing cat across the bleakness. Now we're closer, descending. It's just a lake, one of those things where tourists point and say, *Look at the lake.*

—There it is. Look at the lake.

I look.

—Take a snapshot.

I pull out the phone and take a shot.

—It's supposed to have these rock formations. Maybe we'll see from the highway.

—Tufas.

—What?

—Limestone formations, little bumpy spongy rocks, like if you piled dumplings on top of one another. They form underwater, but then the water level drops and leaves them standing there like ancient ruins. Like Babylon.

And I could tell him that Mono Lake is twice or three times as salty as the sea. That there's billions or trillions of brine shrimp there. That once I'd tried to write a poem about tufas—splotchety blotchety warts and hickeys, jags and squiggles, nodules and knobs, scars of acne or chicken pox, lost cities emerging from primal ooze, sand castles nibbled by ducks—but it was all just calisthenics. Maybe the skinny man was a tufa. Like ancient ruins. Like Babylon.

—Maybe we'll see some.

Dad's voice is as bright as a little girl's. No way would we see tufas from the highway, but no point telling him that—he already knows it. We've looped around Yosemite without seeing a splat of scenery, but he's saved his thirty bucks and had a meaningful heart-to-heart with his almost-only-begotten son. I look over, see the tight corners of his mouth, thin desperate nostrils, furrow between the brows like a double-yellow center stripe. Honor thy father and mother, they say, but how do you honor a man you feel so damned sorry for?

He tries one more time—

—Those clouds, layers, hills—put together all the slivers of lake you've got an amazing . . . Once in high school they took us, I remember, whole senior class to hear classical music. Whose idea that was . . . Omaha Symphony, and they threatened us with prison time if anyone let out a fart. And it wasn't anything I'd ever listen to, but I couldn't ever forget it. Music like clouds coming in, layers on layers, dark, light, lightning flash, rain. I tried to forget it, couldn't ever. Never heard it again.

We descend toward the lake. I think we see it together. Another promise.

—11—

Vernon

Where was it? I woke straight out of a dream and fumbled to see the alarm. Four a.m. Cross-hatches of light on the ceiling. Somewhere a toilet flush. Where was I? Denver? No.

The dream went skidding away. Railway station, Denver, dusk, but like a desert with scrub trees. A sandstone outcrop, and I saw a body lying there. The head was uncovered, but I was crying so hard my tears smudged out the face. If I ever stopped crying I'd see who it was. It was so real. When I woke I still smelled the salt.

That woman with the grapefruit in her brain, even after they found it she still believed that her visions were real. Like God sent the tumor to get her attention. Merna said I should get to the dentist for a checkup. And people should have colonoscopies after the age of forty, or was it colostomies they needed?

My mind was running on like the place with the smoke alarm and we tried to fan it to shut it off, but— Four a.m. but what day? I'd better call Merna. Seventy bucks the night before, thirty-five for dinner and eighty-five tonight— Seventy thirty-five eighty-fi— Geniuses do it all in their head, or retarded kids, they—

When I woke up at night my brain would get the trots, and I woke up a lot. At home I could go out to the kitchen, sit there. I guess people read books so they won't just scowl at the linoleum and wonder who designs the little squares and squiggles. But reading books would just make you jumpy, wondering who the killer was. Zach read lots of books and maybe that was his problem, but I couldn't tell him not to. The guys that write books make a lot more money than me.

But the damn motel, there's no place to get up and go except the bathroom and I couldn't sit on the can for three hours. Pay eighty-five bucks to lie all night in a cage with chintzy curtains that let in the yellow floods from the parking lot. I had a flash of the train station, Denver, the Indians off to the west, the mother's face, the toddler staring into the— Staring at me.

It was after nine when I woke again. How could I be lying wide awake adding figures in my head and then slide into sleep and not know it? I must have turned off the alarm again. Zach was lying on the other bed channel-surfing. At least he had the sound off, which was thoughtful of him, but we needed to get on the road.

—Jesus God, I guess it's morning. I slept good. Did you sleep?

—I couldn't tell. I was asleep.

More jokes. Always jokes. I got out of bed, did my stuff, thought about changing my underwear but didn't. We walked out to the cafe across the parking lot for breakfast. The waitress had dark chestnut hair in a bun, curly squiggles down from the temples, and a tattoo just visible up the back of her neck that looked like it ran down her shoulder. She gave a nice smile when she took our order, but she moved around so slowly that she maybe had something wrong. I could ask about it, but she might think I was calling her a gimp. Beautiful hair. When we got back to the room it was after ten.

—I forgot, I better call Merna. I forgot last night.

Zach flopped down on his bed and went on surfing the universe. He wasn't studying his history, but it was too early to have a squabble. I dug for the cell phone, made the call. Eight or nine rings. She didn't work Saturdays unless for some reason she had to go in. Finally she answered and as usual we stuttered through the hellos and how's-it-goings and I-thought-I'd-better-calls. Neither one of us was good on the phone, but Merna gave it a try.

—Well, so how was the drive?

—Well yeh, we had to go clear up around Yosemite. The roads were closed for snow, but all these big slabs of rock and then these mountains, even though you couldn't see Yosemite, but it's pretty amazing, it's really God's country. Although we're not so crazy about God's motels. Eighty-five bucks for a room.

—Well, it's blowing here, we might get some weather.

—So we're fine. And Yosemite is truly amazing, although we didn't really go through it, but still you can see the mountains, not those particular mountains, but mountains are mountains, I guess. We oughta visit some day, see the waterfalls, whatever.

How it would feel to look up to the waterfall . . . The sheen on the lake . . . The waitress's chestnut hair . . .

—You take pictures?

—Zach took some pictures, but maybe when we're coming back we'll go through there. But it was strange, we're driving up over nine thousand feet and all of a sudden we come out down to this—

Railroad station. The mother is trying to comfort the kid, but she looks like she wants to kill it, and I couldn't remember how old was Lannie when— Falling into a well, down inside myself and—

—No, I was just thinking how—

—What?

I remembered I'd been describing Mono Lake, trying to, coming to Mono Lake and the layers, the shimmer of steel, but she'll think I'm—

—Huge flat lake. Mono Lake. Just flat.

—Flat. Well, lakes are flat. I never saw a hilly lake.

—No, but— And then it's just desolation, just— The hills are scorched black. Like the preacher, Finch I guess it was, preached about Sodom and Gomorrah when the fires came down, like somebody dropped the bomb, and you drive mile after mile through all this black cinders, or maybe they had a forest fire, I don't know, but even that, I mean even when you don't see a bit of scenery, still you feel like it's God's country. Like the Promised Land—

—Scorched black?

—No, but just the size of it. In school we used to sing *Purple mountains' majesties*, it was like that.

—So they're not purple any more.

—What?

—They're black.

—You sound funny.

—You sound funny too.

I heard myself say all that, but I couldn't believe I said it like that. I tried to say, *Hon, Mono Lake, it's the closest thing to a vision of God. The gleam on the water, miles and miles, and the layers of mountains behind. We have to come and see it.* Why couldn't I tell her that?

We had come down and driven along the edge of the lake, the road along the lake, just before sunset. We couldn't see the rocks or the tufas that Zach talked about, but we saw the lake and the hills, mountains, the layers of blue from gray-blue to blue to purple. It looked like other worlds and what you couldn't see from the road you could imagine—lost cities up from the lake.

I couldn't say it on the phone. I had to say it when I was holding her. When I was home and we were naked at night because that's when it really counted. I wanted to burn it into my mind so I wouldn't forget like I always do.

She asked about Zach. I looked over at Zach. His book was open but I couldn't tell if he was reading or just channel-surfing the garbage inside his head. I waved to get his attention, pointed at the phone, if he wanted to talk to his mom. Zach turned back to his book. I guess he was reading his history. It was important that he learn it for the test.

—He's good, he's fine, he's doing his homework. This place is what, Mountain Lakes, kind of a resort area, I guess. Just a little one-horse town, but it took me three stops to find a motel that wasn't an arm and a leg. Eighty-five bucks is really cheap here. But he's fine. We had a pizza last night. We're doing a lot of talking.

Merna was silent. I wanted to tell her things. I wanted to say we'd be driving through Death Valley tomorrow and I was scared about maybe a tumor in the brain. I wanted to tell her my visions, or not so much visions as flashes that looked so real. I wanted to say how my head was clenched tight in a fist. The mother had got the toddler settled and the Indians were moving west. Silence over the deep and across the miles.

—So anyway tomorrow we get into Las Vegas, or maybe late today if we ever get outta here, cause I overslept this morning. I thought I'd set the alarm but it didn't beep. And the guy's schedule—Stubblefield, I don't even know his first name, funny—he's busy, obviously, but that'll give us time to see Las Vegas. There's more than just casinos, I think there's a circus, magic shows— So I'll call you tomorrow.

—Okay.

—Well. So. Love you.

—What?

—I love you, Merna.

—You too. Bye.

I punched off the cell phone and took a heavy swig of air. No more railway station or squalling kid, thank God, but I could smell my mom's row of four-o'clocks. They opened at twilight, and huge moths hovered like hummingbirds, and it all faded into the mottled tan of the motel wall. I was still half asleep. I heard my own voice, raw, squeezed—

—I think she's drinking again.

We were back on the road. Zach was deep in his shell. I kept my eyes on the center stripe, thinking of all the thousands and millions of dashes down the middle that somebody had to paint to keep me in my lane. I couldn't stand to look at mile after mile of desolation. Why couldn't I talk to Merna? We could still joke around and come up with little endearments, but whenever it got serious, things that mattered, then it either hit the fan or just ran out of gas.

I knew there were books about how to be happy and get along with your wife, keep your blood pressure down, make lots of money and scream at your kids constructively. Those books sold millions of copies. I wondered if people ever read them or felt that just buying the book would do the trick. At least she hadn't freaked about the eighty-five bucks.

—Why'd you say that?

Zach was staring at me. His face was pinched up like a little kid about to cry. I made some kind of a mumble but he cut in.

—You blame her for anything. You tell her you love her, then turn around and say she's drunk—

—I didn't say—

—You said.

—Zach, it's not so simple. We've had rough times. I don't know what you remember from when you were little, but if—

—Nothing. Nothing before last week. Okay, no, I remember Interstate 80, I remember taking pills, I remember my brother once—

—Well, you've blanked out a lot of stuff. Times when you were sitting there and we went on pitching a fit— I thought maybe that's what gave you the problems later on, but—

—You're blaming her for—

—Not blaming her. I'm blaming the both of us. We're both responsible. Both of us.

Zach turned away, looked out to the gravel and sage and greasewood. A sign said *Caution* but didn't say how to be cautious or if something was about to fall on our heads. The car rumble filled the air, then faded behind Zach's voice. Tiny, distant, girlish almost—

—Why can't I see my brother?

—What brother?

I couldn't last long in a contest of pain. As a kid I couldn't hold out when Richie twisted my arm and yelled at me to say, *Vernon's a cocksucker!* I could never endure Merna's tears. I couldn't stand when my son shut up tight.

—You can see him. Nobody said you couldn't. I don't care if you see him. He's, what, maybe in his thirties now, you wouldn't have nothing in common. Just don't tell your mother. For her sake, I mean, don't tell her. And he's not your brother, he's your half-brother, dammit.

—Half a brother. Half empty or half full.

—He was a mistake.

—Well, but what's the big deal? You had a kid with your first wife, so what's the big deal?

—Not my first wife. I broke up with her when I met your mom.

—After you had a kid—

—I didn't have a kid. What is this, Twenty Questions?

—Then how did I get half a brother?

—We had a kid later. That was you. I didn't have a kid before, I had an accident. There's no point digging up the past, dammit, we have to look to the future. What made this country great was—

—Dad—

—Get ridda the past—

—Dad—

—Because I was stupid! Leave it at that! I was dumb shit stupid!

The car made a sharp swerve into the oncoming lane, but I straightened out. I forced my eyes onto the center stripe where some pathetic fool had painted those millions of dashes. We chugged down the highway and I tried to change the subject—

—Those mountains are shaped like a whale.

—Walrus-belly hills, hippo humps, herds of stegosauruses.

—That's good. That's poetic. You've got the words, Zach. You'll do okay. You'll do—

—Like imagine God's face is ridges of chin fuzz and whiskery stubble and eyebrows of pickleweed.

Was he trying to be funny or just having fun with his idiot dad? I kept my eyes on the center stripe.

The boy knew more than I thought he knew, but he had it all mixed up. What he didn't know he didn't need to know. Kids have their secrets and so do adults. At fifty-five I deserved a little privacy. In our house when we went to the bathroom we shut the door.

—If you want, ask your mom. You can ask your mom, but you never want to talk on the phone, I ask if you want to say hello and you sit there. Ask her, she'll tell you. I was stupid. At least give me credit for that.

I flicked on the radio. Static. Punch it. Static. Punch static, punch static, punch *Jesus loves you*, punch static. I flicked it off.

—You want to look at the map and check out where we're going?

—Las Vegas.

—I mean which way.

What options for crossing Death Valley? I didn't like Death Valley, the whole idea, why they called it that. I saw photos of rattlesnakes and the old cartoons, prospectors crawling past cattle skulls. Not so much a fear of death but where I saw it as dead as Aisle 14 at the Walmart—all those shelves of Cheerios and Ajax and twelve-packs of Charmin every day. A reign of death, an empire of death, a valley of death, the movie where bats swarmed squeaking out of the mouth of the cave. I tried to stop with the goddamned christalmighty running my mind.

Zach splayed out the accordion map and folded it wrongside back so the map would never get refolded the proper way. But that was the only way to see it. Stuff was always wrongside out. They must have designed it that way so you'd buy a new map. Stuff was designed to go wrongside out.

He said that unless we went far out of the way we had to take the 190 across. In my head I cursed the politicians who'd built the roads so we wouldn't have freedom of choice. No matter where you wanted to go, there was always something screwy. Zach tried to refold the map and I tried to untangle my head.

—Well, it won't be so bad, maybe I guess. What the preacher said once, sometime, whoever, that God sends you out in the desert because the desert has no mercy. There's birth and there's death and stuff has to die off. But then you come through it, and that's what we've always done, we always came through.

Could I for once stop hearing my babble? I must have a god-given urge to babble. I babbled on.

—You're asking about me and your mom, so just remember something. *Yea though I walk through the Valley of the Shadow of Death*, it says, okay, right. So I'm at the air base in Minot and driving a forklift, stacking toilet paper, millions of rolls, while other guys are over there getting killed. But still I'm thinking, this toilet paper is for the guys that are alive, not the ones that are dead. So you better thank God you can still wipe your ass—

I caught myself. I was rambling like an idiot. I was making no sense. I'd tried to poke through my son's dead ears, but I kept taking detours and didn't know where I was or where I'd intended to go. Zach tuned me out. There was no other option except the 190 through the Valley of Death. But at least now when God sent you out to the desert there were highways with Caution signs. Probably rest stops. Park rangers. Souvenirs.

What I clung to in the dark of the desert sun was the faith, the hope, the sure knowledge that Merna was holding me close. She was home. She was gazing at the clock on the kitchen wall and praying each minute for me to find my way. I knew that for sure. I knew that as I focused on the center stripe. I knew it deep in my heart, even though my heart was so fucking far away.

—12—

Merna

Today would be better, I thought. Thursday I'd been up before daylight doing the cooking and packing, and what with Rosella moaning round trip and Old Pinkeye giving us all the hairy eyeball, I flopped into bed that night as soon as I'd finished gnawing a chicken wing. I was cranky enough to eat it bones and all, but I said to myself, *Hey, no, Merna babe, don't take it out on the chicken.*

And then I woke up at 5 a.m., panicked it was so quiet, and couldn't get back to sleep. It felt good to stretch out in the bed and hog all the covers, but the only sleep I got was between little rag-ends of half-awake dreams. Scared of something but couldn't tell what. Finally got up Friday morning and called in sick to work, said I'd see 'em Monday unless I was stone cold dead.

At first it was almost fun, like playing hooky. I tore into the kitchen and cleaned up after cooking for their trip, did the whole nine yards. I had to laugh at all the grease there was after I'd groused about fast-food grease, but frying chicken meant grease. And I'd cooked a bunch of bacon to crumble up and stuff into their baked potatoes. They both liked bacon.

After I scoured the kitchen I thought I was off and running. Whole day to myself. Eat whatever I wanted, sleep if I felt like it, no sonsabitches shoving invoices into my face. And so here I was sitting at the table like a toadstool for half an hour before I remembered I hadn't had breakfast and hauled my butt up to cook myself an egg. Flopped it onto the toast, made coffee, chomped and sipped.

Next thing I knew, I was in Zach's tiny room, prying around in his stuff. This was my chance and he'd never know. What was I looking for? Some teenage secret? Something to kill himself with? Some key to unlock his head? I started to straighten his bedcover tangle but gave it up. I picked up three dirty socks and a t-shirt strewn on the floor, typical, tossed them into the hamper, opened the top drawer of his dresser. It stuck and squawked, and a dog bark startled me, but then I had a surprise. His room was always a total mess, but here was his underwear and socks and tee-shirts all folded neatly, all by him. No dirty magazines underneath, just some memo pads with finicky little doodles that looked like faces in dreams. One drawer was full of books, every which kind, even an old Dr. Seuss. Nothing that told me a thing except that I had not a clue. I went back to the kitchen. I don't know what I needed to know, but I knew I didn't know it.

Lunchtime already. I warmed up a can of chicken noodle soup and crumbled a fistful of crackers in it. It tasted okay. Thought about going for a walk, being a nice sunny day. Might even go out to a movie, but then I'd have to take the bus and someone from work might see me—even though, no, they'd be at work. My brain was on vacation. But officially I was sick, so I'd better stay sick. Last time I'd ever stay home from work.

I lay down on the couch and took a nap. When I woke it was nearly dark. Vern hadn't called Thursday night, so I thought sure he'd call Friday. I could have called his cell phone but I didn't. I wondered where they were. Did they eat all the food? Was the bacon good? What would they eat tonight? Hell, what was I gonna eat? Salad would be good: eat healthy. So I got off the couch, rummaged in the cupboard, found the makings of mac and cheese, fixed it, ate it, felt like a cow, fat but full, washed my dish and went to bed. And then, just before blotting out, I saw Zach's face. I'd never touched a drop.

Then it was Saturday, and a weekend free and clear. Vern called in the morning. I'd been dreaming hard, so my brain wasn't right-side-up. I must have sounded goofy, but he was never a champ in the talk department. Sometimes he sounded at least like he's got past third grade, but with me we both sounded like total fools. I guess there'd been snags between husband and wife going back to the day when a caveman threw a bone across the fire at his cavegirl—Mom said that once in a rare blurt of wisdom—but that wasn't a lot of comfort. Things were fine, he said, but he told me nothing, diddly, zip.

I was nursing a hangover from the dream, Zach's face, something. Now it was past noon, there was a plate in front of me, so I must have eaten breakfast, and the clock was saying 12:20, lunchtime. Strange how time condensed or expanded the way water boiled or froze. Or in chemistry class, the chemicals would mix and then suddenly flare up or crystallize. I'd loved chemistry, but now the chemistry was just cooking dinner and I was pretty sick of it.

And sick of living in a trailer house, but that's what we could afford. Mobile home, they called it now, but where I grew up they called it a trailer house. Every day up the four steps, and I'd think if only we had a little porch, but all we had was four steps and a wood rail to balance the grocery sack till I got the door unlocked. Kitchen was okay, even though I hated electric stoves, but not storage enough to stash food for two grown men. The kitchen opened to the living space, so you got lots of togetherness whether you wanted it or not. And over the table a dinky chandelier. The realtor called it *super cute*. He'd pointed out the wood-grain linoleum floor—wood-grain linoleum, wow. I'd seen in magazines how to pretty up a trailer, but I wasn't big on plastic flowers. One thing I knew for damn sure: cooped up in a trailer house, people went nuts.

I'd always led a pretty balanced life. When I worked I worked, when I cooked I cooked. When I fixed Zach's lunch bag I tried to put in something special. When I cried I tried to stop it.

Why Zach? Why, *Bring along your son?*

Better fix lunch. Warm up leftovers, something. I got up and went to the fridge, dug in the salad drawer. Better have salad, start to eat healthy like I'd resolved yesterday, so I tore off some lettuce into a bowl, dug for onions and radishes, and we still had a tomato. I cut a thick piece of cheddar cheese and wolfed it down and went on fixing the salad. By the time it was fixed, tomato sliced, I'd eaten another hunk of cheese and a leftover cold potato and a fistful of salted peanuts, then left the salad on the counter while I sat down at the table and put my head in my hands and went right ahead and cried.

After a while I went into the so-called living room, picked up the *TV Guide*, took it back to the kitchen table. Stared at a photo of smiling goons from some reality show. *TV Guide*. The image came into my head: fat cow slouched down gorging on TV. *The Price Is Right, Judge Judy, Dr. Phil, The Young and the Restless, Days of Our Lives, The Bold and the Beautiful*, and they even brought back *Let's Make a Deal*—all this stuff from twenty years ago still bulging out like hemorrhoids and people still watching it, people like me. And old movies, baseball games and the news news news. Some kid got shot, some new war, somebody won the Lottery, and all the candidates bellowing like bulls with the bloat. I threw down the *TV Guide*, tried not to look at the clock. Would it be any better if Vern struck it rich and I quit my job? What would I do with the time? I had free time right now this afternoon, but here I stared at the clock, serving my drippy life sentence without parole.

Zach's face again. I could see him but I couldn't see his eyes. Sometimes he'd be reading a book and I'd rub his hand, the back of his hand. Just saying I was there. When he was little I'd clip his fingernails, brush his hair. Kids grow out of that stage, but still he'd let me rub the back of his hand.

And then I went and sat down in Vern's chair facing the TV. I had a pile of books from the library. I used to read books, and I still tried to read when I could, always checked out two or three and never finished one. Picked up the first and skimmed the jacket blurb. The heroine is twenty-nine, she's whip-smart but depressed, and finding her long-lost mother uncovers a family secret. Tried another: she's a top-flight CEO with a gritty past and in the midst of a corporate merger discovers a family secret. Another: she's in love with a guy, but she's written the novel that burns within her, revealing family secrets. And the photos of the gals who wrote the books: nice hairdos, nice smiles, floral bouquets of words. *Zora brushed her thick auburn hair slowly, languidly, imagining the urgency of his fingers in it.* That's all I needed: urgent fingers in my mousy hair. And maybe some way to pay the Visa bill. Who reads this crap?

And how many of those finger-lovin' heroines had teenage sons? Full-time job trying to keep up with Zach. New girl friend, Rebecca something, sweet but kind of plain. At least he wasn't in with a bad crowd, kind of kept to himself, so of course I worried about that. There must be some mom somewhere who's not totally clueless. I thought I heard his voice saying *Hi.* Must have been those feral cats.

The birth was really hard. The miscarriage hadn't put me through so much, although in a way it was worse. But after that I'd given up hope. I couldn't bear more punishment for what I didn't know I was guilty of. But suddenly, age forty-two, I was pregnant. They told me, some little twerp named Dr. Deets or something that made me think of tits, that there might be complications. I was sick all the time, but I took care of myself, read all the what-to-do books. Fourth month I had this huge flood of energy, and I never cleaned house so much in my life. That didn't last long. At seven months everything hurt, it hurt to stand up, to sit down, ankles and feet swollen, I couldn't breathe, and when is it gonna come, when when when? Once Vern said, *Well, some people never show up on time,* and I had to laugh, but whenever I laughed I had to go pee, which got me mad at him, but I had to admit it was funny. Vern used to say funny things.

They shot stuff in the IV to make the contractions faster, and it tore me to pieces. I didn't get to see Zach, the baby, the evil little demon, that whole first day, and then it was like seeing God. They'd asked, *Would you like to see your son?* and it was like the first time I'd ever heard the word *son.* People say baby this, baby that, but then you see your son. He was born on Election Day. I forgot who got elected, and I couldn't care less.

Then forward a bunch of years, and he's curled up kneeling in front of the toilet, clutching the rim and writhing around dead white, vomiting out his heart. Wow, he's a big boy now, he's old enough to kill himself. I'd seen it in dreams, like a flash, a nightmare you feel its heartbeat. You can't hear for the roar of it, just hearing yourself think think think think think. Like a fist.

—Damn you! Damn you, Zach!

My own voice startled me. Horrible to speak it out loud, but such a relief. I could say whatever I liked alone, as long as it couldn't be heard. I hated to hate the son that I loved.

I wiped the wet off my cheeks, picked up the books I'd tossed to the floor. Look on the bright side. Celebrate. They were out on the road, promises, brighter days, father and son. Good reason to celebrate. I needed something. I got up from the chair heavy with afternoon, pulled the step-stool up to the kitchen cabinet, reached the top shelf and took down the bottle of Johnny Walker. Elegant ring to the name, elegant guy.

We kept it for celebration, though we both knew we had to watch it. We'd been through times when Vern fell way off the wagon, right to the edge of alcoholic although he wouldn't admit it. I'd had a few binges too, but not after Zach was born. The bottle was there for special occasions, and I kept a little mark on the level. I had a bottle of cheaper stuff behind the clutter under the kitchen sink, but it felt too weird to drink that, so I used it to top up the Johnny Walker if I took a sip. Exactly what Aunt Lettie did. So stupid to lie to ourselves, but that's what we do. I was too damned busy to be a drunk, but there were times I sure did want to be.

One sip would do it. Vern didn't need to know. I never lied to him—or I told myself it wasn't a lie because he never listened. I tried to keep the home fires burning bright, tried to be a mother, tried to top up the Johnny Walker. I poured my coffee cup a quarter full. I knew that after a while I'd pour it another quarter full.

—No, dammit, we love each other!

My voice again. I couldn't shut up. I sounded like a lady walrus, big stocky blonde dyed black, a big belching horse. I took a sip. Remember to top it up. Another sip. It burned. I was drinking now, and for the first time in seventeen years I knew I wouldn't stop.

Denver. It wasn't only his fucking that woman. It wasn't the first time for that little dance. It was meeting the son. Even though I had Zach and the older kid was history, eighteen or so, it was like a fist. Like I was still barren, lost one and now she had it. Ripped me so deep in the gut I could hardly feel it, could only scream inside. But we lived through it.

The phone rang. I got up. The booze made me heavy. I knew who it was. This is *Bridget from Cardholder Services—* My favorite robo-call. *Hi Bridget.* Bridget warmed my heart. Some would-be actress with bleach-blonde hair got paid fifty bucks to record her little squeak, and her words went out to the billion fools in the world to screw them out of a buck. I'd read somewhere that Bridget was a goddess or a saint. A goddess phoning me, amazing. I clicked off and took a full swig.

I needed a goddess or a god. Church wasn't the same any more. We still held on, a bridge between us, and thinking it'd be good for Zach if he ever went. It might give him hope, some reason to keep plugging, some lies to live by. But the terrible thing about God was how easy it was to lose him. He'd flit off like a moth or burn up in the candle. He must be watching the news right now thinking, *Screw them all!* But the pastor now, it wasn't the same as with Reverend Bud. With Pastor Finch it was God God God, every third word was God because God seemed so far away. With Reverend Bud you felt that God was just sitting there in a pew alongside you, laughing at the jokes. You'd feel God's love like a mother loves a baby. Babies know they have to make their moms go nuts, just crazy with love, and they sure know how to do it. First three years with baby Zachary, and then he started growing into Zach.

It would only take them one swerve in the road. Head-on crash. I might not know it for days. Some stone-faced cop at the door. Just another half cup now.

You hear the news to start off your day, all the doom doom doom. Some kid gets killed, and always some mother going wacko. The car slams, the gun spits, and nothing's left but one big gob. Last week's sermon I couldn't get out of my head, Finch's little asshole-pucker lips telling us God says, *Kill your son*, and the old man says, *No problem, God*. That just about curdled me on the Bible. That idiot Finch: on and on about Abraham's faith, and who give a shit for the mother back in the tent? She watches them disappear, she sits there in the tent morning, afternoon, night, no phone call. Blank stare at the wood-grain linoleum.

Mommy! I jerked awake. Sounded like Zach about six years old. Damn cats, it must be, the scrawny yellow tom and the big mangy gray fur-ball that might be female. They sounded human. I felt my head shaking. Opened my eyes, confused, sitting in Vern's chair, and the TV going on about spices and gunpowder and indigo dye. *The Silk Road*, some educational thing. I almost had to laugh: here was Merna Orcutt with her eyes popped open, watching camels and Arabs. Or now she was Merna McGurren.

—You are so drunk!

My voice again. More amused than mad. More like a party floozy, like the old days when girls powdered their faces and every year the powder got thicker and thicker till they were in their fifties and it all fell off in chunks. No, yes, okay, drunken ramble. You're drunk mid-afternoon and watching camels and Arabs and how we got guns from China. Vern had a gun, I said, N*ot in this house you don't!* At least now I knew where we got indigo dye, which might come in handy if somebody asked me a question about indigo dye. I'd lost an hour in my life, but good riddance. I laughed a dried-out laugh.

Nothing funny about it. But for Merna, me, myself, laughing was better than crying and those were the only two choices. Up to me to hold the fort, keep the faith, hold that belief in my two fine men gone out to spear the woolly mammoth and cart home the woolly mammoth chops. I'd better steam veggies for dinner, clear my head. I drank too much, and the drink hit hard. Some poem in my head from English class. *Half a cup, half a cup, half a cup onward . . .*

And then the laughter grabbed me the way it almost never did, but when it did it grabbed like a bulldog shaking me and shaking me till I was all emptied out. Drunk didn't work. I needed to get incredibly stupid.

—13—

Stubblefield

More than once I regretted this deal. It made me feel like the asshole I am though in fact there are guys who almost force you
to be an asshole. A con man has a general plan but the specifics are
improvised. The mark's quirks guide the story. Effect induces cause.

I can't even remember what got me to Chico. And totally off the
top of my head I said *Bring along your son*. I didn't plan a thing. A
conversation starts and you flow the way rainwater floods down the
time-gouged wrinkles of old Mother Earth. You imagine the clouds
form this vast conspiracy of cumulonimbus to fuck up your weekend
but that's not how weather works. There's a mountain a lake a front
moving in from the north and thinning the air and it all comes down.
Insurance companies blame it on God of course but a wind isn't like
some geezer puffing out birthday candles: it's high pressure here low
pressure there and the suck between. Likewise commandments like
Bring along your son. Just one quick suck.

Vern was heavy into commandments. The more the merrier
if you're crying to change your life to be anyone else but Vernon
McGurren. He told me about the Sunday when his Reverend Bud

said *Don't let your ignorance hide your Truth*. He struggled with that. The *ignorance* part he knew pretty well. His teachers his bosses his sergeant had drilled it into him plus his dad's belt strap before the age of five. He was a whiz on ignorance.

The *Truth* part was harder. Reverend Bud explained it so beautifully but then it would slip away. Every man had God inside like what the Quakers said and God was Truth and that was the meaning of *The Truth shall set you free*. You could learn stuff from church but you had to see what God showed you every day. Look across the table. Look what the wife puts on your plate. Look what's there to love. It sounded almost as good as riding a snowmobile.

It seemed so simple from Reverend Bud. Jesus wasn't some honcho saying *Look at me I'm a big shot so kneel down and kiss my ass*. No. Jesus was saying, *Hey I'm like you I feel pain I'm despised and rejected of men but you know what? I think I see the way. There's a path through the wilderness right up to the top of the mountain. Come on. Up ahead. Let's go. Follow me.*

It was all so clear. Vern remembered telling the Reverend things that he never knew were in him, making a frantic grab at Truth but still stocking shelves at the Walmart—as if the little Vernon inside himself had fallen into a well and was groping for a ladder out.

If he could only talk to Zach. Zach was smarter than him but Zach was grappling at the monkey bars and slipping off. Like the time on the playground when little Vernon swung on the monkey bars and his fingers slipped off and his arms got scraped in the gravel and his babysitter didn't know what to do so she took him home and rubbed the scrapes with Lysol and he heard his own screams but couldn't stop and he wasn't sure if he'd ever stopped.

Try to get Zach to talk. It might open him up the way it did for Vern the time he talked with Reverend Bud or even the way he talked to a stubby stranger on a barstool. It was the talking that helped. He wanted that for Zach. He wanted that more than some crazy job in Vegas. Though it wouldn't hurt to make some money as well.

But the fact was that his son— his legitimate son named Zachary after his mother's grandpa—thought a lot about God. God for him—my impression at least—was the mass grave where they bull-doze nameless meat. God was a mouth with sore red gums. God was a great black snoring oven. The son's words twisted like a tourniquet that cut off all flow. Men like Vernon spawned sons like that.

Some of this Vern told me late at night on the phone when he was puking drunk but I already knew the gist of it. That of God was inside him like the Quakers say but who knew what big fat append-age of God was shoved up where?

All which is to say that I had no grand plan, no masterplot. I was as clueless as Vernon. I move in mysterious ways, my wonders to per-form, but I'm always surprised how things turn out. You drive where the highway leads. You start the ball rolling and get out of the way.

There are in fact rapists who truly believe they're the victim. *She made me do it, her thing down there, it sucked me in.* There's the effeminate little kid on the playground you're forced to beat up because he's so frail. Or the pokey old driver you have to rear-end he's so unbearably old and pokey.

I was the victim of Vern McGurren. I was the fantasy begotten of his itch. My words were spawned from his heart's leaky throbs and its backwash of blood. I was tucked tight up to his amygdala. I was along for the ride through sand and dust and Caution signs. I wanted to tell him *Asshole, turn back, you're roadkill.* It wasn't a tumor the size of a grapefruit. It was me in his brain repeating *the promise the promise the promise.*

—14—

Zach

Highway 190. Dad sees the neat little brown sign that marks the border of Death Valley National Park. He shivers. Because of the death part or because he hadn't known it's a national park and we'll have to pay? An old movie flickers across his face, where the Indians appear over the ridge and the wagon train sees all its hopes lost.

We traverse miles of black rock rubble and clutter and shatter. Now the scrubland gives way to sandstone slabs, buttes, mesas, switchbacks, a naked mountainside stripped of green, baring its layers. Ravens, crows, whatever they are, light on the oncoming highway like fingers touching skin, then flinch away the way Rebecca does.

It's a landscape chewed by big dogs. I think of the vacant lot the west side of the trailer park, beautiful in a way. Half acre of broken cement blocks, tangles of brambles, a heap of old tires, a ditch that a bulldozer reamed out but forgot. Little kids could crawl under the brambles into the backyard of Hell.

Here, it's a natural waste, untouched by human hands. Redrock gravel, creosote brush, dried-blood gashes in basin flats, flash-flood gullies of thirst. a steady upward descent into a yawning god's gullet—my brain dribbles out words like a runny nose. Senseless sharp glittery fragments, as if God tore up the floor of his playroom, scattered his Legos, left this mess. Too much like daily life.

Odd overcast, a dark sky rising up in my eyes, and then the sun flashes. It's the kids at school, sitting there dull dull dull, and then somebody farts, there's a cackle, a glitter, a gleam, and then they go dull again.

—You bring something to read? I always see you reading. You should've brought a book.

—I already read it, Dad.

—Read what?

—It's all the same book. You plow through it and at the end it says, *Okay, now read the book.*

—You lost me on that one.

And me. I don't really know what I meant, but it sounded smart. As long as it flummoxes Dad it makes perfect sense. But he knows what I'm saying. He only wishes he didn't. I see it in his face when I can stand to look at him. If only I could go five minutes without a sneaky glance at his dead-fish eyes.

I hunch my shoulder against the passenger door and try to stretch my legs. Try to blank out my brain, try to think of center stripes, think of trees, think of the skinny man. Somewhere in my head there's a blurry face that might be me, but the mirror's fogged. Try try try. Try to recall an old movie I'd never seen, but the title stuck. *The Man Who Knew Too Much.* I feel as if I know more than I ever wanted to know, but I can't get a fishhook into the mouth of it.

I know my dad. I know my dad hated his own dad and wanted to be a different dad, a dad that his son respected. I know that my wisecracks and even more my silences sting him like nettles. I know this trip for him is make or break. And I know I can't stand another chew of the stale tasteless gum. But I probably will.

—You were asking about Denver, that stuff.

Dad's going to start to talk. How fast are we going? Could I open the door and jump? It'd hurt like hell. I can try to crawl down deeper into my cave, wedge in so he can't pull me out, fill my lungs with shadow.

—So me and your mom, we've had some rough patches but we've always come through it. We're pretty good now. I'm not gonna pretend everything's peaches and cream, but there's nothing to worry long-term. That I know for sure. I just want you to . . .

Please stop the talk. Denver. I already know about Denver, every twist and turn, although who knows what— From old letters. From quarrels in the kitchen while I lay in bed trying not to hear. From Dad's evasions. Like catching a fish and it's not big enough, so you throw it back and catch another and throw it back, and they're down there swimming free with their gills torn by hooks. Now Dad needs to say it, whatever it was, and I can't stand to hear it, whatever it is.

But suddenly he's mum. I glance at him. His nose. Broader than mine but that same little hump in the middle as if it imagined growing huge but chickened out, then poked out to a little point. Elf ears, beady eyes, widow's peak. I look out the side window again. All the boring fluorescent linoleum death of Death Valley.

Suicide, I thought, might flatten the landscape, nothing to either side, the way Nebraska runs on. I had so many reasons. Part of it was school, but not the biggest part. School was just waiting out your sentence while trying to glimpse nipples down girls' blouses and thinking where Cynthia's tattoo at her midriff was wandering down unto. Trying not to antagonize Mrs. Coad, who was mad at me for being smart and not giving a shit about it. And homework asking me to compare and contrast Jefferson and Jackson, both of whom were exactly alike, being dead.

Other reasons, okay. Stupidity. In English we read James Baldwin, who proved that African-Americans can be geniuses. But Wilfred Holmes could barely spell his own name, sat in the back row poking out little illiterate tweets, so what good did it do him that Baldwin was a genius? And filthy-rich lily-white Rodney was just as dead stupid as Wilfred, which proved that all races could be equally dumbshit stupid. It was contagious: sit across from Rodney and come down with a fatal case of stupid.

Other reasons: sex. I got into Luann's pants but wasn't quite sure what to do when I got there, nor was she. I'm still about two-thirds virgin and she's probably the same, except now she's going with Reggie, so it's only a matter of time. I could have said to her, *Hey, we need to practice this, cause I'm not very good at ping-pong either, but I just beat Philip, so all things are possible.* Instead, we both got this hangdog look, like Adam and Eve caught bare-ass, and couldn't meet each other's eyes. So I must be two years behind my age level, with scant prospect for closing the gap in playing *Hide-Little-One-Eye* or whatever cute name now for doing it. Rebecca is way above my league, and Catholic, though I keep up my hopes that some day she might have to come up with hotter stuff to confess.

But I guess that all my reasons came down to simple boredom. A boredom so fat and deep that I couldn't breathe. I needed a big circus act to jazz up my fans. A hammer smash to the mirror. The shock of dead meat on the bathroom floor. Some way to stop sneaking glances at Mom and Dad.

Even so, I see now that death while two-thirds a virgin would be so humiliating. Instead, why couldn't I sign for an AP course in Crazy? Read the textbook, words fall clattering to the floor, the teacher springs a leak, and the class chants headlines every morning till we start tearing out our hair. We bring old shoes for lunch and sit there licking them. We stand stark naked, but nobody notices till someone passes a note around and then the wild rumpus begins. I've just had little nibbles of Crazy, but I savor the taste. (Miss Plankett would jot, *A bit much, don't you think?*)

But Mom had it right: I read too much. *You'll hurt your eyes,* she says, but there'd be no problem if reading left you blind. But no, it opens your eyes and you see the world. Then you see that it isn't yours. You meet these amazing people—philosophers, pirates, painters, pimps, pyromaniacs—and then at page 275 or 863 they vanish into the fog. I guess it's the same as Burger King ads or porn sites or televangelists—all the great hopes dangled just out of reach, the tease that makes you scream. You read about Yosemite, the history of Yosemite, the wonders of Yosemite, and then you roll up the windows

to keep the fresh air out. *We'll come back and spend some time.* Dad
works so hard at never touching it.

—Dad, could we make a pit stop?

—Sure, watch for a pull-over. Should I make sandwiches? They
didn't have much at that little store, some lunch meat, slices of cheese.

—Whatever.

We're in some ancient bed of a lake, like the skin of a withered
crone. It's flatter than flat. A scatter of sagebrush, creosote, greasewood—can't tell them apart but I know the names. Dad looks for
a place to pull over, but he never sees a pull-off until it's past. He
slows down at a place that says *Scenic View* but veers back onto the
highway. He's not the most decisive guy.

Now he pulls off to a wide spot the side of the road. I roll down
the window. There's not enough breath in the world for even a wispy
cirrus, but the clouds have followed us here. Thirty yards from the
car, in the deathly floor of the desert, a huge oblique slab of sandstone
juts upward, three men high: Lot's wife looking backward to Chico.
No, she wasn't sand, she was salt, but it's the thought that counts. I
get out of the car and walk toward God's porta-potty.

—Look out for snakes!

I give Dad a wave like an astronaut off to his moonwalk. I see
him reach back for the grocery sack—sandwiches of cottony bread
and slices of meat like pork-flavored Jello, from maw to belly to
sewer. No, stop thinking and look out for snakes. My brain is full of
horseflies.

Up the slope, where the scrub brush thins, a black ridge bares its
saw teeth to the sky. *That's a sight,* Dad said as he pulled to a stop,
or thought it—I didn't listen. What an idiotic catastrophe, being
a father. What kind of father would let his son wander off among
rattlesnakes? What kind of son would give not a shit what the old
man feels?

I walk toward the up-jutting sandstone. I know who's there. I'm
expecting him, and just before coming around the edge of the rock,

I see the shadow. A shadow more squat than I would have thought, but the sun through the clouds is high and no one is tall at noon. I make my way around a scruffy brown bush, step over the dry cut of a rivulet, and see the skinny man.

His shadow lies south, toward the sun.

He leans his back to the rock. The same mirror shades, but now he's wearing a straw fedora. His skin has a cast to it, Mexican, Italian maybe, something dark. He looks at his feet, not at me, but a thin finger wags in acknowledgment of my presence. *Yea though I walk—* He's my hallucination, so I ought to speak first.

—Hi there.

—And you.

The voice is high and thin. It comes from somewhere inside the rock and vibrates through the skinny man. His lips move out of synch with the words. I put my hand to the rock.

—Are you— I'm trying to— Lannie, is it?

—Call me Ishmael.

—I read that book last year.

—All you'll ever need to know about whales.

—But no, isn't it Lannie?

—Call me the Firstborn. That's more Biblical.

My brother must be in his early thirties. Taller, darker than Dad, narrow blade of a nose. Skinny, but his leaning back on the rock gives a hint of strength. I wonder will he kill me or curse me? I lean against the rock like a very cool dude. Not wanting to wake up. Say something pointless, silly, flip—

—I always hated beer, except once I dreamed I liked it, and then after that I liked it.

—Sorry, no beer.

I smile. Long time since I remember smiling. His face crinkles, the faint start of a grin. I want to see his eyes behind the reflectors, but I dread the thought of eyes. I look down at his shadow, then up. Now his face is smoother, lighter, but his voice has the guttural bite of lemon rind.

—No wind today. You blew here without any wind.

—Dad. The one and only.

—Great sense of humor, Zach. Careful the jokes don't snap back in your face.

Lannie is like the cat we had whose name I can't recall, but it always licked itself as if it had a little secret that it'd never tell. It died under the porch and I felt like I'd always be a little boy, no matter how I leaned against the rock like a very cool dude. My brother speaks in that distant citric voice—

—Remember the canyon?

—Yeh, you came to visit, we climbed down the canyon.

—I was eighteen, you were four or five.

—I asked Dad why didn't you live with us, but he never said.

—Cause Daddy got tired of fucking my mom, so he fucked your mom instead. Simple as that. A chronic mom-fucker.

Shadows don't go that way. But no big deal if you're crazy. They even let you murder people then.

—So pull up a chair, baby brother.

—Chair?

—No chairs in Death Valley? Hey, it's all pretend. Want a joint? Sorry, no joints.

My brother's face has changed again—yellowish sandstone, sculpted—and his lips never move. I'm hearing his words like a podcast. I need to speak, say anything—

—So what do you do? Like for money.

—I'm a night manager.

—Of what?

—Just the night in general.

—I mean where do you work?

—I sell mementoes.

—Mementoes of what?

—Stuff you forget.

—No, seriously, what do you do for a living?

—Professor of comparative mythology. I compare all the lies and decide which to recommend. Sorry, no straight answers, Zach. Read the Bible: I'm a wild ass of a man.

My fingers feel the stone behind me. Smoother than sandstone. My brother's reflectors show nothing except my faces.

—I had a red tricycle then. You tried to ride it.

—You had the advantage. I was eighteen, you were four or five.

—I tried to kill myself.

—Well, it's a popular hobby, Zach. And granted, it looked like her sleeping pills and you couldn't read the label without your glasses but didn't want to live long enough to find'em. But was that worth hearing the paramedic cackle when she checked the bottle? You need to take a course in suicide, my brother, maybe a college major. But frankly, there's no future in it.

He smiles. The sun flashes off his shades. I want him to be real, but you don't meet brothers in the desert. Dad talked about visions and I asked him if he meant like mirages, but he shut up about it. Maybe this is Dad's vision and I'm inside it, like the wormholes I read about in the cosmology book I couldn't understand. Whole parallel worlds an inch away from ours, but nothing gets through, not even the neighbor's yapping dog. If I pass AP Math I could maybe understand. Or if I had sex with Rebecca.

—Don't count on it, my brother.

It's seepage. Like something seeps through the strainer. Even black holes have seepage, and they theorize tiny black holes that can't be found, but what if we carry them in our brains and that's the last place we'd ever think to look? Not even Heisenberg ever knew where his particle was. But suddenly it spews out stuff that seems so real, that casts a skinny bass-ackward shadow. My dark brother spurts through a wormhole into my head and smiles.

—Because you're funny. You don't have to try to be funny: you just are.

I shut my eyes tight and blink open. Lannie is still here. His name is Lannie. I can almost see his eyes behind the sunglass glare. The wind is so sharp I can't breathe, and then it's as still as bone. I try to get back on whatever track we lost.

—We went down into the canyon.

—I was eighteen, you were four or five.

—You told me don't look at the sun, you said it burns out your eyes.

—And so it did.

—I wish I could talk to you.

—Do it like grownups do. Talk to yourself and pretend it's me.

A raven squawks into the sun. My brother is leaning beside me against the rock.

—Hear me, baby brother? You were a cute little kid, and you weren't the only one who thought, *Hey, I've got a brother.* You weren't the only one. So why is your heart so full of stink? Why not open a window, let in the breeze? Who would you be if you weren't always sucking your sour little pickle? You look in my eyes, you see your own reflection. That's all you ever see.

—What's that supposed to mean?

It stings like a spider bite. He starts to take off his shades, and in the breath before I see his eyes, he's gone. The desert stretches, shivers, throbs, and I'm standing here. Far distant, the sheen of a lake.

I'm alone behind the big slice of rock. No goodbyes, no nothing. My hand feels the rock. Not sandstone, not granite, more like the limestone tufas I'd read about, rising out of the lake with thousands of little rat-bite pocks on the surface. My fingers feel the pimply face and pull away. *Yea though I walk through the Valley of Death.* My own shadow puddles at my feet. I turn, put both hands against the rock and push, leaning my body into it, yearning the craziness back, but a gentle breeze is up and my brother is gone.

I'd better pee and get back to the car. I said I was going to pee, so I unzip my fly and then zip it back up. Another attempt at Crazy. For the span of a month or so, when I was eleven or twelve, I had an obsessive compulsive urge for symmetry. If I scratched my right ear I had to scratch my left, or clean my left thumbnail, then clean my right. Not only an urge but a screaming nag till I did it. Then I looked it up: there was a technical name for that condition and a list of idiotic things that people did. It was so tacky to be doing stuff that had a psychiatric name that I stopped. But I still had these moments like unzipping and zipping my fly so God would think I had peed. His eye is on the sparrow.

From the distance I see the passenger door standing open like a tongue stuck out for the doctor. Another comparison, faintly hoping that Miss Plankett might molest me. Simile, metaphor, personification, I learned in grade school. I still wonder why. Why compare one thing to another? Everyone seeps into everyone else.

I read about a kind of desert toad. Spadefoot toad, this little brown bulge-eyed lump of gristle that hibernates underground, maybe for months, until it rains. And then it goes wild, digs out of its burrow, cavorts in the puddles with its classmates, and they fuck up a storm. Then the girl toads spew out billions of tadpoles, till the dryness rolls in and they dig back into their bedrooms. If Rebecca and I were spadefoot toads, we'd listen till the weatherman said, *Chance of showers*, and get ready to roll. I'd like to give it a try. I'm a long time waiting for rain.

—15—

Vernon

Zach opened the door, got into the car but left the door open, like he was letting the silence in to suck out the air between us. My head was coming up with all this stuff. Weird shit.

—Shut the door? Sandwich?

He had already shut the door when I said to shut the door. I was still holding my cell phone from the call. I didn't know how I made the sandwiches while holding the phone to make the call. Or no, I didn't make the call, I got the call. Zach stared at the sandwich I held out to him. He shrugged, looked confused, didn't move. I reached it out at him.

—You okay? You look kinda funny.

—So do you.

He took the sandwich, looked at it as if it had bugs. I waved the cell phone.

—That was just him checking in. He's funny sometimes, funny sense of humor. Weird guy.

Weird guy. That wasn't the half of it. *More indirect route.* What did he mean by that? Last time I took a more indirect route it was joining the Air Force to get rich like Bob Dylan.

—No snakes?

Zach didn't speak. We stared down Highway 190, straight as the road to Hell. Forget the big honcho, I thought, the opportunity, the promise. Just turn tail and head straight home.

But the car was pulling onto the highway, and it was me behind the wheel. I drove straight on. The rocks rolled by. Basin land tilting and bent, falling away to badlands, and big bites out of the hills like dinosaurs chewed it out. But some people would call it beautiful. Layers of whites and browns, grays and reds. Chunks of black rock, long streaks the color of gold in the sand. Trees with knobby fists and low brush up the slope of a mesa like scruff on an old man's chin. Distant blue mountains in ranks, armies of clouds—

And another brown sign for Death Valley National Park, as if you'd never guess it. It said we'd have to pay, but I knew that much already. Eventually they get you. If I wanted to turn around I'd better do it right here and save the bucks. *Farther east*, he said on the phone. What was that all about? I looked for a turn-around.

We passed a sign pointing to Cow Creek. A couple of houses and a wad of trees, just a wide spot in the desert. Those little dirt-track roads, off one side or the other, nothing for them to go to, nowhere to go. It almost made you thankful to live in Chico, California, where at least we could go to the ocean if we ever did, though we didn't. Cow Creek. Maybe people went there to die.

—Think of living in one of these little places? Not have to see so many people, I guess. Little shack in the middle of nowhere.

—But for sure there must be a Walmart.

Zach was funny sometimes, but I tried not to laugh, it only encouraged him. There was always a darkness to it, and lots of comedians killed themselves. I could never tell which way to react. He had a funny streak.

Then across the valley I saw a lake, what looked like a lake with a sheen. Or might be a mirage like in the cartoons, but it looked real, and not far away. It might be close. If it was really a lake.

—Is that water there? It couldn't be water, it must be salt. But it looks like water, I mean it rains here sometimes. But not a whole lake. It must be salt.

—We could stop and go see.

—It must be salt. But amazing, all that salt.

—Yea though I whiz through the Valley of the Shadow of Death.

He was right. I was hitting eighty-five. I was thinking about the phone call, what Stubblefield said. *Test of faith*, he said. *Indirect route, farther east.* I had to get to Las Vegas and call him and ask what's up. Okay, I get it, he wants people who follow orders. But not to turn over and wilt. Okay, I'm a fly in the spider's web, but if I buzz loud enough the spider had ought to show some respect.

We passed some kind of a resort or inn with tile roof buildings and palm trees scattered around and another sign saying that we could rent a Jeep.

—We could rent a Jeep there, Zach.

—Okay.

—But I don't have a great urge to rent a Jeep.

Not true. I had an urge to rent a Jeep. A Jeep meant freedom from the ribbon of concrete they laid down to trap you. I used to think driving was freedom, but it's really just waiting. The car hits seventy, eighty, eighty-five, and it seems like you're going somewhere, but you're just perched in your little box watching the world whiz by. A thousand miles of pavement, and nothing changes along the way unless you turn off to Cow Creek, which doesn't have much appeal. Taking you where somebody decided they wanted you to go. The sun beats down until it goes black and you cringe in your little box.

Up ahead was the ranger station and a building for souvenirs. I knew they'd eventually nick us for money. I pulled in, but no rangers, just a yellow machine on a post to put your money in. I wondered if I could just ignore it and drive away or if they maybe had cameras. I shouldn't risk it. I parked, got out of the car, checked the instructions. Only twenty bucks, not thirty. I stuck my credit card into their goddamn slot. The Feds did all they could to drive you crazy.

Right then a ranger appeared around the corner of the building. He was a little rabbity man in one of those Smoky Bear hats. I guess my twenty bucks bought him his hat. He looked like the TV comic we used to see, this whiny chicken-faced guy.

—Good morning, friends. Or afternoon, whichever.

—Oh hi. What is it, twenty bucks?

—Unless you have a Golden Eagle.

—What's that?

—Well, that's for seniors. I'm joking.

—Well, I might get there pretty soon.

He was friendly but never cracked a smile. He looked at you the way they do in the movies, like at the camera over your shoulder. The machine spat out a slip. Good thing I hadn't blown it off. The Feds are always keeping track.

—Well, I thought it'd be hot in the desert, but it's not that hot.

—We vary. Are you driving around? Camping?

—No, just right through. Business in Las Vegas.

Was he trying to charge me extra? Or no, I shouldn't judge people by their hat: maybe he's just keeping track so we didn't get lost and die. Although the old lady jamming the parking lot: she wore a blue blouse with flowers, big blossoms to keep her alive, and driving a white Ford pickup. Little old lady driving a pickup. But if her husband just died on the couch and she drove out for help and had to stop for dish soap—

She wasn't driving a pickup. My brain was doing it again. Maybe I should write TV shows, they like that crazy stuff. I waved the slip to say thanks and got out of there fast. I rubbed my forehead to see if something felt funny.

Twenty bucks just to drive straight through, like the ticket price to Hell. Hell after they dropped the big one. Burned-over mountains, black rock, slag heaps, then this long yawning valley, down below sea level according to the sign, rock and rubble, demolition, a land still roasting from when the angels tore down the Garden of Eden and left a vacant lot.

We drove through miles and miles and miles of that vacant lot. The flatness gave way to steep grades, switchbacks, tall ridges where the highway cut deep through the rock. Clumsy hatchet job. The overcast was gone, no clouds, no haze, just cold blue sky. Zach was lost somewhere in his head.

Test of faith. I could see my so-called benefactor's eyes from way back at the bar in Chico. After three beers, a snake's eyes would look friendly. *They will instruct you.* I couldn't shake that damn phone call. *Slice across the throat.* What was that all about?

And the dunes. I'd always thought of dunes as blowing and shifting, sea waves like corn meal, but these were just pointy hills plastered over with sand and scrub. They ran from deep brown to gray and dead white like piles of chemicals, limestone, borax—we studied that in chemistry class, stuff that reacts with aluminum. Funny thing to remember. Old Mr. Cozad wore a bow tie, the kind that you tied, but he never tied it straight, it always drooped down like an old dying dog—

That I saw on a back porch in Omaha with a swarm of flies and then one would get in the bedroom and buzz all night but I'd have to get up early—

To get into Las Vegas tomorrow and call whoever the hell his assistant was and say I damn well had to talk to the boss and ask what he meant by—

Seeing the dentist because yes it's been a long time but I don't think I need a colonoscopy, I don't have a problem—

With that red pickup coming the other way, first thing for miles, and I could swerve head-on—

To swat these flies in the brain. What's going on with my brain?

The road made a twist between redrock hills, and then in a heave the mountain reared up and I saw the face of God. A rock like the face of God. Not the God that Reverend Bud knew, the God full of love, but God like he was at the blaze of noon. Great slabs of granite hatcheted into cheekbone, brow ridge, snaggle-tooth teeth, ruts down the cheeks from the tears. God from the Bible. Huge bristle-face Daddy. A couple of seconds and I was past.

—Uh, Dad?
—What?
—You okay?
—Why?
—You were making sounds.

I was making sounds. So what if I was making sounds? When he got to be my age, he'd be making sounds.

—I'm fine.

A sign said we were leaving Death Valley. Twenty bucks for nothing. Fifty-seven varieties of garbage dump. They didn't even check if we paid. Then a sign for Death Valley Junction, some kind of town— here if you found two buildings you called it a town. Flat wall of a two-story building with a big block-letter sign, then a long low white motel, it looked like, with arches along its face. A couple of cars out front. I took a sharp left. We were past.

—State Line Road, I think this gets there faster.

—Make sure we get there faster, Dad.

—Funny building.

The one we passed. Zach got talkative. He'd read about it or seen it on YouTube, something. *Amargosa Opera House,* it said on the side. Some lady from New York, a dancer he thought, had bought the building and moved there and put in a stage, made it into a theatre in the middle of nothing. No audience, so she painted her audience around the inside walls. Kings and explorers and socialites, Vikings and Indians and clowns. And she danced for the people she painted. Pretty soon the locals came from miles around, and she put on a show. You see the stars on TV that are totally fake and get watched by millions of nitwits, but this lady just painted her walls and did her dance. Some mornings I wanted to feel like that. To feel like it's enough. I did enough.

Zach didn't know what happened to her. Some time we might stop there, if there was time. If there was ever time. What if you walked the whole stretch of Death Valley and saw what was really there?

—Funny thing, Dad.

—What is?

—All the stories, they go into the desert. Looking for something. Moses, Elijah, Abraham, Jesus, Mohammed—

—In the Bible?

—Well, I guess Oppenheimer too, but that was a little different.

—Is that a joke?

—Well, even Oppenheimer. He's the one founded the Church of Atomic Bombs. I mean he gave us something very big to think about. Bones and rattlesnakes and mushroom clouds. But no, I'm serious. Indians call it going on a vision quest. You said something the other day. About visions?

—Visions? No.

—You talked about visions.

—Not me.

—But now I guess we do our vision quest at the shopping mall.

He had the last word. Let him have the last word. I wasn't going to take the bait. All that crap about visions, mirages, second sight. Better you look to the future. Look to what's real. I caught myself grinding my teeth.

—So the flyer said there were ruins around here somewhere. Back from before there were people here.

—Before there were people?

—White people, I mean. But all they left were ruins.

—Whereas we built Las Vegas.

We were heading into another squabble. Try not to sound stupid. Pretend I'm intelligent. Keep it light.

—Well, so it's an hour or so to Las Vegas. It'll be nice to see some green for a change. Guess they do a lot of watering there. Amazing how stuff sprouts up if there's water.

—Where the money grows on trees.

—And I need to make a phone call. See what happens from there.

When I was a kid I had a friend, Kenny. We were in Boy Scouts, his dad was scoutmaster, ex-Marine, sour little guy, little rooster. Kenny was a year older than me. We'd ride our bikes all over town, South Omaha where we lived, and I'd help him on his paper route. Do kids still have paper routes? The paper came out in the afternoon, we'd fold the papers, and I'd look at the headlines, try to figure it out. Haven't ever been able to.

One Saturday we rode down to the river and left our bikes and hiked. We were throwing rocks and clods, and he said, *What's the worst thing?* I asked what he meant. *The worst thing you could do?* He was thinking like the worst way you could torture a guy?

I went to the Presbyterian church two blocks from our house, and what came to mind from Sunday School was where God made the father kill his son. Or not actually kill him, but I felt it what it was like for the son. I still remembered the belt strap, but what if you saw your dad with a knife and your hands were tied and your back was flat on cold stone? My dad was already gone or else I would've, I don't know, snuck in with a steak knife when he was asleep and— Whatever. Though what I never thought was what it was like for the dad.

So I told the story to Kenny, and he said that wasn't in the Bible. They were Mormons or something weird, so I told him it meant obedience to God, and Isaac was like Jesus, only they killed a sheep instead. Then Kenny said sarcastically, *So they screwed a sheep?* That was so stupid a thing to say that we got in a fight. He was bigger than me, but I kicked him in the crotch and he made a kind of bark and sat down and moaned. After that we were still friends, but then it trailed off.

Or another time we found a culvert pipe that went under a road. Kenny yelled dirty words, and it echoed like the voice of God, like God yelling *Shit!* and *Fuck!* Sometimes my guy in Las Vegas acted like Kenny, the voice of God yelling *Fuck!* There was so much that bothered me then.

I drove on to Las Vegas, totally clueless. Little baby crawling across the desert—rubble, stubble, asphalt—and can't see where it's going. Totally confused, can't focus, but up ahead it's like a water mirage, it opens up, layers of light, lake, snow, green mountains. Or is it all salt?

—16—

Stubblefield

I get lost in people's heads. Some carnival they had a house of mirrors where you tried to find your way out of the maze but all you saw was five reflections of yourself converging like one-way streets. You could get lost in there for days.

These people did that to me. The son talked like he was inside the dad and the dad spoke from far away but it was all a worm-fest of words. To Vern the world was real only insofar as it spat on him. He couldn't tell if he heard the Voice of God or an elephant fart.

I should have warned him. Travel changes you. Check out Moses. Before the Exodus he only killed one guy who was beating up a slave. But afterwards he wiped out whole cities tribes races without raising a sweat—too bad for those dummies in Jericho who'd built their ancient city on Promised Land. And my uncle talked about Vietnam and the dead meat he saw after napalm. No question but travel broadens your perspective.

You wonder. Does the father truly desire to be a role model and a moral compass and a bank account for his son or is he looking for any excuse to crash and burn? Does the son want to fly on the wings of an eagle or die as fast as he can? Do they really need a bird chirp in their ears to tell them what to do?

Vern I pictured sitting there by the roadside waiting for his son to come back from a pit stop. He would watch the boy walk up behind a huge slab of sandstone watching for rattlesnakes. He would have been surprised when his cell phone burbled. Reception in Death Valley? Burble burble. It took him a while to find the phone that might have slipped down the side of the driver's seat.

—Hello?

Bad signal. My own voice sounded tinny.

—Doing okay, Vern?

—Oh. Hi. Yeh. Good. Great.

Silence for a breath. Had I lost him? Say something, Vernon. Talk. Expound.

—Oh yeh, we were just stopping for lunch.

—How's your boy?

—Fine. He's there, taking a pit stop. I just fixed sandwiches. Funny, cause the cell phone's working now, middle of Death Valley, middle of nowhere and I couldn't get a signal— Or no, I was gonna say I couldn't get a connection before, but that's not true cause I never actually tried, I thought what's the point—

—You know what causes global warming? Too much talk.

A beat of chagrined comprehension.

—Right.

And here was me not really knowing what I was going to say until I said it. But always trust the quantum dimension to fire the quark that shoots up our ass and drives us on. I could hear him breathing like a bicycle pump.

—So here's what you do, my friend. I have a meeting tomorrow in Dallas. These things happen. So you get to Las Vegas, check in somewhere, save the receipt. Then call my office, my secretary Wendall, he'll be expecting the call. You may be asked to drive a more indirect route, which would be farther east or thereabouts, and so we would not at this point intersect directly in Las Vegas. Although that will happen. But just do what they tell you and follow the dotted line. We'll take it from there. Think of it as a test of faith.

—Farther?

—East.

—So you're saying—

—I just did.

—East, okay. But so I'm— I'm just wondering—

—As you should.

—It's funny, the signal is funny, your voice is—

—This is the age of communication—

—Right—

—Meaning it sucks.

I could imagine Vern glancing out the side window looking for his son toward some huge stone slab where the boy went to piss. I saw the boy walking back dead white from seeing a ghost. What I said next was pure inspiration. No notion why I said it though my premise was that people go limp in the presence of a lunatic. No predicting what's next. No logic to cling to. Nothing fits. It's the surefire way to boggle a mugger: tell him *I need to know what time it is*. Scrambles his yolk.

—Tell you what, Vern, here's a thought for the day. The Jews have this thing about kosher food. Kill the beast in a Biblical way. One slice across the throat gives you happier beef. Slaughter like mad as long you keep it kosher.

That stopped his clock. He was trying to fit my words into his world of reference. Burble burble, am I satanic, anti-Semitic, what? I slipped another bedbug into his ear.

—But I mean, Vern, check out all the killing in the Bible. It's kind of educational, right? Ten Commandments, okay, but what it really says is *Thou shalt not kill unless I say so*. Your descendants will be as the grains of sand and the stars in the sky, first-rate killers all. Just one quick slice.

Vern was hanging on the ropes not sure what hit him. All this stuff about driving east and slitting throats—gibberish defying all logic. A bullshit avalanche. Bunkum by the shovelful. Suddenly I sounded to him like God because only God could be so fucking nuts. And then the first glimmer of killing. First whisper of a Beethoven theme—I'm heavy into Beethoven—and it grabs you. In a minute it blossoms up and thunders.

—Question, Vern.

—Huh?

—Who do you think I am? Or who do people say that I am?

—I'm sorry, what?

—Just kidding. World without end, amen.

I do have dreams of redemption. If we could get all the world's sonofabitching bastards all the serial rapists the mild-mannered terrorists the money-grubbing swine the hypocritical scum of Planet Earth to tell us the simple facts that are in them to tell—how we've come to stand in shit swim in shit dine on shit get born on a tidal surge of shit—we might build our wistful utopias on firmer footing. We might achieve the new millennium. We might escape the Death Valley that spreads over our mucous membranes.

It won't happen any time soon.

The boy came back from the rock and got into the car and Vern drove on or so I imagined. It wouldn't be far once he hit the 160 but now it seemed like Las Vegas was only a stop for the night at just another motel then on to wherever the Powers That Be would direct him—that royal road to nowhere. He surely had the urge to turn one-eighty. *Turn back! It's a scam! Go home!*

The raw throat of the landscape growled at Vern. Needle and thistle and weeds. Saltbrush and bloodroot. Ledges and spires and slabs and arroyos he remembered from Westerns as a kid. They passed a rock shop in the shape of a big pink blob that was someone's idea of a rock. They passed a sign marking a spot where history happened. Vern turned on radio static and then for the nth time turned it off. He remembered in grade school that after the pledge-allegiance they sang *America the Beautiful* but the song never mentioned the rubble. Parched lips. Mirage. A blister beetle's scuttle.

And I had brought up the image of cutting a throat. I could see where this was going. I almost wish I didn't.

—17—

Vernon

Three motels, he said. He was counting motels. What did he
expect? Sack out in the car?

—What's this business with motels?

—Just keeping track, Dad.

We came in the door. The Las Vegas motel didn't look any different from the other motels except for just one king-size bed and over
the bed a picture of wild horses. Guess people couldn't tell they were
west if they didn't see wild horses up on a ridge with a cactus. We'd
never seen any horses on the trip: they were all in motels.

We drifted into the room like detectives looking for clues. On the
nightstand were flyers advertising a casino, the cartoon of a cowboy
riding a bucking slot machine. Zach set his doggy bag on top of the
cowboy.

—Your mom wouldn't be too happy, you having a burrito for
dinner and not even eating it.

—If you tell her.

—Your mom and I don't lie to one another.

—Awesome.

He pulled off his shoes and rolled onto the bed. No point pursu-
ing it, because anything I said . . .

—Anyway I've got my doggy bag. I'll eat it after a while. I'll be the happy doggy.

I picked up a flyer with the bucking slot machine. Casino just the other side of the diner and the motel was cheaper than I expected, so we could go and spend a few bucks. Or maybe Zach would want to hit the sack and I could go out for a walk. I checked the back of the flyer. This showgirl, cheerleader type, arms outstretched, smile so wide she could catch gum disease. That stuff was so fake. Somebody thought it was sexy, but all the movie starlets my so-called buddies thought were hot stuff were that same hysterical fake. Thank God Merna was real. She'd never win a beauty contest, but when we made love it was real.

But sometimes you didn't want real, you wanted fake. I wondered how many girls started out real, then put on their lipstick and did up their hair and practiced their cute little smile in the mirror. I fell for that more than once. And tonight, the waitress at the diner: twenty-five, twenty-six maybe, dishwater blonde, a little eye-liner and lip gloss, but she smiled when I said how hungry we were. She looked directly at me in the eyes and she smiled. Eyes that hadn't ever seen me at my worst. Maybe that's what guys were looking for: a girl that hadn't seen them at their worst.

Good thing there wasn't a way. If Zach sacked out and I went back, she might smile, and this time I'd give her a smile instead of looking down at the menu. I had wanted to look at her walking away but didn't want Zach to see me ogle a lady's rear end.

The phone call. I was still stewing. *Test of faith*— I was thinking crazy. That's not what I was here for, and Zach wasn't ready for bed. He was watching a golf match. They plop a ball in a hole, then walk five minutes and plop it into another. Made as much sense as the stage play they said on the news, where guys just stood there doing nothing. The newscaster made fun of the pointy-head jerks who'd pay to see it, but it made total sense to me. It was pretty much what people did every day, trying not to get shit-canned but hoping they'd get somewhere. And here I was driving a thousand miles to scratch the itch, not even knowing where it itched.

—You gonna call Mom?

—When I do.

—When's that?

—When we know what's going on. We'll find out tomorrow.

At least Zach was talking now. He'd sat there while I was eating dinner, staring at his burrito and taking maybe two bites. The waitress asked if he wanted a doggy bag, and he smiled. Looked at me sideways when I ordered a second beer, and for a moment I wanted to smack him. I knew other fathers felt that way, I'd seen a movie like that. Movie, hell, I remembered my dad. At least I did better than Dad.

—Dad, you said you'd call Mom when we got to Las Vegas, so we're here in Las Vegas, so why don't you call her?

—What's this whole Mom business? I call her, you never talk, you just wave it away. Are you watching that?

—Yeh, they hit the ball in a hole to kill gophers. They want to preserve the lawn.

I sat down on the bed. Not the time to go out for a walk. Maybe coming back I could see her. Her name tag said *Catherine*. She wouldn't like *Cathy*. There was something in her face that was starting to age. You could already see the old woman in the girl, but it made her more real. Her voice was back in the flat of the mouth, but the voice was nice. *You ready to order?* as if she really cared. First time I might stroke her shoulders and we'd look in each other's eyes. This fantasy crap—it kept running in my brain.

—Anyway we just got here.

—So tomorrow you see this guy and then we'll be rich?

—Don't get smart.

—Could you call Mom? Dad, I'm just seeing her sitting there waiting and how she must feel, and I'll talk if you want, although I have absolutely nothing to say. But I'm just feeling like—

— Well, we've got the whole evening. We could go out and see Las Vegas, casinos, I mean we don't need to gamble, but they've got shows, family stuff. Or stop back at that diner for a piece of pie? I mean we've got all this big sky and mountains and rocks but we're in these little boxes twenty-four hours a day, the car, the motels, or sitting here watching a little box—

We sat watching the little box. The sportscaster built the tension up down to a whisper, and the golfer putted and missed. A low moan. Why were we watching this junk? *Gophers*—that was funny. Goddamn phone call. *World without end*—

—Or we could take a walk, Go downtown, take some snapshots. They say it's lighted up like daylight. Your mom wanted pictures, so we better take snapshots— You want to see Las Vegas?

—Not really.

He rose up sharp from the bed, his back to me, slapped both hands flat to the wall and stood there. Did he think he was being funny? Best if I didn't say a word.

—Zach, I don't know what's going on with you, but I think you could be halfway civil—

—Okay—

—I'm sorry about Death Valley. One big nothing. They could cut it up in five-acre chunks and sell it for parking lots. Make that thing a national park so you can't just drive through, you gotta pay twenty bucks. Like buying a ticket to Hell. I'd imagined the Painted Desert, I saw a postcard once, it was beautiful but that's not Death Valley—

He had his head in his hands. It hit me I shouldn't be talking negative stuff, I was talking him into depression. I should be cheering him up, but sometimes I had to spew it out, the stuff that had to be said or just lay there and rot—

—And then coming into Las Vegas, it's supposed to be so great, but what leads up? Desert. Worse you get closer, little concrete shit piles, roads going off to junkyards where some poor sonofabitch is trying to live—

—Well, Dad—

—Buildings, these wire mesh fences, and somebody builds blocks of these cracker-box houses jammed up like a city, then sand, miles and miles there's nothing but sand—

—Dad? What are you talking about?

—This whole damn trip!

—I wonder whose idea was that.

My mouth had the runs. I shut up. The golfer lined up another putt. The sportscaster did his breathless inhale. The ball found its hole. Polite applause. Zach tapped two fingers together like an elf applauding. *Farther east—*

A knock at the door. Zach surprised me by getting up to answer it. He opened the door, and a low stuttering voice said something about towels. Zach mumbled and took an armful of towels and closed the door.

—What's that?

—The motel guy gave us towels.

—We've got towels.

—Now we've got more.

He took the towels into the bathroom, came back, and flopped on the bed.

—What'd he look like?

—He looked like a motel guy.

—Mexican?

—I dunno. Skinny guy.

—They're all over.

I caught myself. I was about to say that you can't find a white man's motel, but Zach would jump on that. That wasn't how I thought. Air Force, you learned to respect a guy for doing his job, even though people assume if you're white and live in a trailer and work at Walmart, then you're automatically a bigot. But it was a fact that you couldn't find a motel where there wasn't some guy at the desk with an accent—they had a corner on it.

—I just mean it's funny how they're all foreigners.

—Bring us your tired, your poor, your huddled stack of towels.

—I mean we fight all these wars, spend billions to blow up their country, then turn around and bring'em all over here.

—Except for the ones we kill.

I didn't have an answer for that. He always stuck up for the little guy, which I was glad of, but I wished sometimes he'd stick up for me. Then he surprised me.

—We're a lot alike, Dad.

—How?

—Lotta ways. General outlook.

—Difference being maybe I've got more perspective. More sense of the possibilities.

—More bull.

Another dig. He'd always find some way to twist the knife. Open the door and then slam it shut. All I could see of my son right now was the little twisted smile and his eyes closed off, back in his little box. But I didn't have to say what I said. Who did I think was slamming the door? *More perspective . . .* I tried to change the subject, as if I knew what the subject was. *One slice across the throat—*

—Your mom said she was having dreams.

—They'll be out on Netflix.

He sat staring at the TV, muting the sound to watch the flicker of ads. I opened my suitcase, dug out the tequila. Sometimes I needed a cheer-up and sometimes more.

—Hey, if you eat that burrito, if you like you can have a little tequila with it. You're old enough.

—Interesting you were saying that Mom was drunk.

—I didn't say she was drunk, I said she sounded like it. Like she was drinking. I wasn't blaming her, I was just worried. Times we were both screwed up. You just never lose the worry about it. There's always the scar.

He stayed glued to the flicker.

—Does it go both ways? Does she hear you and wonder what's going on?

—Nothing going on.

—How was she all screwed up?

—You gonna eat that thing or take it to bed with you?

Zach reached across, picked up the burrito bag, and threw it on the floor without shifting his eyes from the flicker.

—Pick it up, Zach.

He didn't move.

—Pick it up.

—Suck my dick.

It came out very simple, flat, something he said every day like *Pass the salt*. But he never said stuff like that. That was so unlike him. He turned up the sound long enough for the announcer to say, *Hi, I'm Bradley James and I'm*— but flicked it off. Then he looked at me for the first time that day.

—Dad, I'm having trouble here, okay? What you said, these mountains, big sky, but we're in these little boxes, like you said, and really, seriously, I'm like stop it, please stop it, stop it, stop it—

—You don't talk to your father like that.

—I'm sorry, Dad—

—You said you wanted to come along.

—I never said I wanted to come along.

—You said you wanted to come along.

—You said I wanted to come along.

—You never said you didn't.

—You never asked me.

—Blame it on me, blame it on your mother, blame it on God—

—I don't blame it on God. God doesn't give a shit about me or you, any more than you ever gave a shit about my brother—

—Half-brother.

I was on my feet, grabbed my suitcase, threw it on the bed, opened the lid, slammed it shut. *Thou shalt not kill*—

—All right then, we'll turn around and go back. We'll fucking get up in the morning and turn around and go back. Up to you! Opportunity, fuck it! Go back home!

—Dad, I'm sorry—

—And I don't want to hear that language!

I stood there shaking, huffing and puffing, ridiculous, then got my voice back to where it sounded like me.

—So I need to brush my teeth and get to bed. Be sure you brush your teeth. I told your mom I'd tell you.

—I'm sorry, Dad.

I set the suitcase back on the chair. I hated getting mad, my voice pinched up like a girl. Zach, in a tiny voice—

—Did you hear me say I'm sorry?

The cell phone needed charging. I found the cord in the side pocket of the suitcase and plugged it in under the cowboy's night-stand. At least my son was talking now and I had to acknowledge that.

—Well, I'm sorry too. Okay, so, yeh, sorry—

—One thing, spending time together, we apologize a lot.

—That's true. That's right. We do.

There were times it felt like we were really talking. Like my mom said once, though I never caught the gist of it at the time, the words were being counted and spent. We might be fighting, but the words were counted and spent.

—We better sack out. Or it's early, maybe I'll take a walk—

An angel walked over my grave, or maybe a goose, my mom used to say. I waited for Zach to say okay, but he was eating his burrito, so I pulled back my bedcovers. *Grains of sand and stars*—

—We oughta go to the ocean, I mean back home after the trip. It's not that far from Chico, I guess. Kinda roundabout, but we could take all day and still get back. Mendocino coast, tall cliffs. Course the pictures are always better, I guess.

I watched him eat his burrito. So much I could tell him if he'd keep his mouth shut and listen. If he really wanted to hear, I'd be honest. But it's hell to go outside our dreams. As a kid I'd go out in the backyard and pretend I was hitting home runs. New world record for the most home runs over the backyard fence. And dreams of dropping the bombs. Early morning, look out over Omaha, fire in the sky, and I'd run out into the road, a little ribbon of road like the ribbon my cousin wore in her hair— It's those little broken bits that make up a life. But if I tried to be honest with Zach he'd think I was talking crap.

—Tell me about Denver.

Denver. The word was a fishhook. He couldn't shut up about Denver. All that could be said about Denver had been said, and the rest of it couldn't. He probably knew it all and wanted to twist the knife. Study history, fine, but there's no way to change it.

—You know it. I told you. All there was to it, I already said.

—Well, you kinda left stuff out.

Zach had folded one of the flyers into a paper airplane. He tossed it. It glided around and hit the horse over the bed.

—Scuse me.

He got up, went into the bathroom, shut the door. I opened the suitcase on the chair, dug down the side, pulled out a fresh pint of tequila, took a pull—cheap stuff, burning—and set it on the nightstand. The TV was off, but I was still seeing the golfer line up his putt. I took another pull, and the bed wobbled under me like a rowboat. The first bottle had been fuller than I'd thought. I heard the toilet flush. Who invented toilets?

The next thing I knew was Zach coming out of the bathroom, but after that I couldn't keep it straight. Zach standing there, and then it was all crazy traffic noise, skid screeches, rats in my head. Like in high school Mr. Stuelke describing the Battle of Gettysburg—how nobody knew what was going on, just explosions and horses cut in two, men with faces torn off, the canister shot, the cannonballs. Not even so much the blood, you were ready for that, but the hideous confusion, poor bastards not knowing which way to run, and Mr. Stuelke talking low and steady, like lining up the golf putt. I never forgot those fifty minutes the Wednesday before Thanksgiving, and I needed to shut the suitcase, but I was chugging tequila and Zach was talking or me telling it out loud or the grapefruit in my head?

—*Name was Gayla, Gayla Krelle, German name, older than me, but then I met Merna, your mother Merna, got her pregnant so I left Gayla and married Merna—*

Who was the slurry voice? Who was the father here? Somebody asking, somebody telling.

—*But no baby then, left the Air Force, toilet paper, moved back to Omaha. Drinking a lot and started with Gayla again, but she got pregnant, November '86, she moved to Denver, had the baby, I never saw him, or later I saw him, and Gayla married a plumber—*

I wasn't drinking, but the pint was half gone, way more than half. I couldn't help it.

—*'93, went to Denver to check out a job, but I knew Gayla was there, we started up again and Merna found out, your mother—*

The pint was empty already, my words were slurred. I couldn't make out what was being said. It wasn't the way I meant it. I could hardly hear what I said for the slur. Something got said. Something about my binges and one-night-stands. Something about getting fired. The time I puked in the bed. The time I hit her in the breast. And then church. And then pregnant. And then a son. I didn't know which way to run.

—That was Denver. That was the story of Denver.

—Well, it's all in the Bible, Dad.

Merna, before I lied she'd know it, even before I knew it myself. We do these con jobs on ourselves. She'd heard the promises, promises, and California, *Hey, honey, there's mountains and oceans in California*, but all I ever did was flop down at the tube and then get up, go to bed, go to work, go to Hell. Even with Jesus, me letting Jesus into my heart, she knew it was crap. She'd get these flashes. She called it a fist.

—Dad, I don't need to hear any more.

There was more. Lots more. I got to my feet to prove I wasn't plastered, and I must have knocked the suitcase to the floor. It was all scattered, however neat she tried to pack it, shirts and my shaving stuff, underwear, necktie that I never wore, and there was the pistol in his hand.

—Dad? What's this?

—What? What does it look like?

I was slurring like a drunk comedian. It must have been packed in the suitcase. I must have packed it in there after Merna packed. He was holding the pistol by two fingers, like a dead mouse. He was in this tiny voice again—

—What have you got a gun for?

My head was blank, but the words came burping up.

—Browning twenty-two, semi-automatic. I had a nine-millimeter but I left that in Denver. She didn't want a gun in the house. The Browning, I've had that for, I don't remember, I—

—Is that legal?

—Couple years. Sure it's legal. Legal to have it, you can't do concealed carry, or in some states you can, but it's legal to have it, it's a free country, for now, goddammit—

—What the hell—

—Don't swear! For protection. Chrissake, this is Las Vegas, right next to Mexico, immigrants coming across. Desperate. Motels, find people in bathtubs, they cut out your kidneys to sell.

—That's an urban myth.

—It's not urban, it's everywhere. Protection. I promised your mother. This is a different world. People hate us.

—Mom knows you have that?

He wasn't holding the pistol. It was lying in the suitcase open on the floor. With my kit bag open, tube of toothpaste, toothbrush, razor. I needed to tell him remember to brush his teeth, but we were on vacation so never mind, unless he really wanted to. We could have a good time. Talk like father and son—

—Is that loaded?

He was talking about the gun, but I wasn't holding the gun, I was holding the toothpaste and he was yelling, *Call Mom!* But I couldn't call her now, she'd be stinking drunk, and there hadn't been one day since the boy tried to kill himself when she wasn't thinking, *Where is he, what's he doing?*

Zach stood there staring. He looked lost.

—Dad, should we better go to bed? It's early, but we're tired. Maybe get some sleep?

His hands were empty. I was sitting in a chair. Maybe I hadn't brought the pistol. I'd remembered the cell phone. Call Merna in the morning.

—Try to remember, Zach, just remember, just— Everything comes from God. Not just the— But everything, I mean all the—

—Thanks, God.

—Long drive tomorrow. We should talk. Important stuff in the world. Not politics, they're all crooks, but we're father and son . . .

—Good. I'd like to. Let's do.

But no more words were left in the day. I was on the bed. I heard the voice somewhere in the back of my head. *More indirect route—* And the cowboy, the bucking slot machine.

There must be a wind made of curses. Rises up from the fruited plain and you don't feel a breath, but it's curses. Promises, plans, impossible lies, and I fell for it all. I believed my own lies, and that took some doing. I couldn't stand the sound of my voice, but I saw the waitress smiling, Catherine, Cathy, the way she smiled, I liked the way her lips came to an edge. She bent down in the night and kissed me gently. And then I was christalmighty dead out.

—18—

Stubblefield

The public has a misconception of the nature of the sociopath the torturer the kid who pulls off the legs of frogs. Lack of empathy. No feelings. But there's a spectrum. Certainly for some it's a power trip being sole master of his little screaming universe. But at the other end of the chart is the hyper-empathic madman who tastes every sip of fine emotion. Those are drawn to Vern and his like. I felt acutely what he felt though our perspectives differed.

Vernon told me this. The longer ago the tighter it sticks. He was a kid, he hit his dog Ragsie with a pillow and then Ragsie snarled and he hit her for snarling and she barked so he kept hitting to make her stop and he hit her right on the nose with his fist. She gave a big yelp and ran out the door. He was sorry for that but Ragsie would never accept his apology. Why he told me that I have no idea.

I knew that poor Vern was tired of the desert—all that red gravel baked rock and chisel teeth. Like the old pioneers he hated stuff that you couldn't make money from like land that just sat there with Indians loafing around atop it. It offered no amenities like food for his family or the promise of young waitresses' butts. And yet—

He held hope. Something higher than himself. Las Vegas. Las Vegas towering up from the desert this sleek neon cancer this joyous toxin this tumorous boogie that turns every brain cell to mush. God's labyrinth. A labyrinth isn't a maze where you choose your directions. You just follow where it leads. You're marching into the heart but suddenly it twists you farther east but then you slowly wind your way back to the promise. And yet—

Vernon's motive was deeper than winning the Lottery or cadging some gratis nookie. There was love in his heart for the wife back home who was possibly drunk and for the son who must hate him. And yet—

Every consequential act involves tiny gestures. You take the cap off the pen to sign the warrant. You stamp your seal on the royal decree. You punch the button to start the world war. Those fingertip twitches vary with the times: nobody uses a fountain pen or a wax seal. But it's still the tiny gestures that get the job done. Flick your Bic and tap your screen and poke your spindly digits and check out what happens. And so my directive to Vern McGurren was foreordained.

—So if you would write it down, please, Mr. McGurren. Specific directions, which I hope will not be inconvenient.

—So lemme go outside so I don't wake up my son. He's asleep.

Vern apparently found a pen and notepad compliments of Longhorn Motel and stumbled out to his car to scribble directions. I'd envisioned he might scribble the holy words on the vest of the bucking cowboy, but you can't always get what you want, as they sing in the song.

—You know, Mr. McGurren, I'm not authorized to say this, but you are far ahead of the game. I have to confess an envy. It took me much longer to earn his confidence fully. It's really a matter of trust.

Wendall's voice had a blandness you could only call digestive. He recited the directions all the highway twists and turns but the poor guy felt the walls shake with an indrawn gasp inhaling the whole big sky. In that moment he glimmed what it was all about. He saw the end of his journey. No word was spoken but the numbers added up and the image locked into focus with the knife coming down.

Come on Vern. Write it down. The directions were clear though I had only seen photos of the monster cathedral ascending above the flat. The gigantic stone wings of Shiprock.

—19—

Vernon

I woke up early and checked voicemail, even though it would have beeped if there were any calls. But I had missed the beep: the guy's office left a message. I listened, listened again. Zach was still asleep. I got dressed, slipped on my shoes, went out to the car and called on the cell phone, then back into the room for a pen. Zach was awake, but he didn't stir. Back out. Directions. Clicked off, sat there a while, grabbed the atlas, back into the room, sat on the edge of the bed, studied the maps.

Another five hundred miles. I never agreed to that. When the guy's assistant gave me directions I nodded automatically, but he couldn't have heard the nod. They couldn't just assume. I was being led on a snipe hunt. Boy Scout camp, they'd take the new kids out in the woods at night to hunt snipes, they said. Point being to get the tenderfeet lost in the dark. I never fell for it then, but it was my turn now. Though there really is a bird called a snipe. Or they say there is.

Breakfast with Zach at the diner, but of course my waitress wasn't there, the one who smiled. I hadn't even really looked at her, she could've been a dog, but that's not what I was there for: I was there for bacon and eggs. Zach just stared at his pancakes. Two tables over, I watched a young couple, Chinese tourists maybe, with a cute little boy that looked like a chipmunk. Would he grow up and stare at his pancakes? He looked at his dad and smiled. Nobody smiled these days unless they were selling toothpaste.

Back to the motel, and I packed the bag, checked around if we'd left anything—Merna called it *the idiot check*—and walked down to the motel office, nobody there, and left the key. Got into the car, Zach looked at me.

—Aren't you wearing your suit? When you see the guy?

I didn't reply. I was the father, dammit. We drove out and I turned east, thinking we'd have to run into a freeway.

—See the sign there, Zach? What's that?

—Flamingo Road.

—Watch if you see any signs.

—Signs for what?

—This is just suburbs, I guess. They stick a few palm trees around so you know it's not Omaha.

We crawled through stretches of houses. Nothing was going right. The jam in the parking lot, Yosemite, the desert, the nutty phone calls— But then the street widened and blocks away I could see skyscrapers catching the morning sun.

—There they are, you can see'em.

—See what?

—Casinos. Caesar's Palace, The Palms, Bally's, they're famous. What's that one, big white one? Look at that, shape of the Eiffel Tower. There's big money there. They say it's not just casinos now, it's a major center for lots of stuff. It's where the action is.

Probably stuff we don't even know about till it hits us. I didn't say that. It was the kind of thing Zach would say.

—Where are we going, Dad?

—Somewhere farther east. We'll run into something. 15 North, let's try that.

—Didn't he give you directions?

My turn to be silent. I turned onto the freeway. Zach watched the last gasps of Las Vegas.

—I thought the destination was Las Vegas.

I nodded my head, choosing the right moment.

—Change of plans.

I sounded like the action hero. Tight-jawed blunt stud with a mission, a man of few words. Long shot of the car merging onto the freeway into the clog of rats in the maze. After a while the morning traffic thinned out. Once you're on there you drive to where it takes you, and I drove to where it took me.

Zach could never stay silent for long. He started probing. He should be a dentist looking for decay. Maybe a lawyer, jumping on every word.

—So, but Dad, I mean, didn't we come over on the Mayflower and cross the plains in a wagon train and fight the Viet Cong so we could strike it rich in Las Vegas? Wasn't that the plan?

—I'm following directions. That's how you do it. Specific detailed directions. You better learn that. You don't ask why.

—Dad, I'm sorry I sounded sarcastic. I'm just . . . confused.

And I didn't mean to sound pissed-off, but I was driving against the sun and suddenly hit a blinding glare. I tried to explain to him: voice message, change of plans, head east, I-15 to 9-East then 59-South at Hurricane, wherever that was. I went on babbling directions like a GPS. Zach looked at me funny. He'd never heard me talk that way, like some movie with secret agents or Navy Seals. I didn't tell him the crazy stuff, no point in that, like about Jews cutting throats. The honcho's assistant sounded more normal—kind of a sweet-talker, kind of a prick.

I tried to explain. This was a job of consequence. *Not a school assignment, Vern, where you write your little paper and nobody reads it except the teacher who gives you a C. This has consequence.* I believed that. I had to believe it. This was how history happened. I felt a shudder, from me or him or somewhere. Zach laughed.

—What's funny?

—Nothing.

He was right: nothing was funny. I felt his stare when he heard me mention Shiprock.

❖

Out from Las Vegas it was giant mole hills, gopher mounds, huge brown pimples on the face of the earth. Rock gnawed away by big rat teeth. Layers of yellow and tan and the color of salmon pink, then a long streak of brown like the back of a highway patrolman—I had to grin at the thought. Then colors I'd never seen, a dark copper cliff, a lavender ridge, butterscotch rock, I could taste it almost. Then the highway ran down a wide-open gullet, slabs rising to either side, and the layers, veins, crusts, whatever you call it, tilted up so you thought the mountains were charging each other like bulls. And then nothing, just scraggly sagebrush, gravel, empty parking lot for miles and miles.

I never thought like that. *Skies are blue and trees are green* was as much as I ever noticed. A wound was opened raw.

—Sign there, mileage to Kanab? Funny name.

—Must be where kanab-us comes from.

I frowned at him, then realized he was joking, funny in fact. Some people laugh when they're making a joke so you know it's a joke. Zach never did.

Back into hills again, and around a switchback I saw a dark blob in the road, roadkill maybe, the size of a cantaloupe. I didn't want to swerve, so I ran over it and bang, a crack and shatter. Omigod, a rock. They had these signs that told you to look out for falling rocks. I guess I found one.

I hadn't thought we were riding so low. I should have stopped to look under the car, but I didn't know what that would tell me. I didn't know cars. High school, my buddies talked cars cars cars, and I would nod and fake it. I sort of knew what a carburetor did, but I got pretty good at pretending. Not much different than talking about girls, pretending you knew every nook and cranny, you could take her apart and put her back together. But every time you nodded your head, *Right, I know*, you cut yourself off from ever asking a question. Only dimwits asked questions. Never thought I'd hit my fifties and be nearly as dumb as I was at age fifteen. At least with cars and women.

Maybe a hundred miles outside Las Vegas, middle of nowhere, it started making a funny popping sound, and I thought I smelled exhaust. I pulled to the side of the road, sat there a minute to let it settle, and when I started up it seemed to lose power. We limped into a little town and stopped at the only service station I saw.

Wonder of wonders, they had a mechanic. He was a stubby guy in gray coveralls, moon-faced, tiny black eyes, looked to be Mexican, with his name embroidered across an upper pocket: *Bruce*. He didn't look like a Bruce, he looked more like a Pancho, but I didn't have much choice. At least he spoke English.

—Might be a cracked manifold. I could solder it, weld it, but to replace it I'd have to get the parts.

—So how long . . .

—One job to finish, then I'll take a look. You in a rush?

—Kind of.

That didn't send him into any big hurry, just stared glassy-eyed like I was a mile away. If I'd known more about cars— But how would I know at the age of fifteen that I'd fall into the clutches of a beady-eyed Mexican that called himself Bruce?

Where were we now? Some godforsaken place with a Coke machine outside the door. I put a buck in, got a can of Coke, went into the tiny office with a couple of plastic chairs. Sat down, picked up an issue of *Guns & Ammo*. I didn't really want a Coke or the magazine, but it was something to do. Zach was walking outside.

The sun was up bright and the chill burning off. A big bastard fly kept buzzing me. I swatted at it, but the fly was better at buzzing than I was at swatting. Made me want some wimpy little moth to squash. I had a flash of the fighter pilots at the base in Minot. They never spoke to me—they were officers after all—but from what I heard them talk, they didn't want to go up against the Russians or Chinese. They really wanted to dogfight some candy-ass North Koreans they could swat out of the sky by the dozens or to waste the air force of Peru. We all want to stomp the weakest kid on the playground, stomp him into the dust, but that damned fly was giving me the finger. And the phone call—killing, cutting throats—came back in my head with a louder buzz. Crazy stuff. I wanted to scream out *I'm doing my best!* but who would I scream it at?

I stared at the cluttered desk, swivel chair behind it, and on the wall by the door to the shop was a pin-up calendar. I hadn't seen one of those for years. When I was five, six, my mom left me at the barber shop and went for groceries. They put a booster seat on the chair and lifted me up. Old guys were sitting around waiting for haircuts or their funerals. The barber faced me at a calendar between two mirrors, this girl in a bathing suit striking a slinky pose, which even then I thought looked fake. I heard an old guy talking about his wife. I couldn't tell the words, but the tone of it was dirty, like he was saying she stank. And I felt the calendar girl was dirty and tried not to look, but the chair faced me to her. The old guy talked about *doing it* and I didn't know what it was to do it, but it must involve the girl. When Mom came back to fetch me, there was stuff I could never tell her.

The Coke tasted more metallic. Maybe they made it different for the desert or maybe it was me. Zach was outside, so I wanted to call Merna before he came back in. She'd be at work, so I could leave a voicemail, which would be a lot easier if I could say it right. Finish the Coke and punch the number. It tasted awful, but it cost me a buck, so I was going to drink it.

—*Hi. Leave a message. Beep.*

—Hi. It's me. Sorry I haven't called. I know you're at work, but I thought I better call. The cell phone was outta range, but now it's not, or if it was there's a pay phone here, but so I'm calling from, I don't know, just a little one-horse town. The car's had a problem, but we're okay. Might be the manifold, cracked manifold or something, but they're looking at it, and this is just a little town in the desert, which was lucky for us— So anyway, we're fine. I just didn't want to call till I knew what was going on.

Not that I knew what was going on. My eyes went up to the calendar. It felt weird looking at tits while I talked to my wife, but I couldn't help it. I was still in that barber chair pointed straight at the girly-girl. I guess for guys you're always pointed there.

—But anyway we're someplace between Las Vegas and Four Corners, which is where four of the states come together, the only place, I guess, where— Colorado and maybe Utah, I get mixed up which state is on top of which, but— Little town here, like about four buildings, but so the plans are changed. We came through Las Vegas, but now we're being told to go to this place at Four Corners, but I guess it's the protocol. I mean I can't drive a thousand miles and turn around, but— Although that's maybe what I oughta do—

I grabbed for words but they wouldn't come. I looked away from the titty girl. On the desk was a half-full coffee cup, ashtray, open pack of Camels. And a propped-up frame of a woman and little boy looking Mexican, Indian, something. Cute little boy. Those people had families like we did, maybe even closer than us, the cute little boy. I looked out the window. Cliffs the red of raw meat.

—So we're south of Grand Canyon, or maybe north, but I was thinking it might be nice on the way back to stop and see it even if it's just a big hole in the ground—

I lost track. Outside I saw two guys talking, looking across the road, laughing at something. One in his forties maybe, cowboy hat, leather jacket, fur collar, strange for the desert although there was chill in the air. And an old guy in a brown fedora like my dad wore before he ran off. He might be the ghost of my dad. And my words were coming out jibber jabber, yammer, no sense, just buzz, but I couldn't stop it. Part of me was hearing it, part of me was just flapping my lips and I couldn't stop.

—I mean I wasn't expecting this crazy wild goose chase. I mean it's unreal. That thing on TV, was it Montana, that asbestos mine? Where the air was so clean, they thought, but this dad had lung disease, couldn't even pick up his little son without going into a fit— But the point being— Sorry, I got off track—

The two guys were talking close together. Clouds, fly buzz, nipples, a Coke sharp as acid— If I could find words—

—I should just forget it, I guess. Turn around, come back, come home. It's maybe a test of fate— Not fate, I mean faith, but— Although, hell, we've come this far, and I don't know when this guy, this Mexican I guess, is gonna look at the car. Out here they can charge whatever they want, they've got you over a barrel, but— I don't even know what town, or if we have to stay over—

I was lost again. I knew I was sounding nuts, rambling up one alley, down another— The words were all fly buzz. Did I still even have a signal?

—Funny, I noticed— Merna, hey, hi, I'm trying to—

She'd be listening to this, she'd be thinking I'm drunk. Or worse, I'm not drunk, I'm around the bend.

—I was a kid, we took a trip, we had a bug screen in front of the grill, we'd drive and bugs all over the screen and smashed on the windshield, all the glop. But now there's nothing. No bugs. Great, I'm not seeing the guts of a bug for a hundred miles, but you wonder what's in the air, the chemicals, what if you're the bug. Sorry, but—

I stopped. I was looking at the floor. It was a red brick tile, dirty but real tile. Beautiful if you mopped it. I couldn't talk. I knew that Merna would wonder *What's wrong with him?* but I couldn't talk. The tumor grew to the size of a grapefruit before you knew it.

—Well anyway, Zach's fine. He's doing his homework. Sorry I'm sounding goofy, but it's a long haul. You know I miss you, hon, but I'm doing this for us. It's our future, I hope anyway. But so I'll call when you're there. And hey, how about beef stew and mushrooms when we get back? Anyway, love you. Bye.

I clicked off. The men outside were gone. The sky was overcast, bruised black and blue. I took a sip at the Coke, but I'd finished it. I tossed the can in the wastebasket, looked out the window for Zach, then into the shop. The mechanic had started to check the car. Mexican, or he might be an Indian, if they knew about cars. I looked across the highway to see what the guys had been laughing at, but there was only a tractor-trailer parked and the red shelf of rock above it. A crow perched on a fence post, a raven or a crow.

Inside the office door hung a sign saying *Closed*. That was always funny to me, where they had the sign on the door that said *Open* from the outside so the inside said *Closed*. Now the whole outside world was closed, it was saying. Till closing time, and then it was open. Then I guess you went out.

I sat down, picked up the magazine, thumbed it, looking at ads. Some of those things could blow you in half. Who needed a thing like that if one bullet would do it? They used to have stories in magazines. I remembered reading one where a guy was fighting a bear and killed it. One where a kid won a race in spite of the odds or made the winning touchdown. Stuff that felt real though it never happened. If it did, they wouldn't have to write stories about it.

Then I noticed a little bulletin board by the door. A little kid's drawing tacked up. First grade maybe, the way little kids draw a man with big hands coming out of the head and a brownish-red scribble face. It might be the mechanic's kid. On the paper was printed *shizhe*. That didn't sound Mexican. Maybe Indian. I thought, sure, there are Indians here, all over the place, the mechanic is maybe Indian and maybe it means *my dad*. He might have a son that drew the picture. It might mean *my dad*. I could ask him if that was his son, but he might not want to say.

No sign of Zach.

—20—

Zach

There must be some actual human beings out in the so-called world, not just the aliens I live among. Once I've served out my sentence, released from solitary, graduated, hopefully I'll find them. Meantime, I'm thankful for five minutes to breathe free of Dad. At breakfast I stared at my stack of pancakes, glanced up at him, felt a stab of love so strong—which I can't remotely account for—and wanted to kill him just to put him out of his misery.

But now I amble into the open air. Strange to go out the door alone, a toddler toddling off from its mommy. I feel a monstrous silence clamping down its hand over the desert, over these little towns, over the eighteen-wheeler across the concrete rumbling its gut. Big block letters on the side: *STARZ*. Somebody's name? Who would want their name on the side of a truck? I can see a redrock ridge, but the semi cuts it off. The rumble deepens the silence.

I like barren places. An empty parking lot, a stretch of gravel, the skin of the Earth scraped raw—they say to me, *Don't fret your emptiness: we're bare too.* I can find peace in staring at the classroom floor to let all thoughts of Rebecca dissolve. The print of the textbook flakes into soot, and the teacher's voice devolves into chicken clucks. It's all okay for a while.

Not that the open desert is peaceful. It's pure terror. Something so bereft and yet so rife with beauty—is that a phrase from Keats? No, he was *fairy seas forlorn*. What could I write to curl Miss Plankett's toes? *Deep earthen claw marks cauterized by the sun. Great red heart pumping blood through rock. Centuries piled like the corpses you see on the news—thousands of terrorists dead, terrorist mommies, terrorist babies, terrorist sheep.* I can't look at more desert today. Cement and gravel and *STARZ*—those give me comfort.

Fifty yards off, I see a flat brick building with a faded tobacco ad on its side and a rusted-out water pump. It might be a store or one of those things that just got built and left there when some dad decided the pickings were better in Denver or any place other than where he was hanging his hat. Maybe a camouflaged missile site. Here the highway turns south, so I'm staring into the sun. Cold sun. Out by the road there's a sign for motor oil. *We can't promise you love, can't promise a meaningful life, but we'll sell you all the motor oil you'll ever need.*

I might walk around that building and find an old Indian squatting there, his back against the brick. He's seen the spirits. His heart is cupped in his hands. He'll take pity on this white boy and lead me down into the kiva pit deep in the Earth where the water comes clear and the water speaks and all is revealed. Or maybe not. Maybe he's drunk. Maybe he's only a metaphor.

I cut across the gravel. A couple of trailers in the distance, a concrete foundation weeded over, a half-built cement-block wall. One lone Joshua tree, all knobs and elbows. Distant hills, streaks in the sky: two fighter planes waltzing a waltz, training for death. A phrase in my head, *death needles*, not bad. Just a typical post-apocalyptic afternoon.

Why was I thinking I love my dad? I guess because I'm stupid.

I knew where I was coming. My brother sits on the concrete ledge of a ramp up to nothing. It must have been for loading cattle off to the death camps, but now there's nothing to load. I expected him. He's watching a crow flying north, or a raven, I never can tell which. I come closer. He looks the same, tall, skinny, mirror shades, and his face never fits together. Now he wears an olive drab army cap and a denim jacket, jeans, low boots, dried mud on the toes. His voice comes to me from a long way off in my head.

—Hey, little brother of mine.

I sit a couple of yards away on the concrete ledge beside him, waiting for more to be said. Nothing comes. I finally hear my voice.

—I can never tell if you're looking at me.

—Well, you see one you've seen'em all.

—Somebody mentions their brother, like at school, and I think, oh yeh, I've got a brother. More or less.

—We're all brothers, don't they say? That good stuff? Brotherhood?

—I told somebody once: *I never had brothers or sisters: good thing for them.*

—That's pretty good, Zach. That's funny. Right, brothers kill each other.

—Not always.

—Never miss the opportunity. Don't you read the Bible?

—Not much.

—Just the dirty parts?

—It's all lies.

—A swarm of lies. A herd of lies, a pack, a gaggle.

—A pride of lies.

—An extended family.

We're laughing now. I see he's missing a cuspid. It's an odd feeling: I try to say funny stuff, but I never laugh except to make people think I'm happy. I can't recall if I've ever laughed together with someone, but I'm laughing now. Whatever we say sounds funny.

—In Bible times you'd have been the Firstborn. That was a big deal then.

— So you do read the Bible.

—Wanna see how it turns out.

More giggles, then we settle. Now I'm sitting not more than a foot away. I know he's not there, so I need to say something to make him look at me.

—It's a big deal being the firstborn son.

—Watch out for that Bible. There's a king goes down on his knees and eats grass. Imagine the President eating grass? There's a lady turns into salt. A prophet lives in a whale. That Bible's a lotta laughs.

—My mom said I laughed when I was born. Or my mom laughed. Somebody laughed.

—Sure, why not laugh? It's always nice weather in the Holy Land. Except for the Flood, or when the veil of the temple gets ripped, or they burn up cities.

When I talk he seems real. If I talk him into reality he'll tell me the truth and the truth shall set us free if it doesn't kill us. I look up at him. The army cap he's wearing. A dark reddish stain on his jacket sleeve. A day's stubble, which makes him a lot more real.

—Did you like Dad? The time you came to visit?

—Zach, I regret to say that I hate the pathetic bastard.

—He's born again.

—Born again a bastard.

—He's . . .

What's to say? That he's hateful but I never manage to hate him all the way? That he's why bright guys despise the working class? That I'm so much like him? Can sons put up with their fathers, ever? My brother looks at me with this owlish twist of the head.

—Judge not that ye be not judged.

He's grinning, so I guess he's kidding me.

—Okay. You too.

—Why not!

I must be thinking about the Bible because of Dad. They all go into the desert, it says: Elijah, Abraham, Moses, Christ, rattlesnakes, lizards, the Magi who built the atomic bomb and blew up Baby Jesus. I turn to my brother. His face is in shadow. Cold sun, cold shadow. I tell him—

—They all go into the desert.

—Yep. Great place to start a religion. There's nothing else to do.

He holds out a pint of whiskey to me. I take it, it's empty, I hand it back, but he motions me to drink. I unscrew the lid and put it to

my lips. It burns. The two fighters streak over the sky in a deadly
game of celestial tic-tac-toe. The sun glares on the cracked weedy
acre of concrete, gravel, and desert-themed linoleum. It's all hallucination, a movie where you're the action hero riding the starlet's
thighs and then sinking into the depths of your crying need. Miss
Plankett would say that's really pushing it, but if I could lose myself
in metaphor what a sweet drowning that would be. The empty liquor
burns my tongue. I talk to numb it.

—It's dry here.

—The desert is dry. That's why it's a desert.

—People go nuts in the desert.

—And everywhere else, my brother. But it worked out okay for
Jesus. Forty days and forty nights in solitary. Slowed down his heart
to the rhythm of rocks. Wild things watched him and wind clawed
his eyes while those horny spadefoot toads romped in the rain. If you
don't find it there, little brother, you won't find it anywhere.

We sit there. I can't look at him. He's making no sense. He's
telling me something I need to know, but it all jams up in my head.

—I don't know what you're telling me. It's all jammed up. I have
a very high I.Q. or I wouldn't be so stupid.

—You think you're joking.

—Please stay with me.

—Why sure. You swallowed me, I can't get out.

—Look at me.

—I don't see how that's possible, kiddo. That decision was made
about three thousand years ago. Those wild crazy patriarchs, whatta
sense of humor.

—Would you look at me, please?

I'm talking to nothing. He's sitting there in my head and I'm
screaming at him and can't even hear myself. He grins.

—You want to see me. Okay, you see me. See me now. Look at
me. See me. Who am I? Hit man for all the snotty little suicides you
can't quite pull off? Come on, Zach, you're imagining this heartfelt
family reunion. That's the advantage of being an only child. You
construct a world with you as the hero, the romantic heart-throb

or misunderstood artiste or cheerful quadriplegic. Those purple mountain majesties and juicyfruited plains, those are your birthright, kiddo, despite the technicality that I was the unwanted Firstborn and you just came skidding in on the afterbirth.

That isn't his voice. His voice has a sour sting but gentle. This cackle is mine: the poisonous wimp pretending to be a stand-up comic pretending to be a thug.

—Well, Zach, I tell you. I'm so fucking jealous. You and me both got begat by the old huff-and-puff and squeezed out of the toothpaste tube. But, hey, the birthright, the principle of primogeniture decides who inherits the penis. Only one to a family, passed down from father to son. *Dad, can I borrow the penis Friday night? No, Son, you can have one when you can afford to operate it. Aw, Dad, please, all my friends got their own.* But then little brother grabs it and takes off down the road yelling, *I got the weenie, I got the weenie!* and then suddenly, *Oops, sorry, Dad, I totaled the family penis.*

I wait for the riff to end. He's funny, but I can't laugh. I'm hearing the whimpery kid inside me. I babble whatever words are adrift in my head. Right now I want my mommy.

—I have to do a book report.

—Right. Abraham. Very fucked-up daddy. His seed shall be as grains of sand if he cuts the little brat's throat. Who's the little brat, Zach, me or you? Which of us is it? Who sticks out their wrists for the Binding?

The liquor is rushing through me now. I drop the bottle. The bottle is plastic and bounces. His voice whines like mosquitoes. Like Hamlet I'm going insane but think I'm just faking it.

—I'm sorry, I'm sorry, I'm sorry—

I try to speak but the words won't come to the surface. The liquor's burnt out my tongue. I'm in a panic to get anywhere gone. In a moment I'll start blubbering like Orpah, the little fat girl on the playground, third grade, when Richie pulled down her panties.

My brother's face fogs over. The desert air hollows his voice. The sun is blistering cold. His reflectors look directly through my eyes. My voice is a five-year-old's—

—I tried to kill myself.

—You need practice.

—I took pills. Wrong kind of pills. My mother's hormone pills.

—Girls do pills, guys do neckties. But only God totes that big eraser.

—I love Mom.

—Well, Zach, and my blessed mother died a year ago, while yours made supper for Dad. Breast cancer. You and me both, we really went after those breasts, I bet.

—I love Mom. I mean I love Mom. I wish to God I'd never done what I did because it hurt her so much. I can't stand her to talk to me, telling me she loves me, and I can never repay the debt.

—That's the function of bankruptcy, buddy. Just saying, *No can do.*

—He talks about her drinking. That's a lie. If there's anybody that has it together it's Mom.

—Moms are vastly overrated, my brother. They strained out a big turd and called it you.

I hear this. He didn't say it. It's my voice. A voice in me.

He was eighteen, I was four or five. I guess he showed up one day, I never knew why, and all kinds of whispers ran through the house like when the cops brought Daddy home drunk. Fake cheery voices, shivering walls, cracks in the air. *This is your half-brother, Zach,* said Dad. I wondered what half a brother was. I still make that joke.

He must have asked if he could take me out for a walk. Mom agreed, maybe to get us out of the house so she could scream at Dad. I had a red tricycle on the sidewalk in front, and he tried to ride it with his knees up to his ears. Funniest thing I'd ever seen. We went and climbed over some rocks and down to the canyon. That's all I remember. I loved him.

For a moment I see my brother dead. On his side, then turned face down, seeping out. In that flash I know the whole story. I get extra credit in history class for knowing what killing feels like.

He's not dead. He's looking at me. He's looking at me still, a blur. The mirror glasses are gone. His eyes are dark brown, negroid eyes, yellow flecks, a scatter of blood. The eighteen-wheeler rumbles under the western skies. I try to hold the image of my brother, but he fades by half and then that half goes on fading. My brother's voice, Lannie's voice, the rhythmic slur of my heart valves, is a whisper across the gravel.

—You believe it? You believe all this drivel and drool? You hear how you sound? Zach: you're hearing the dark dirty shit you dribble out every day. Listen to your gut, little brother, and don't believe a fucking word.

—Lannie?

—Keep in mind, Zach, you might have to face the gross indignity of surviving.

—Lannie?

—Ever listen to country music, little brother? Sure, it's mostly guys squeezing their lonesome junk, but I kinda like this one:

I fell in love tomorrow
Or I'm going to, yesterday.

—Lannie?

—So we meet at the next crossroads.

And I'm alone. No trace of my delusion. I've been scuffing a little gray weed shoot with my shoe sole the last five minutes, and now it's a piece of rag that will never seed a forest. The crow, raven, whoever, hops around searching for beetles or crumbs. One fighter plane, in a clean white slash, writes an epitaph in the sky. My eyesight comes back in heartbeats.

—21—

Vernon

A whole day of marking time. Waiting, breathing, hearing your stomach growl. Chop that day out of your life and you'd never miss it.

I sat in the godforsaken office. Good to know there were worse places to work than Walmart. Waiting, breathing, damned fly buzzing, buzzing, batting against the window like it was trying to swat itself. I couldn't ignore it. Maybe God made flies so your brain latched onto little stuff to keep the nightmares out. Why bat against the window? Something so great outside? Some tasty pile of dogshit? Maybe it didn't know what else to do. Same as me.

I thought what Reverend Bud said once, which seemed true at the time. Of all living creatures it's only us that wants something more. The dogs, the fishes, the birds, the bugs, they eat and screw— he didn't say it like that—and that's all they need. But men have a thirst—humans, he said—for something higher. It might be Heaven, it might be a million bucks, but you want to be more than a bug. Funny, though: here was this fly beating itself on the window to smash through and get sucked up into the sky. Same as me.

I felt sorry for the fly, but I wanted to kill it. I rolled up the *Guns & Ammo*, made a couple more swats, like when I was twelve I'd grow up to be the World Series all-star. Finally, the fly got tired of buzzing and I got tired of standing there. This greasy grimy office was where we both had to squat.

Waiting, breathing. You sat there and got a flash of the miles that brought you to this chintzy plastic chair in Arizona. The roads you took, turn right, turn left, the folds in the roadmap. If you hadn't got into the bar fight. If you hadn't forgot the condom. If you hadn't called Lannie's mother in Denver and said, *It's me.* If you hadn't ever seen a damned speedboat or struck up a chat with some con man in Chico after you'd had three beers.

I knew from the start it was some kind of scam, but I couldn't see the point. What could he get from a loser like me? Some serial killer they find with body parts in his freezer? Recruiter for the CIA? Space monster wanting to stick a tentacle up your rectum? Or some honcho who sees hidden potential in the way you chug your beer?

I kept looking at the drawing pinned on the bulletin board. Somebody's kid. Whose? The Mexican? He must be about five years old, the way he drew the hands coming straight out of the head. The dad would think the kid's great, he's proud of his son, and *shizhe* maybe means *my dad* in Navajo. I wondered if Navajos, Mexicans, whatever, go after their kids with a belt. But the kid must be older or else he couldn't spell. Or maybe it means *asshole* and the Mexican thinks it's cute. Or maybe in fact they treat their kids better than us, although I never beat Zach. I could ask the guy if that was his son, but maybe the kid is retarded.

You drive the miles under a dead white sky, make the turns, and here you're the big dumb horsefly banging the window. No wonder some kid takes a gun to school and does his homework there on the spot. I thought what if Zach did that? Once, I was drunk, I don't even know why, I called him a chickenshit. I was totally ashamed of saying a thing like that—not to my son, for godsake. Maybe I was too slurred to be understood, but I heard it come out of my mouth, and so he must have heard it. One more road that brought us here.

Waiting, breathing. After a while the Navajo, Mexican, the little brown guy, looked in.

—Not the manifold.

—Great.

—I'll check other stuff, it shouldn't take long, only I don't work from one to three, I can do it after that.

—After three?

—You can wait here. The boss is around.

He pointed outside. The old guy was sprawled in his trashy wicker armchair like a bum or a billionaire, taking off his fedora, mopping his bald head, putting his hat back on. Life was simple for that guy. He didn't look like the talkative type.

—So I'll finish when I get back.

Damn lazy Mexicans—although if I could get away with taking off two hours who wouldn't do it? I only worked part-time and lived off what Merna earned, so I couldn't talk about lazy Mexicans. I nodded okay, but I felt like whacking the spic with the *Guns & Ammo*. I never call them spics—it just came into my head.

I should go out to see what happened to Zach, but I didn't want him to think I was spying on him. Not much he could be doing out there anyway. I should have asked if there was a diner or something, and I could ask the old guy, but there was something funny about his wearing a hat if he was sweating. So I was stuck for another two hours. The fly was gone. I missed its company.

They had a candy machine, so I bought a thing with nuts and sugar and salt and goo. It said it filled my daily requirements, at least my requirements for goo. Funny what you find to fill the time. In school I used to play with my fingers, sort of wrestle them around and make up names for the wrestlers and if they were good guys or bad. Or count the times Mr. Kaltenborn said, *What I mean is*. Or study the bluish birthmark on the back of Kathy Bogardus' neck. Once I told Zach, *You don't have to be smart to be bored to death*. I don't know why I said that, but sometimes I had to talk just to hear what I thought. Like staring at the glare of the window glass to see some vision, like second sight—

The glare gave way. I saw Zach. Out across the vacant lot, the gravel and weeds, he was perched on the edge of a concrete ramp, kind of a loading dock. Why I hadn't seen him— Or if I was seeing him— No, he was sitting there, waving his hand, like talking.

I wondered if sons ever spoke to their fathers unless the dads yelled, *Talk!* I never did to mine. Every day when I looked in the mirror I saw my dad. Every time I spoke to Zach I heard him. Sins of the fathers pass down to the sons, and God gave his only begotten son, but nobody ever said if the two could have a conversation. *My God, my God, why has Thou forsaken me?* Not a very supportive relationship. I should have had a daughter if I needed to have anything. I never wanted a son, though I never told Merna that. But still the first time I saw him, I thought *Wow!* Through a plate glass window in the maternity ward, though I couldn't hardly see him for the glare—

All of a sudden I was standing. The old man outside in the wicker chair took off his hat and he was bald as a bowling ball, and that did it for me. I saw myself raise both fists to smash the glass, but I never did. I knew I was acting silly. The pinup girl with the tits would be in a giggle fit. At least I was on my feet, and I had to talk to my son, whatever smart-ass cracks he made. He was flesh and blood. I went out the door.

Zach sat on the concrete ledge, his foot kicking at something, maybe a weed. I walked across the concrete, gravel, weeds, this pathetic piece of the Earth we'd come to. He saw me coming, sat there, stopped kicking. I gave him a jolly grin.

—Where were you? I was looking.

I hadn't been looking, I'd been swatting a fly and eating a candy bar, but I felt like I should have been looking. The sun was bearing down, though I still felt the chill. Zach sat there, a cactus, all bristles.

—So I called your mom. Left a message.

—When are we going to be fixed?

—Couple hours. The guy's on break. No big problem, I guess.

—Cancer of the carburetor?

—What're you doing here?

He didn't say. He stood up and walked toward the garage, staring at the ground in front of him. I followed. The old guy sitting outside never looked at us. He was just living under his hat, like other old guys in hats, waiting for life to get tired of him. Once I tried to wear a hat, but I felt too much like my dad. We went into the office to wait. The fly was on its lunch break. Zach found a magazine I hadn't seen, started leafing through it. He never mentioned lunch.

—What are you reading?

—*Popular Mechanics*. Tells how things work. Guy's gotta know that. I mean what if nothing worked? Life would be a very boring movie.

For some reason that hit me. He just said it off the top of the head, the way he does, but here's a little kid sucking at the breast, and next minute he's saying that life is a movie, like it's all made up.

—We're not a movie, dammit. Life is not a movie. This is life, right here. You're always saying you feel like you're in a movie—

—I never said—

—A movie, they just make up what they think is gonna sell. Reality is where you don't just make it up—

—You don't just make it up, but it still has to sell.

—I'm saying what's real. Faith is real. Hope is real. God is real.

—I'm not going to go there, Dad. You go and tell me what you find.

All that smart talk, he knew it always got to me. It seemed like the only way we could pass the time was have a fight. Maybe that's what it would have been with my dad if he hadn't run off. We both shut up and the heat drained out of the gulf between us.

—So what's with Las Vegas, Dad? What happened with Las Vegas?

—Change of plans.

—Shiprock?

—It's a big rock. It's famous.

I could hear the grab in his breath. He was about to start in, get me worked up, but then he went quiet. The car, I thought if they couldn't fix it, then we'd turn around and go home. But my head was screwy: we couldn't go home if the car didn't run. Zach read his magazine, I watched the old guy in the wicker chair. The fly ambled up the window glass, a perfect target, saying, *Here I am*. I could pick

up the magazine and smash it, but I thought no, let it be a sonofabitching fly, it's trying its damndest.

Waiting, breathing, I nodded off. Finally the Bruce fellow stuck
his head in, woke me, said it was done. I'd expected him to charge
me an arm and a leg, but it turned out that all he did was change the
spark plugs, fix some clamp that was busted off, and pull out a weed
that got stuck underneath. Even then it was less than I would've paid
back home—there they'd have replaced the weed and charged me
for it. I felt ashamed for distrusting the Mexican and mad at him
for making me feel that way. Nothing wrong with Mexicans if there
weren't so goddamned many.

—Is that your kid's? The drawing there?

He looked where I pointed but stared as if he'd never seen it.
Maybe he hadn't put it there. Maybe he didn't know the meaning of
shizhe. Maybe it was an inside joke that only Mexicans or Navajos
knew, if they ever told jokes. He wouldn't tell me, and I would never
know.

It was after four when we got back on the highway and through
these so-called towns, Indian towns, bunches of buildings or trailers sprinkled over dirty brown slag-heap hills. I would be bitching
how ugly it was, and then suddenly we'd come to a mesa with layers like chocolate and cream, late afternoon light that took away all
your words. Nothing said, nothing to say. What did roadrnnners do
before we had roads?

And then we both had a laugh. We passed a billboard, big medal-
lion like a sheriff's badge, bald eagle embossed, and a slogan across
the eagle: *Live Wild!* It was an ad for bail bonds, saying, *Live wild,
go to jail, good business for us!* We both laughed. First time that both
of us laughed.

We stopped at a little greasy spoon. Pretty hungry, we hadn't
had lunch. The diner was like all the others, knotty pine veneer, and
over the pass-thru window a bull skull with horns. Little paintings
scattered wherever they had a space on the walls, flowers and cactus
and trees. Must be some local artist, maybe an Indian, they're supposed to be artistic. Waitress, forties, fifties, kind of a cute fat face,

frilly apron over blue jeans with little Xs cross-stitched on her buns, and a couple of pens stuck in her back pocket, so she must not ever sit down. She hung out at the counter talking to a younger guy, red bill cap, sweatshirt that said *EMT*. Was that medical?

—No, I checked out this ad for SWAT team. Cops on a SWAT team, you know what they make? I couldn't believe it. Joey said ninety-six thousand a year.

—No way.

—In California they do.

—Well, that's California.

—But you gotta take tests. Maybe kill people.

—I'd do it for that kinda money.

—Who wouldn't?

But what if he had kids and told them he shot somebody? I didn't want to think about it. He was a nice-looking guy, but it was always the nice-looking guys that did it.

And this old couple in a back booth. There was always an old couple in the back, him reading a newspaper, her staring off in the years. Maybe the same ones moved around, diner to diner, bar to bar, just to let you know your turn is coming. Zach had meatloaf and gravy, drank a Pepsi. I had chicken-fried steak and wanted a beer but did coffee.

And another young family. On their way out the dad held the one-year-old up by both arms, walking him along. The kid's knees would buckle, but Daddy was holding him up so he could do these long lopes like dancing on the moon. Then his dad swooped him up in the air and he crowed. Maybe that's why we have dreams where we fly, the times when our mom or dad swooped us up off the floor. Once the kid could really walk by himself he'd never feel it again. Was it right to do that with a kid, when he'll never fly again?

We were in the midst of limbo as darkness fell. I pulled to the side of the road behind a tractor-trailer that was parked, still running—some reason they keep them wheezing all night—and we stretched out half-upright in our seats. Zach folded his jacket into a pillow and leaned against the side. I took a couple of pulls from my pint—I'd remembered to pick up another—not that I ought to be drinking. The desert closed around us. I felt the chill, shut the windows to keep out bats, rats, wolf packs, whatever. Night, they say, the desert comes alive.

—When you were little, still on the bottle when she had to do that, your mom called your bottle a titty-bottle.

Why I said that, it must have been the swig, two swigs, drinking way too much. I mumbled something about getting there tomorrow, finding out what's up, but my words came out all knotted up. Not a whisper from Zach. I needed to pray, but forming words was like walking in slush. I tried to think *Dear Lord* and *Name of Your Son* to jump-start a prayer. Pray to be able to pray. Hour or so, maybe, I drowsed into the snore of the eighteen-wheeler.

My head kept churning. The glare came up, Merna's eyes, the whisk of bat wings, then no sound but wind and rumble. Drift off, wake up, the brain sifting crazy things—the phone call, nutty talk, directions, fly buzz, Shiprock—the way a cat rags a mouse, tormenting it, not killing it, just killing time. Gut, heart, fingertips, lips peeled back, breathing, waiting.

Once I talked with a guy, Frank something, one of those bar-stool chats. I asked him if he had kids, just one of those things you ask, but it got him started. He had told his wife he didn't want kids, no kids ever. But then she got pregnant, and all she cared about, he said, was the kid, the damned kid, so he left her. *I told her. She couldn't say I didn't tell her.* Took up with another lady and wound up with four daughters. The joke was on him and he laughed about it. But in fact no sweat: he worked oil rigs all over the world, so he'd come home long enough to plant another kid and then off he went. *Best of both worlds*, he said. He was pretty funny about it.

But he couldn't stop there. When they all grew up—he was like in his sixties—he made his daughters promise, hand on the Bible, that they'd never ever have babies. And they never did. None of them ever did. And he told me this, he sounded proud of it. What kind of a guy would do that? And why would you tell a total stranger what a fucked-up SOB you were?

I wanted to talk to Zach, tell him the stories and blessings and shame. Be honest with him. In the morning I'd say it all, every damned bit, if I had some way to remember whatever I had to say. I didn't want to be like what I was. I couldn't see for the glare.

—22—

Stubblefield

So many ways it might go from here. Imagine the story conference for the blockbuster pitched as *The Ten Commandments* meets *The Shining*. Under the blistering desert sun the great stone buzzard Shiprock takes wing and lofts the boy upward as Daddy waves goodbye. They're beset by scalped Spanish friars and find a dead virgin in the bathtub denuded and disheartened. Under the shadow of the rock the father and son face off with snarling chainsaws but see their sacred kinship and fall into manly embrace as the sunset reddens the West.

Or add comedy. They meet a nutty Navajo who leads them down a ceremonial kiva to a frat beer bust. Dad makes it with a squaw who turns out to be a guy. The son joins a kachina punk band The Shiprockers. So many ways to spin a legend.

It goes any direction that sells. As in politics: fuck truth. Credibility is a formula. Hone the motives and slap on some mythic dimension and plant the gun and build the illusion of inevitability and then spring the surprise. Don't get distracted by reality. In reality they take a wrong turn and wind up in Phoenix. Or the kid breaks out in shingles. Or the mom elopes to Haiti with her Negro dentist. Real life is an amateurish mess.

But you never can tell. Some old patriarch writes a shoot'em-up. His hero eats an apple and it all flows from there. Family feuds genocides plagues messiahs—all from eating that apple. Moral: don't snack between meals. Total crap and yet it sells billions. One thing he got right when he started off with brother killing brother. Family kills family is the norm.

Time to get things moving. I had no clear intent except to yell *Fire!* and see who shits their pants. As Vern said: *waiting, breathing.*

For practice I'd tried making a rasp into the phone. Tongue grating against the hard palate: *Kkkh*— And I had an electric pencil sharpener—stick in the pencil it grinds—so I found a pencil somewhere and stuck it in: *Kkkh*— Silly but it sounded amazingly true to life.

Most practical jokes aren't worth the effort. It takes you an hour to catch the frog and stick it under your roommate's pillow and block it off from escape—all for three seconds of his reaction—not to mention how stupid you feel for doing that. But there's a compulsion and so you do it.

I clicked on the speaker phone. It would hollow out my voice and leave my hands free for the pencil. I called Vernon and got his voicemail. This was the moment. What you might call the tipping point. *Please leave a message* said the little sexless robot and beeped its wee beep. Okay baby I will.

—Well hello, Vern. Sorry plans changed for Las Vegas, but all things come round, which is why God invented the future. So I was hoping to talk to you, but—

I made my rasp of static mechanical and humanoid both. *Kkkh*— Sounded silly but silly stuff was more credible.

—Bad connection, sorry. So this is the drill, my friend. You're headed to Shiprock, the reason for which you have no idea, am I right? Okay. Shiprock— *Kkkh*— Shiprock is a volcanic remnant towering seventeen hundred feet from the floor of the desert near Four Corners, the intersection of Arizona, Utah, Colorado, and New Mexico, and this is where you're headed, my friend. So here's the drill— *Kkkh*— Static on the line, I hope I come through okay— *Kkkh*—

No question but this would be comic relief if they ever make the movie of Vernon McGurren's excellent adventure. To my ear it sounded convincing. God moves in mysterious ways.

—So, specific instructions. Now we're not talking obedience, like obedience to a boss or some Lord God Almighty, but just responding to the future. Like sensing what flows in the veins and where gravity draws the trickle. So you're heading right now to the town of Shiprock, the town being maybe fifteen miles from the actual rock, the actual Shiprock, but you do see Shiprock from the town, it's visible for miles, it's seventeen hundred feet, for chrissake. Somebody thought it looked like a ship. As if Navajos ever saw a ship. So— *Kkkh*— Hang on—

I counted to ten. I was just going by instinct. A fly buzzed at the window. I should call Security.

—So you're with me so far? So you look for the Four Corner Motel. Easy to find, it's a little tiny bump in the road, the town is. Four Corner Motel. *Kkkh*— Check in, put it all out on the table, out where it's fully visible. Hold on—

Another silence. Let him mull over what I just said and try to figure it out. There was no such motel but it added specificity to the quantum entanglement.

—Next morning, okay, you take 491 South to Route 13, take a right. This runs along the south of Shiprock. You'll see the rock, it's huge, like a shark fin up to the sky. When you're direct to the south of the rock itself, there's a volcanic ridge up from the desert like a row of rotten black teeth, pardon the— *Kkkh*— But a very sacred site for the Navajo, who never go to the dentist—

Again I waited for Vernon's brain to shift into low gear for the steep ascent to comprehension. Was he primed for visions? Ready now? Staring naked into the glare?

—Turn there. Turn right there. Gap in the fence, little dirt road, two tracks, take it slow, very slow. Nothing but ruts, quarter mile, a mile, it seems like ten. So take it very slow and when you get to the foot of it, you and your son, then that's where you do it— *Kkkh*— Down on the— *Kkkh*— And both wrists, make sure both wrists, and— *Kkkh*— Just behind his head, behind the ear, so that— *Kkkh kkkh kkkh*— I know that's hard, that's so goddamned hard, Vern, the hardest thing you'll ever have to do, but some things, cause we all make sacrifi— *Kkkh*— Then carry him— *Kkkh*— Call me when you've done it.

I clicked off. That's it buddy. That should fry your bacon. Try that on for size.

—23—

Merna

Monday at the office was a clown show. Rosella was sick, so I had to take the bus and was worried I'd be late. But then Old Pinkeye was late, so nobody would know about me being late except Joanie, and she wouldn't say anything because she was the one who started calling him Old Pinkeye. The boss's name was Pinkel and the salesmen all called him Pinkie, though of course to the office girls he was Mister Pinkel and a total sonofabitch.

Business had been slow, as it always was in the months before the new models came out and they couldn't cut prices low enough to push leftovers out the door. When business was bad the salesmen got goofy and flirted a lot, although they might have been freaked if one of the girls had called their bluff. And Old Pinkeye got meaner. Take your full hour at lunchtime and he'd find some way to make your afternoon miserable if he possibly could. I was always afraid I'd lose my temper and get canned. A number of times I was sorely tempted, but we couldn't afford it.

That morning the new salesman Gerald laid a gadget on my desk, a plastic windup gizmo shaped like a pair of tits. When he set it off it made a burst of eeps and scurried around the desk and fell on the floor. This was the kind of thing they always pulled on Rosella because they'd get a reaction—she'd blush and swear at them in Spanish—but Rosella was sick so it was my turn. They never bothered Joanie. Something in Joanie warned them off.

—Gerald, that's stupid. Get outta my face.

Gerald snickered and beat a retreat. Places were supposedly cracking down on harassment, but harassment was the only thing that kept those guys on the job. Take harassment away and they'd go postal. It was like that all morning.

Actually I liked Gerald, but he'd never be good selling cars. It was like he was playing a salesman on a sitcom. He smiled so hard you thought his teeth would shatter. I could have been pretty good at that job because people seemed to trust me, but the day Pinkel hired a female salesman would be the day they played hockey in Hell.

Lunch hour I went into the ladies' room and called home on the cell phone to check voicemail, thinking Vern might leave a message, knowing I wasn't home so we wouldn't fight. I listened to his call from Sunday again. Not Las Vegas, okay, they're past Las Vegas. Four Corners, where the hell was that? Talking about bug screens, carburetor, asbestos in Montana—he sounded nuts. I played it back twice. Zach was doing his homework, that was good at least. I started to punch his number, but what was the point? I knew word for word how the conversation would go, how he needed to do what the big shot told him to do. Here we're paying the cost of two cell phones plus a land line and still couldn't make half sense to one another. And Zach was whining for a phone of his own. *I'm seventeen, Mom!* I had a flash of Zach. Zach looking out a window, streaks across his face.

I walked down the street to get a cup of coffee at the corner stand, waited in line behind a girl in her twenties with a dragon tattoo crawling up her neck. The dragon's mouth was wide open to chomp her ear. With that thing crawling up her neck I wondered what kind of stuff she had crawling down below. I rubbed my forearm. Whenever I saw a tattoo, I had to do it. When I was six or seven I'd found a ballpoint pen and drew our cat Tigger on my arm. I showed it to Mom who freaked out and rubbed it and scrubbed it till Tigger was gone and so was most of my skin. I still felt poor little Tigger being scraped off. *The times are a'changing*, the song went, which I guess meant that now they get tattoos all over themselves. But maybe the kid was smart to act nutty when she's young, cause at my age you can't really do it right. I got my coffee, splashed in some half-and-half, and walked back to work.

Twenty-five minutes and I wasn't going to rush. I sat down to eat at my desk. I pushed back the keyboard, reached in my bag, set out my BLT and two squares of chocolate, my daily treat. Pinkeye didn't like you to eat at your desk, but he didn't want you to sit in the showroom either, and that left only a couple of plastic chairs by the vending machines. When Joanie told him, *My ass is too big for those chairs, Mr. Pinkel*, he knew he'd better not push it. So I sat to eat at my desk. My ass was as big as Joanie's.

It wasn't that bad a job as jobs go and lots better than sitting around the house trying to be a drunk. I didn't mind fending off the salesmen, and I got along fine with the other girls, although Rosella was a whiner and Joanie was a bitch but never to me. At least I wasn't on my feet all day with a waitress job or carting bedpans for old geezers trying to die. A car dealership wasn't as evil as a gun shop or a fast-food heart-attack joint or selling giant TVs to drooling cretins. The only thing that got to me was what I felt around me every day—the desperation.

One salesman had been laid off, and Gerald was next if things didn't pick up. They'd joke around, but it all smelled sour. If Gerald smiled any harder he'd sprout his own pair of tits— Damn, that's what I should have said to him. I worried they might start cutting office staff, and if that happened Rosella would be toast and most of her work would land on my desk. You could hear the tension in the voices and see it in their eyes like little slivers of glass. I thought of Ray.

This little round jolly guy with a big nose and always a cheery word was a born salesman. He was married to an old battle-ax and always flirting, not the way guys do that makes your skin crawl but in a way that made you laugh and even made you think twice about the possibility. Ray had only been at Pinkel's maybe a year when he left to start his own used car lot. He'd been their top salesman, so Pinkel wasn't happy to lose him, told him, *Well, Ray, you're great selling cars, but you don't know shit about business.*

Pinkel was right. Ray's location was bad and his cashflow was worse. His clientele were all the low-life who couldn't get financing, so he'd carry the paper himself and spend most of his time repossessing junkers that'd had the wheels run off. Once in a while he'd stop into the dealership to joke with the salesmen and flirt with the girls and rail at the politicians he blamed for it all, but he always made you laugh. And then he killed himself.

Word was that his grown son was a gambler, and Ray tried to pay his debts out of money he wasn't making. On the side he sold car insurance and he'd write policies for customers and then just pocket the money. He bragged about it. *Niggers don't need insurance,* he'd say, *they don't have nothing to lose.* But then he got into some double-mortgage scam with the senile biddie that worked at the title company, and when the bank found out then jolly big-nosed Ray was on his way to the slammer. They found him behind the wheel of a '99 Ford Mustang, hose from the exhaust. Gerald told about it, tried to joke—*Nice car, clean, real classic, and he shit in it!*—but it was like all the laughs had been repossessed.

It stuck with me. In Vern, the same desperation. I'd wake up and see him staring at the ceiling. They tried to take the final exam, but all the words fell apart. They wanted to be men, but they were little boys with a hard-on and didn't know what it was.

Zach again, suddenly, just a flash. It grabbed like a fist. Some terrible thing grabs hold. My heart was racing, my head was a mess, and there must be some way to keep the goddamned bacon from falling out of the BLT.

—Merna, hey, when you're finished, I know you're still on your lunch hour, but would you take care of that stack on Rosella's desk? I need that stuff for the end-of-the-month report. Don't rush, I know you've got stuff left from when you took off Friday, but just so you get to it in the next hour or so, okay?

—As soon as I can. After lunch.

—As I said, I'm not intruding on your lunch hour, I'm just saying.

—I heard.

—Fine. Okay.

Prick. He always timed it. Last bite of the sandwich, my mouth was full, so that was the time for him to spout orders like some general with a bug up his ass or claws on his balls. (My mother said that once when she thought I wasn't listening.) Rosella dealt with accounting for the parts department and Joanie knew her work, but I would have to look up all the journal entry codes, which would take me all afternoon, so I'd be that much farther behind. All for Mr. Pinkel's end-of-the-month report, which went directly to Mr. Pinkel.

I still had five minutes. Better get started. No, let him stew. Maybe that wasn't the Christian thing to do, but Jesus never worked an eight-to-five job. Some church hymn said pry open your heart, but from where I sat I didn't see that happening at Pinkel's Quality Fords. Five minutes to space out the sips of my coffee. Flash of Zach. The fist.

Think happy stuff, Merna, like Vern taking snapshots. But what did I care about snapshots of rocks? We had snapshots of parents, grandparents, friends I didn't remember, and all the cars and front porches and Christmas trees with people smiling in front. And the clog of unsorted photos in my head. The apple tree. The dead bird. Going all the way with Bennie. The one time Dad cried. Vern bandaged up. Our ratty little lawn in Minot. Zach home for lunch. Mom wheezing at the end. Sunset in the Rockies. The smoke when the rice boiled dry. All of that stuff should go in the trash.

End of lunch break. Old Pinkeye would be popping out of his nook any second. I took the last sip and dropped the paper cup in the trash and went over to Rosella's desk, brushed away shreds from an old burrito and sat down to a clutter of invoices with a *People* magazine underneath. I flicked on the computer, logged into Rosella's accounts with the password *Rosella*, and launched into the afternoon.

Afternoon, the mind wanders. The invoices were hateful but restful in a way. They took my mind off things. Like a road full of potholes: whenever a thought would grab, then the bumps would break it up into little blurts. Vern was driving with my son a thousand miles without the foggiest notion, and I was doing the same just sitting there at the desk.

The mind wanders. Vernon, I didn't hate him, I loved him, but the hate was there too, like the stink of that dead cat under the trailer that lasted for months, even though Vern crawled under and took it out. I knew he loved me enough to stop drinking and go to church, try to change his life, pursue his dinky opportunities. He loved me enough to get away from that woman who gave him a son while I lived for fifteen years with a womb stopped up. And sometimes I screamed, but I knew how to scream without making a sound. There were times I wanted to die, and maybe that's why at last I bore a son who wanted to die. It passed through my blood like the babies with AIDS. I passed the longing to him.

Three o'clock. Ten-minute break. I got up and went out to the sidewalk for a cigarette. I was trying not to drink so Vern wouldn't have the excuse, but that pushed me back to smoking. I hated the taste but couldn't help wanting to taste it. It made me think of dried-up cat shit. A couple of teenage girls walked past giggling at something. Must be fun to get out of class and walk downtown twitching your butt. Not knowing what's in store, not knowing the clench of labor, the tearing, the years of watching your baby grow up, up and away. I had the sudden urge to run after them, cry out, tell them that before their first labor pains, before the water broke, they'd better win the Lottery or something, anything. But they would only roll their eyes and smirk. That was my daydream at 3:08 in the afternoon.

End of break. Back to Rosella's desk. Her journal entries were all messed up, repair costs assigned wrong or figures wrong. I didn't know what to do. If I left it the way it was I might be accused of the fuck-ups, but if I told Pinkeye then Rosella might get fired and I'd have all that extra work. Vern would have said this was the time to pray to God for guidance, but I didn't think God cared a fart for Pinkel's Quality Fords.

The mind wanders. Was there still the hate in my heart or only the smell? Smell of Aunt Lettie, smell of the hospital, smell of the

Sunday after church when Daddy shoveled the snow and laid down on the sofa and died with his eyes wide open. Every time they talked about the face of God, that's what I saw: the wide dead eyes and rigid mouth and the stink of shit. I knew why God never answered one single prayer: the old fart had suffered a heart attack, he'd kicked the bucket, he was worms. My son tried to take his life and my husband was a train wreck, and no amount of *Dear Lords* was going to do a thing. God was just a big joker who loved to pull a fast one.

Even saying that, I loved the church. Like my auntie's lap where I could crawl up and feel safe, even though she stank. I didn't care about commandments or sermons or such, but I loved getting up Sunday mornings and sitting to hear the choir and letting the pain drain away. And that was a bridge between us. It brought us back together. *I love you*, Vern said, *I want to make it up.* He asked God's help and really believed it at the time, so I believed it, and we saw that glimmer of sunlight. That was sweet. That was so sweet, and then it clouded up and started to drizzle away. *Nice, honey, I'm sure God loves us all, but I wonder what's that smell?*

The mind wanders, then lunges, all claws. Right then, out of the blue, it hit me. What are they doing out there? What's happening to my son? His face came at me. I could see him, five years old, crying. His hair was still blond. I crumpled an invoice so as not to scream. Then I smoothed it out.

First time, when I lost the baby, I thought I'd never want to risk it again. And when they told me I was pregnant I couldn't believe it. Couldn't be. Me? Forty-two? Inside me? Then I felt him. Like a wiggle, like a whisper, what they call the quickening, like a fish. He was real. And then everything for me was babies, babies born, babies fighting for life, babies making their moms go nuts with love so they'd live. Thousands of years ago they learned how to do it, and suddenly there wasn't a day or an hour went by without my thinking, *Where is he? What's he doing?* He was my whole world, my life, and then, by days and by years, he grew up.

Men yowl if they cut their finger, but women crack wide open to make a baby, and women know how it feels to lose it. Women on TV every day, they've lost their babies, these women crouched over and screeching like somebody shoved their hand right up in there and ripped the baby out. They lost them in war or starving or drive-by shootings, all the ways you could do it. Every day women screaming between the commercials. When Jesus was born they killed all the other babies, but nobody talked about those. They were nothing special, just roadkill, whereas the good one got saved.

But these mothers, it was their own damned fault. They didn't hold tight enough to their kid, but I could hold on. I was his mother and I would hold on, I told myself, even though he was out there beyond my reach. Four Corners. Four corners of what? At three-thirty I came near to screaming on company time. But I needed to call the trailer park office about the septic system. I'd wait till Old Pinkeye was out of the office. Just ten more minutes to wait. He always went to the toilet at three forty-five.

—24—
Zach

Outside the door of Unit 23, Dad fumbling with the key in one hand, suitcase in the other, I hear one long drawn-out squawk that splits the sky. It's the crow, the raven, the fierce black feathered hunk of gristle portending doom. I count on my fingers for dramatic effect—

—One, two, three, four. Fourth motel. As I said. Fulfillment of prophecy.

Dad opens the door, flips on the light, looks in. I step around him through the doorway and come face to face, over the bed, with a stately pinto stallion overlooking a copper mesa beneath the turbulent desert sky. Somebody must paint these by the hundreds, stick a wild horse in every motel west of the Mississippi. Dad follows with the suitcase, which he makes sure to carry ever since the pistol rose to the top.

—It's the same damn room.

He's right. Every motel is the same motel, every room the same. One size fits all, till further notice. The only difference being that they might trade the wild horse for a bronze Indian or a cactus. Always lots of neat stuff to do: you can channel-surf, walk across the asphalt to the Burger King, fling towels around the room, flush the toilet for laughs—all the same, wherever. And the weather, you don't know if you're north or south cause the air conditioner blows right through your head.

Dad swings the suitcase onto the bed. Nice big wide kingsize bed, but that's nothing new. Every motel room with a pinto stallion also holds a smirky son and a clueless dad with a pistol in the luggage to save their kidneys for Jesus. I resist the urge to start running my mouth, but resistance is futile.

—So, Dad, why'd you say we were going to turn around and go home but then just drive on?

He goes into the bathroom, either because his bladder is full or his brain is empty. I can't keep my mouth shut now. I talk to the door.

—You know why? Cause that's exactly what I knew you were going to do. Is that amazing or what?

A flush. He comes out, moves the suitcase from bed to desk, then to the luggage stand, looking around for something to do to hide the fact that there's nothing to do.

—Well, we'll see when we get to Shiprock.

—This isn't Shiprock, Dad. This is Farmington.

—Well, we went through Shiprock, there's no motels, you saw that. This is Farmington.

—Your guy said the motel was in Shiprock.

—There isn't any. We looked. We asked.

—You said he was very specific. I mean, there was a Taco Bell, maybe he meant to bed down at the Taco Bell.

—So we're twenty miles past. We'll go back in the morning, same thing.

—Go back where?

—Shiprock. The town of Shiprock.

—And then we'll be in Shiprock. Amazing.

We finish that little tap-dance. He talks about going out for dinner but just opens the suitcase and takes out his bottle and sets it on the nightstand his side of the bed. He studies the pinto, then jerks his thumb at the door.

—Guy in the office there?

—Who?

—Another Mexican.

—Well, Dad, there were Mexicans here long before we invaded. We just drove down from Chico before they had time to turn white.

—I was stating a fact.

He'll never own up to being a bigot, and some time ago I realized that he's not. He's just trying to sound like one of the guys. I goad him into it, so he has to spout idiotic stuff just to prove he can.

—Damn tailgaters. However fast you go it makes 'em go faster. They can't help it. They just need to push you.

Where did that come from? Just another blurt from the complaint department. Once he starts he has to feed the grinder. One more way we're alike: we say whatever burps up. Nothing connects. Maybe he's crazy. I know I am. I feel like saying, *Look on the bright side, Dad!* But I don't.

Tonight will be the same hours of a dumb ox butting a tree. We'll go out to eat and Dad will eye the waitress and try to say something cute, and I'll eye the waitress and fiddle with my fork. At least we'll be thinking the same thought from our manly essence. Then we'll eat a hunk of fat and a pile of glop, and Dad will say, *That was filling but I miss your mom's cooking*, and I'll let the silence stifle us both. Then back to the room and he calls Las Vegas. Mumble mumble, and Dad stands there with a half-open mouth like a toddler who's pooped his diaper but isn't sure what happened. Then after he says, *Dear Lord, don't let the bedbugs bite*, we go to bed and I try to dream of Rebecca but sit in the limbo of AP Math with the minute hand climbing up the miles.

He surprises me, punching the cell phone, calling Mom or pretending to. He'll tell her we're stuck in a little one-horse town. Right: up there is the pinto stallion, the one horse in the one-horse town. But either Mom isn't answering or Dad's actually dialed the weather report. He clicks off.

—Well I don't know where she is. It's after six there. Maybe she went out on the town.

—Maybe she went out for groceries.

—Probably.

—You know, Dad, you guys sound pretty funny even when you're not talking.

—Well, I'm not as much of an asshole as I sound like sometimes.

I don't know where that came from. Sometimes he surprises me. It's easier to think of my father as a kind of withered turnip than to accord him a bit of self-knowledge. Once, the bathroom door was open when he was shaving and I heard him talking to himself in the mirror. It sounded like a person trying to tell himself the truth. Or maybe just making noise to avoid hearing himself think think think—as we say in our family. It was that way the last time I talked to Rebecca. I kept talking—quantum physics and Dostoevsky and baseball—a brilliant spew of words to hold back our knowing each other. The more I talked the less chance she'd have to say what I wanted her to say. So she didn't.

—She gets this feeling—

She meaning Mom. My father was talking to me. I didn't want to hear it. Once, years ago, I'd seen Dad naked.

—Hears noises—

And when I finally got naked with Luann and she looked at me, she got this far-away look in her eyes that might have been ecstasy or stomach distress. I didn't want to be naked, ever again.

—She gets this sense, before it happens, she can tell when I'm lying and I don't even know I'm lying, cause I can believe any crap, even my own. When I strung her along with my other— This other person, my— Your so-called brother's mom, and even with letting Jesus into my heart I still kept seeing the first one off and on. And your mom knew. She gets these flashes. She calls it a fist.

He's sitting across the room, his back against the wall in the only chair, revving up to tell his life story in front of his son the firing squad. He wants me to hear him open his soul and to be understood and forgiven. *Dear Dad, I love you, no matter who you are.* I know that isn't too much to ask, but it's way too much to give him.

—Promises. It was gonna be speedboats, it was gonna be real estate, California, mountains, ocean— But we never do, we just flop down at the tube, then get up, go to bed, go to work, go to hell. We coulda done that in Omaha. Okay, I'm just running off at the mouth, but—

—Dad—

—And my own mom thought I was so goddamn special—

—Dad, I've already heard this crap.

He jerks as if I'd slapped him with a fish. He shuts up. I feel sick. This man is my father, and I'm a budding genius who deserves a better dad: poor me. He chases big bucks in Las Vegas, I try to feel up Rebecca, and father and son sit in a dark motel room in New Mexico, feet in the quicksand, shoulders slumped.

Dad rubs his forefinger with his thumb, then turns on the table lamp.

—He can wait.

—Who?

—I'm not his servant. We're going home.

—Home?

—Turn around, go home. I know I said it before, I said it a dozen times, but I mean it. Just turn around, go home.

—Okay—

—Promises, listen to promises, you think it's from God, but it's a joke. Believe in the future, believe in the lies, believe all the bullshit. I oughta kill the bastard.

—Okay then—

—He's a nut! Just some bullshit joker in Las Vegas!

—Dad—

—Shit!

—Can we get something to eat?

—Sorry . . .

He's apologizing for saying *shit*. We're sitting on opposite sides of the kingsize bed, backs to each other, The turn-around-go-home stuff echoes into space, and our heart-to-heart is lost in the music of the spheres. Miss Plankett would question-mark that metaphor. I wonder if she'd correct a lover's choice of endearments. I would never risk it.

—So should you call Mom, say we're coming home?

And I know he's already forgotten what he said. That's what they mean when they talk about freedom and fight the wars to defend the land of the free: to forget what just got said.

—I should have asked the guy at the desk, the Mexican, about Shiprock. I mean the rock, the best way to get there, if that's where we go, if we— I mean we saw it off a ways when we were coming across, or you saw it anyway, but I guess maybe go back to the town of Shiprock and then call him from there and see what he wants us to do. He gave directions but it was kind of a bad connection—

I could say, *Well Dad, you were just saying let's go home.* But why expect anyone to mean what they say?

—Sounds like a plan.

—I mean what we're supposed to do— It wasn't clear, it was—

—You got a message, right? Voice mail? You checked it, you listened a dozen times—

—Shiprock, that's all I— The connection was— I mean you know the damn Indians never would've called it Shiprock, cause when did they ever—

—Call Mom?

—I did that five minutes ago, goddammit— Or no, that was yesterday, I guess, I get mixed up— But no, I just called— Or I guess she must have been taking out the garbage. Okay, I'll try.

He fumbles for the cell phone, finds it on the nightstand, gets up, goes into the bathroom, leaves the door open. Click, buzz, then on the other end—

—Hello?

—Hello, hi, it's me.

I can barely make out what he's mumbling, and I can't hear Mom at all, but I know every word they say. All the words have been said time and time again, plastered on billboards, chiseled into rock.

—Where have you been, Vern, dammit, why haven't you called, I've been trying to—

—I'm calling now—

—I've been worried sick. Why didn't you call?

—I called five minutes ago and you were out—

—I was taking out garbage. It doesn't take out itself.

—Well, I called.

—So where are you?

—Motel. Sitting here.

—You sound funny.

I stare at the pinto stallion to stifle my DNA's babble. Sometimes I think my parents are really my kids and I'm responsible for their scars and their groping, but how do I qualify to be the adult? And that's exactly what they're feeling: how do they qualify?

—Anyway I didn't want to call till I knew what was going on, so now I'm calling.

—So what's going on?

—Whatta you think's going on? We're sitting here, I'm calling. We're at Shiprock.

—Shiprock?

—It's a big rock. It's famous. I told you this. I left a message, didn't you hear it? He said drive to Shiprock, wait there, so that's what I'm doing. That's what's going on, goddammit!

Again there's a silence that comes from saying nothing but saying it very loud, and they take turns breaking the silence. Maybe Mom will scream the way she did once. Maybe I'll slump over the wastebasket, nauseated by words. Dad revs up to drone on.

—Actually not Shiprock. There's no motels in the town of Shiprock, so we're in Farmington, but then in the morning we'll go to Shiprock, and then I guess down to the rock. Or I don't know, maybe we'll just turn around and come back. Maybe that's best, though I always give up on stuff. Think about those Marines that marched into the swamp, somebody said march into the swamp and they marched right into the—

—Marines?

—Marines on the news, for chrissake. Long time ago, which war I dunno, but the point being— Like the wars we used to win and now we always lose, but is that because we give up too soon or because we don't?

Silence over the face of the deep.

—I'm sorry, Vern, I'm just trying to follow.

—No, I'm okay. Just don't ask if I'm okay. I'm okay.

—Can I talk to him?

—Who?

—Our son.

—He's fine. He's busy. He says hello.

—Tell him his mom loves him.

I can only hear, *He's fine, he says hello.* Dad's voice is like the talking toy they gave me once, a fibrillating Santa that croaked *Merry Christmas!* till the battery went dead. They do their goodbyes. He clicks off the phone, comes out of the bathroom, paces back and forth like the red-assed baboon when Miss Young took the fourth-graders to the zoo and tried to hurry us past the red-assed baboons.

—She's fine. Kinda slurry. She's not drinking, but her dentures make her sound kinda slurry sometimes. Wow, you think of a dentist all day looking in people's mouths, see what they had for lunch—

His thread is unraveling. He knows he's lost but he can't find north because it's overcast and there's no way to tell by the sun. He feels me looking at him. He's like me in the junior class play, forgetting my lines but the play goes right on like a tank, rolling right over the rotting corpse of Zach McGurren. Dad sits on the bed, rubbing his forefinger with his thumb.

—I need more faith. That's the whole basis of Western civilization, whereas the Chinese, Hindus, Japs, they're fatalistic, they don't believe in God so why should he do'em a favor? Faith is rewarded is the idea, it's hard to believe but the believing makes it true. Not that you ever can trust whoever's telling you stuff.

—Could I ask you an honest question, Dad?

He nods or it looks like a nod.

—You sound drunk.

He glances around the floor to look for the words he's lost, then looks at me. Stuff swarms into his head like bees, and he wants to say again we should turn around and go home and thank God for the trailer park. How Mom loves flowers but they never plant flowers.

How he wanted to play the World Series. I feel his eyes on me, like he found a strange bug up his sleeve. He could squash it but what if it stung? He's rubbing his thumb and forefinger. It's his trigger finger and hammer thumb. Itching for the six-shooter that won the West. I feel the weight of the pistol, held by two fingers, and the music swells, big splat, and I catch a glimpse of the headline. *Father Charged in Shooting Death of Son.* Photo of weeping dad in handcuffs. Profile of smiling honor student. The cell-phone mystery man. Calls for gun control. Tarentino sweeps the Oscars. End of story. It seems so perfect. Trigger finger and hammer thumb. The sins of the fathers will never fall on the sons if you waste the son. He wants to tell me he doesn't know what the holy fuck he's doing.

Dad stands up and sits down. After a while he stands up again and sits down. I wait for the next time: all things come in threes. He does it again. I understand. He's wanting to stay sane until tomorrow. And I'm crouching in the shadow I carry with me like a soggy sack lunch. I almost start to laugh. The puzzle falls into place. Too perfect. What's the word for a daytime nightmare?

There's a tap at the door. I go to open it. The dark man from the motel desk stands there, holding a stack of bath towels. This happened before. Was it the same towel guy from a thousand miles away?

—I check the towels.

—I think we've got towels.

—I check.

The guy goes past me into the bathroom. Mexican maybe, but I can't quite tell from his accent. Maybe the Ancient Mariner lugging his albatross, or the Flying Dutchman, or the Wandering Jew meandering with his towels, motel to motel, across the American West.

Dad sits frozen, other side of the room, his life passing before his eyes like a cartoon: a weeny duck-faced Vernon McGurren outwitting Sylvester the Cat. The dark man is in the bathroom for about twenty seconds, long enough to plant a bomb in the toilet, then he appears without the towels. He seems to be glancing around the room, no movement except the eyes. Might he suspect we're fugitives, a defrocked priest screwing an altar boy? Or drug smugglers gypping him out of his cut? Or thieves with designs on the priceless pinto stallion? I ask—

—Okay?

—Bueno.

—Bueno, gracias.

I feel odd being spokesman, but I answered the door and I'm the one who speaks *Intro to Spanish*. The dark man has a wart below his left eye.

—Hay un buen restaurante a dos cuadras de aquí.

—Muchas gracias.

A relief. Clearly the Mexican wanted to cut out our kidneys, but he's had second thoughts, seeing how Dad straightens up ready for action. He gives a cheery wave without the trace of a smile and leaves. I giggle at our comedy routine.

—So, plenty of towels. They must think—

—I dunno—

—Maybe gringos need lots of towels.

He looks up at the painting. The pinto's noble stature seems to gentle the riot in his head. So much has happened. He called his wife. His son said he sounded drunk. The Mexican delivered towels. He rubbed his thumb on his finger, and the devils went into the swine. Now he finds a couple of leftover words—

—Hey, let's get some dinner.

So we get some dinner at the diner down the road, or something passing for food. Nothing is said in this half-hour except, *Pass the ketchup, please*. The waitress is a fat wad of wrinkle. A TV behind the counter, and somebody makes a touchdown—they do it once, they shouldn't have to keep on doing it. A deer head, a fire extinguisher, a wood carving of Smoky the Bear, an old man curled in a booth like the crook of an umbrella.

We come back to the room. The pinto is still keeping watch and the stack of towels stands ready. I sit down to my homework while Dad watches a basketball game, murmuring, *Terrific!* or *All right!* He's trying to have fun, despite his finger and thumb. And so time passes in a New Mexico motel, whose only occupants are the father and son in Unit 23. At last the father stretches out with a yawn, rising to his feet.

—Hey you know I'd kinda like it, but if you don't want to, but if we could kneel down together and—

Sure, why not? I'll do what's needed to do. The TV goes mute with a gasp. I close my history text at the point where Pepin the Short begets Charlemagne, which surely improves the breed, and lay it on the nightstand and kneel beside the bed while Dad kneels on the other side. Somewhere beyond all traffic, the hatchet head of Shiprock hacks into the starstruck sky. I wish I could write that in my notebook, but I'm on my knees and Dad is talking to God.

—So dear Lord Jesus, we thank Thee for this—what? Opportunity? Just maybe I wish you could give us a clue. It's beautiful coming here, although I didn't much see it. But I always believed in the future. Believed there is a future, but sure, you have to make it. Pull up roots, we pulled up roots from Omaha, we had friends there, we had more of a life— And it's not like fly to Las Vegas and come back rich, but I still— I'm just trying. Goddammit, I'm trying!

Middle of the night, I wake up and lie there with my itchy bedbug mind repeating, *The devils went into the swine.* Must be that you can't kill the devils, they have to go somewhere, so where do they go when the swine all come down with the flu? Fly into our eyes? I lie there watching thin slits of parking-lot light on the ceiling. After a while, in my undershorts, I get out of bed into the night chill and the deeper chill in the bone. The devils are numb with chill.

Dad is trying, I'm not. Or I'm trying not to try. I don't feel I've really earned another suicide. I've spent more time farting around with depression and existential despair than actually getting up to speed on any of it. I don't want my cereal soggy. I don't want to pretend to be stupid. I don't want more movies where corpses pile up to amuse me. I don't want to be my father even if there's nothing else to be. I don't want a future. I'm standing there in my droopy undershorts. I've forgotten my lines and I'm chilled to the bone.

Nor do I want to flunk my suicide again. You can put the gun to your temple like Russians do, or under your chin, in your mouth, and we've got lots of towels now to tuck around the head—that's why they delivered the towels. But it's still a horrible mess, not to mention the defecation. Maybe off the Grand Canyon, or Golden Gate Bridge if we ever get to San Francisco. Or maybe symbolic self-destruction, some hideous atrocity where Rebecca would say, *What? Zach? He wouldn't do something like that! He was such a nice young man!*

By the parking-lot flicker I fumble my way to the suitcase. Open it, feel through the laundry, grope the pistol, touching it very gently. *Hand-gun* sounds more genteel. Now holding it, both hands. Now sitting on the edge of the bed, my side. Now hearing Dad's open-mouth snore. Now seeing the faint yellow light on the blanketed lump. Now feeling the safety catch.

I've thought a lot about killing my father, not really for any good reason, not really hate. Just that things would be different. I wouldn't have to do my book report, and Mom would have more excuse to get drunk. In fact I'm sure that Dad would be happier dead. I find the safety catch but can't tell if it's off or on, so I don't know when I flip it off if it's really on.

All cliches, Miss Plankett would say, *You can do better than that.* Write instead how absurd, ridiculous, exhausted I feel when I stick it into the suitcase, deep down under the laundry—we need to find a laundromat—and go back to bed. On the ceiling I watch the funny slivers of light.

—25—

Merna

I got off the bus, so slow it was nearly dark by then, walked up the steps and it hit me. If I'd been riding with Rosella it'd been her bowels, but now it was mine. I left the grocery sack on the top step, got the door unlocked and just made it to the can in time. Whoosh. Never knew I had it in me.

I sat there a couple extra minutes just in case, but no, just that low-down gripe. Felt like back in high school when I had cramps. I'd get a sick pass from the nurse, perch on the toilet doubled over and groaning, sounding like the steam radiator. Not at all a bad way to spend an afternoon. Even with the pain it was better than Home Ec and Algebra, and between cramps I could read my sci-fi paperback. But there always came the time, like now, to pull up my pants and get in gear.

I cranked open the louver to air the stink and went back out front to pick up the grocery bag. My dinner stuff: onions, zucchini, ragu sauce, Italian sausage, a little bottle of olive oil and the three fresh tomatoes I shoplifted. So weird, shoplifting three tomatoes. Sudden impulse, scary if it wasn't so funny, then paying for all the other stuff while hoping my purse didn't squish. I'd never done that since high school, and then it was mostly those sci-fi paperbacks.

I was bound and determined to fix a slam-dunk dinner and eat every damn bit myself. Fresh tomatoes in the sauce, and theft made them extra tasty.

I washed my hands in the sink. In Home Ec, Mrs. Puterbaugh told us always wash your hands before you handle food, as if you had such red-blooded Wonder Woman germs that cooking wouldn't kill 'em. Silly, but I could never not do it. Now I heard that crusty old biddie's voice like a creaking door: *Schedule your cooking so it all comes out ready on time.* Okay, Merna, schedule to come out ready on time.

Talking to myself. Right, nobody to hear, but who ever listened anyway? The kid in the hospital where I'd worked, amputee, kept feeling an itch in the leg that wasn't there. There was a word for that. Funny kid, he joked about cutting off fingers so the phantom fingers could scratch the phantom leg. Now Vern wasn't there nor Zach, but I kept feeling the itch. Hear yourself think think think, no stopping it.

Chop the onion. Big beautiful onion and they glue on this label that tells you it's an onion, and you can't get it off with a fingernail or hardly even a paring knife. Mrs. P showed us the trick about onions to keep the tears back: don't nick the onion skin, keep those fumes from getting out. Great idea, not time yet to cry, but how to slice it without nicking the skin . . . At least it was quiet for once, except the fluorescent hum. Keep those home fires burning.

Bourbon again in her coffee cup. Drunk never worked for me, but I tried. Half a cup, but then it all crashed in: *Goddammit, no! Pour it out!* I emptied the cup down the drain. Then I emptied the rest of the bottle. Then I shoved the empty bottle down deep under the trash—

And cut my hand on something. Ouch. Not too bad. Get a Band-Aid. *Pay attention, Merna. You! I'm talking to you!*

Rinsed off and got a Band-Aid. Mrs. Puterbaugh would never approve of blood on the onion, and Band-Aids never stuck in California like they did in Minot, or maybe the cuts were deeper. They're in New Mexico. Hold on, make your schedule so you come out ready on time. Water for spaghetti, ten minutes to boil, ten minutes to cook. Turn it on, start the wait. In some motel. That TV show where they knew it was done if they threw it at the wall and it stuck: must have been a sit-com, but these days who could tell? What were they doing for supper?

I couldn't tell if the guy came for the septic system but the smell was worse. I started to make some tea. But no, I really wanted booze. But no, I got rid of it. But no, I still had the Johnny Walker. But no, I couldn't top it up. But no, I'd survive. I had to. That's what I did.

Okay, talk to yourself. Onions, zucchini, sausage. Peppers? No peppers. Tomatoes? Okay. Oil in the skillet, onions, zucchini, sausage on top. She always told us to make the onions sweat, whatever that meant, or if she even knew. Ten minutes for the sausage. Turn up the fire, then lower. Zucchini, just chop it in chunks like the sausage, shovel it in. Ten minutes, then pour on the sauce, chop tomatoes, and right at the last drop them in and try to stop crying— *Zach Zach Zach!*

Sit down to wait. Cooking is mostly waiting, but they never tell you that. How many minutes in life is just waiting? Sit down a minute, Merna, close your eyes, blank it out. And I shut my eyes and it's faces. Vernon and Zach. An old guy in a hat. A dark-skinned man with a stack of towels. A cutie-pie waitress. A stubby Mexican in cover-alls. The cracked granite face of God Almighty.

They never know what it's like, the men. The water breaks, he tore me wide open. *You want to see your son?* Beautiful, and then he kills himself. Tries to, same thing. They never know. They're off across the desert to get a write-up in the Bible. Philistines, Viet Cong, Arabs, however many they kill there's always more. While the mother is back in the tent making the onions sweat. Waits for the phone call, tries not to scream. At least I got to the toilet in time.

What if they kept on nursing, the men? They could pay to nurse at the breast because money makes it important, and they might just be able to see Mommy's eyes. The President nurses, the armies nurse, the bankers, the movers and shakers—take the nipple but don't bite. I loved nursing. How could I be thinking this stuff and not be drunk?

❖

Phone ringing, I woke up. Woke up with the trailer full of smoke, skillet black, pot boiled dry. Phone ringing. Goddamn robocall. Reach, turn off the burner, pick it up.

Vern. My heart in my throat, I sat again at the table. *Motel. Shiprock. Big famous rock. Marines in the swamp.* Fist, grab, yank. *Zach's fine, busy, says hello.*

—Jesus Christ . . .

I hung up. Opened the window to vent it and scraped my Italian cremation into the garbage. Ate the tomatoes as a consolation, took aspirin for the headache, three or four might do it. I should take the whole bottle and see if God cares. Felt like I weighed two hundred pounds. I shuffled over, sat, thought about calling Vern to say sorry but couldn't remember what I was sorry for.

I saw the blackened skillet in my hand. I was holding my cast-iron skillet. I must have carried it into the bathroom, carried it eating tomatoes. I felt the rage hit my face like a spit of hot grease and the lights flared white and I wanted to bring the skillet down hard on something I couldn't see. Down flat on the faces, bashing, battering Vernon, Zach, Pinkeye, Mommy, Daddy, God, and that second-hand green vinyl couch I hated with a passion, bang bang whangity bang, trying to kill, till I collapsed on the green vinyl couch.

But I didn't. I depended on that skillet. Might be nice to go nuts, but then I'd pay for it. I put the skillet on the stove, made a cup of tea. And then, I guess, up late pointing myself at the tube, comedians yucking it up. One made jokes about old people, one about the President, one about some movie star's boobs. All snappy smart guys, too dumb to know which end to pin their diapers on.

I crawled into bed. At least I didn't have to kneel down and pray to God. *He's got the whole world in his hands . . .* Which always sounded to me like he had us in his fist and was starting to squeeze. The mind ran down the dark squiggly road behind my uncle's house— *Yea though I walk through the Valley of Death*— And mixed up with the poem about trees. *I think that I shall never see . . .* And then Alice fell down the scary black rabbit hole.

—26—

Vernon

I saw her chopping onions. A dream, but more like snapshots, flashes, jerks between sleep and awake. I didn't see her out loud—out loud, funny way to think of it—but only her face and her hands and a knife and tape that wouldn't stick.

It was morning again. It struck me that every morning was morning again. Like the pioneers, a big mural I saw in the Denver station, a line of pioneers heading west in covered wagons with angels flying above and scruffy Indians pushed off the left edge except one noble chief on a horse, looking sad. Every morning they'd get up and trudge on toward Chico. Were they happier when they got there?

I woke up shivering with sweat. The sun was sharp on the ceiling. The alarm hadn't gone off, but I saw I hadn't set it. I couldn't feel if Zach was there in the bed, then I flopped over and saw him. He sat in the chair at the desk looking in my direction. He wasn't looking at me, he was looking past.

First thing that struck me: we had to turn around and go back. We could see the Grand Canyon, take time to tune in and talk like father and son. Drive through the Painted Desert, the colors on the postcard I saw. This Las Vegas thing was nuts: what did I know about casinos? I always jumped at something for nothing and what ever came of it? Heartache. I'm out in the backyard tossing up the baseball, and I know it's all fake. I'm tossing up the ball so it's easy to hit and hitting home runs over the backyard fence, cheering myself, but the sun goes dark and I can't even see. We had to go back. Give the joker a call, say thanks, go home.

Zach was still looking in my direction. I don't think he'd even heard me. I must not have said it out loud.

The pint was there on the nightstand. Morning, but this was a special day. We were going home. We were going to see better times, talk like father and son. Take a pull and feel the hard bite, start off the day awake. But his eyes were on me now.

He sat there looking at me. *Do your homework*, I said, but maybe not out loud. Some kind of gap between what I was saying and what got said, and a dumb thing to say before we'd even had breakfast. Zach never moved his eyes. Just looking directly through me, and Merna chopping onions. It must have been last night when I called.

I stood, pulled up my pants, buttoned my shirt, went to the bathroom, came out. Zach was already dressed or else he'd been like that all night. I groped around for the cell phone, fumbled it, started to call Merna. I thought I heard her answer, thought I said hello, thought I passed the phone to Zach. I heard him distinctly talking to his mom, telling how much he liked the trip. *New perspectives*, he said. I heard him talk, the desert, the homework, the tumbleweeds. So eloquent I thought, *Is this my son?* But then he hung up and I knew I'd never made any phone call. The phone was in my hand.

—What are you looking at, Zach?

—Morning.

His eyes were somewhere strange. His fingers made circles in the air. It made me want to reach out my fingers and make circles too. I tried to laugh, a big fake guffaw, but the silence squelched it. We were in the last days. Those were the words that came into my head: *the last days*. It sounded like church but I couldn't say what it meant. Then I saw Lannie.

Lannie stood at the door with an armful of towels, just standing there. It was him every time. All the sooty guys back of the desk. Maybe the kid with the SWAT team, maybe the so-called Bruce. Older than I remembered him, thirties maybe. Olive skin, Mexican hair, soft dark eyes like his mother. Nice smile. Lanford, Gayla Krelle's grandfather's name. It wasn't me who saw him. I was looking at Zach, and Zach was seeing Lannie. It was very real.

He was an accident, one stray spurt, a streak of gristle in the pork chop. He turned up on the doorstep when Zach was four or five and they seemed to get along, but I never had more than a dozen words with him. I didn't remember black hair like that. He showed up and I gave him a hundred dollars and that was enough. It was long ago. I never had a feeling for him, even though I tried to tell myself, *Hey, this is your son.* I never wanted a son.

I couldn't look at him. He was there in Zach's eyes. His voice was low and smooth—

—You can only die once, kiddo.

—Is that what you're waiting for, Lannie?

—It's like dessert. Unless you can't wait and you just gotta bite the cherry.

I heard them as if through a door. Zach wouldn't talk to me, but he talked to him. I wanted to throw myself across the room, whomp with my fist to prove there was nobody there, but I just sat. The figures came into a sharpness, a knife-edge glitter, my son and my other son. My own eyes were seeing him now. Second sight. Low blood sugar made you hallucinate, like the hippies jumping out windows to fly. We had better get breakfast right away.

Zach turned away. There was no one at the door. I hadn't seen the so-called other son for years. I needed breakfast.

—So today we'll be at Shiprock.

My voice sounded hollow. We were in that culvert where Kenny and I yelled dirty words that hooted and rang. I couldn't hear the words, but I saw them printed on air. I felt my zipper half zipped, so I zipped it. It was that real.

—I mean Shiprock, not the town of Shiprock, I mean the rock. I mean you saw it out there from twenty miles away, but when we get right up under it's a thousand feet tall or something.

—Well, hey, Dad—

Zach was talking, it seemed like, but he made no sense at all. The words came spouting like that crazy bum who screamed at cars in the street until someone got out and hit him with a carjack. I couldn't tell if he was making a joke or reciting some poem he'd learned in school. Or else the words were spouting out me and I was nuts. I felt my hand shaking and tried to stop it, but it only shook the harder. Low blood sugar, what Merna said. I needed breakfast.

—We need breakfast.

He was talking at me but not looking. He was looking at the door where his brother, half-brother was, but he wasn't. Zach was talking about babysitters, but that wasn't the—

—One time, Dad, you left me with a babysitter. There were older kids and their mom wasn't there, so they took a gun out of their dad's drawer and chased me all over the house. They said they were going to shoot me because I didn't have a gun. Mom packed me a sandwich, but she should have packed me a gun.

—When was this?

—I ran into the bathroom, crouched down in the tub, and they pointed the gun right at me and pulled the trigger.

He was quiet, thinking up something clever. I couldn't resist.

—What happened?

—They shot me dead.

I yelled to shut him up, but I couldn't hear my voice except in the culvert roaring dirty words. He didn't act like he heard.

—So I've been dead ever since. I just faked it cause I wanted birthday presents.

His voice was crystal clear, but my head was a windy roar. Long breath, low rumble. Words came up like little cartoon balloons and hung there. I needed breakfast.

—We're going home. I'm calling that sonofabitch. What's the number?

I had the cell phone in my left hand without knowing where I got it. I was punching with my right-hand finger, not even looking at the numbers, just punching hard. Zach sounded as if he was grinning.

—Punch *Menu*, Dad. It shows all the calls you've done.

—Fuck it!

I flung the cell phone away, and it hit the wall. I rose up and twisted around to pound my fist on the wall but caught myself. My face squeezed into a pucker, and then my legs went limp. I crumpled into a squat, but I still was holding the cell phone that I thought I'd thrown at the wall. After that it went blank.

It was close to nine-thirty before we went out for breakfast, the diner a block down the road. On the way we never spoke. Same diner, it felt like. Old ox yoke screwed to the wall, and a guy at the counter like the Indian chief without the feathers. The brown-skin stub-nose waitress brought bacon and eggs that I must have ordered, and I ate what I could. She chatted about the weather, grinned, and I nodded. I don't think she really wanted to grin at some flabby hung-over gringo, but if your chest is flat and you want to get tips, I guess you have to grin. She stood there nattering on—good thing the gun was back in the room. Friendly is fine if you're in the mood.

My eyes were the way they'd be if I looked at the sun too long: sharp vision around the edges but the center was gone. And the sounds—the clatter of dishes, the motor hum, somebody's chewing, the waitress's shuffle and pencil scratch—the center was gone.

I had to speak to Zach. Important things to say if I could keep it straight. We came back to the motel, the boy and his dad, opened the door, and came into the room. It was the old train station in Denver, huge, two stories high inside, with pioneers and angels, the chief on a horse, and the echoes wrapping us. It wasn't hallucination—I knew I'd eaten breakfast—so it felt safe, but safe in a terrible way, like a bug on the lip of a beautiful flower. That didn't sound like me.

—Exactly the way I dreamt it.

I heard him talking. He knew what would happen before it happened. He'd finished his history lesson, and history repeats itself, so now we were watching re-runs.

—Mrs. Coad always said, *You'd get good grades if you wanted to.*

—You'd get good grades if you wanted to.

—I get good grades without wanting to.

—You've got a gift.

—And you hit the big one over the back yard fence.

I never told him that, or if I did it was a joke. Any kid wants to be great, and you make up stories from all the crap that you hear. Who doesn't want to be the star, the guy with a million fans screaming out your name? That's freedom.

Zach was holding the pistol. Holding it like a girl would, both hands and pointing to the floor. A Browning .22 semi-automatic, must be mine. The suitcase was open. He was showing me how to release the safety by pushing up with the thumb, which I knew but I didn't know that he knew it. It was hard to hear for the noise. He must not have come with me for breakfast. He sounded like he was talking, or somebody was.

It's just a gun, Dad, that's all. It's yours. It'll come when you say Fetch. We're not like making big changes. We're just facing the facts.

Zach held the gun the way he might hold a wounded bird, cradled like a gentle thing.

Come on, Dad. We're not at Shiprock now, not the rock of Shiprock now, but let's pretend. It's an opportunity, a promise like you said. You said talk like father and son so I'm talking like father and son, but otherwise we just dribble on the rug.

It wasn't the Denver depot. We were in the motel, no pioneers. I laid the room key on the nightstand and tried to think if I'd paid the check at the diner. All I could hear was static. I saw myself tearing open the blinds to let in the sun, but in fact I just stood there.

Holding the Browning .22. I'd brought it for protection, and I held it now. The ad said ergonomic all-weather grip, pleasing feel to the hand. I laughed at that when I read it. Matte-gray finish with matte-blued barrel, excellent for plinking, said the ad. I might do some plinking. I didn't recall how the safety worked, but I found it with my thumb. At that moment my senses were very sharp. I could see numbers clean and clear, but no way to know what they meant. Like the switchbacks on the mountain road in the Rockies, hands tight to the steering wheel, taking the curves like a pro but feeling the yearn of the guardrail pulling us out to the edge.

Zach lay face down on the bed. I was close to him. Now I could hear our voices clear and bright.

—Stop that.

—Do it, Dad.

—Get up.

—Sorry.

—You're crazy.

—Right.

—God loves you.

—Nevertheless.

—You want a drink? You're old enough now, you could have a drink. Let's have a drink, celebrate going home.

—Cheers.

I looked up at the white spackled ceiling and a roar came in, like some rampant young stud gunning his big rig, shooting his wad. I saw a crew of young guys stretching down the road, brothers in rage. They wanted something real. Blood was real, a heart blasted open was real, the voice of a desert God. Thirty miles to Shiprock.

—Does Mom know?

—She's fine.

—She know what's going on?

—She loves you.

I heard the words flung out, spewing out. Bat squeaks, thunder of trucks, the culvert echoing filth. It was in my left hand. He had lifted it out, stood there with it, must have reached it to me or how would I be holding it? He lay face down on the bed, mumbled on in that flat muffled voice like once when he learned all the states—

—Do we have to wait till Christmas or couldn't we open our presents now?

I would have told him not to act smart, but I saw he was crying. I turned my back and sat plop on the edge of the bed. One crack, and the movie would go all red, then black, and the dogs would howl in the hills. I raised it to the head.

❖

None of it happened. The last half hour was wiped. We were driving toward Shiprock. The actual rock of Shiprock.

Nothing had happened. No throwing the cell phone. No sight of the brother, half-brother. No holding the pistol. It was all from some movie and it felt so real, but in movies they chop it up, there's a blast and a scream and you think the blast caused the scream, but there's no way to know. No way to know. That's what made it so real.

They say you create your own reality. *Just like life*, my friend Reggie said, whenever somebody died. Reggie died at the age of thirty-eight. *At least he acted like he did*, Jim said. Jim was a joker.

Back west from Farmington, then south on 491, according to the map. Zach was watching the map. The noon sun was in my eyes. Miles and miles of good-for-nothing land, but as long as you're driving you don't have to be there even. South on 491, then right on 13, six or seven miles and then a break in the fence, according to directions, unless they'd got the directions from some Indian selling rugs. Right now it all felt real.

It was tiny, then bigger, then huge. Up ahead to the right, rising out of the flatland, it was huge. The jags went up to a peak, then down, then up to a higher peak. Dark granite, gray brown rock-color, and its face was flat like the face of a stone-dead god. Some giant bird that flew the Navajo there, you saw why they had to believe it. They were like me, needing the promise. They never asked why their giant bird dumped them all in a burnt-over land of scabs. Looking down to the valley, they never saw it. They only saw the promise.

We were told to come and we came. We did what we were asked. The preacher called it a test. Some preacher, it wasn't Reverend Bud because his thing was, okay, God gives us a test but he shows us the answers. He doesn't want us to flunk, he wants us to pass the test. Reverend Bud would never say that kind of stuff, the killing, the blood, but maybe Reverend Bud was full of shit. I never got shown any answers.

We were at the break in the fence looking up to the wing of rock a quarter mile off, and I was hearing it. Microwaves, they say, shoot right through you, but they must hit something in there. Alzheimers,

AIDS, those kids that just bang their heads on the wall to kill the swarm of bees inside, and Zach must be hearing the bees. The wind is all curses, the Bible says, a wild roar in the sky. The big rigs rumble, the bees buzz, the wind whines out its lies. I was maybe still asleep, forgot to set the alarm.

The car stopped a few yards into the break in the barbed-wire fence. I didn't see any sign that said we couldn't go in. Two tire tracks ahead, just ruts through caked mud. I crept ahead very slowly, bouncing in the ruts. Any minute I thought I'd scrape the muffler off the car. Drove, bounced and jostled and drove, never seemed any closer, but we finally stopped fifty, sixty yards from the base of Shiprock.

I set the brake, got out, stood there. The sun was low behind me even though it was just past noon. My shadow stretched long. The sky had clotted into a brown purple face with an arc of blue framing the crest of the rock. Zach got out of the car.

—Big rock.

—Huge.

Neither of us had anything to say that could come to words. Sacred spot for the Navajo. And for us, apparently. Across the stretch of the waste I saw a vast glitter like a path of diamonds. It was beer bottles, broken glass.

—27—

Firstborn

Other kids had fathers, me just a vagrant sperm. My mother had soft dark eyes, and once in a while she saw me. So I found it safest to keep myself ill-defined, a hard fact with blurry edges. The unborn firstborn son.

I was eighteen, a gung-ho Marine just out of boot camp. I hitched from San Diego to Denver on a ten-day leave to visit Mama before shipping out to the halls of Montezuma or the shores of Tripoli. She said I should go see my dad.

—He should see you in your uniform.

—Who?

—Your dad.

So I met the man named Dad. He wasn't wild to see me, nor his wife, who looked doubtful I might shit on the rug. But their kid, this amazing kid. Four or five years old, but he could read, he was funny, he'd make jokes. He made me ride his trike. I tried, with my knees up to my ears, and we laughed. Two days with nothing to say to Dad, but the kid, we were brothers. Two days.

Thirteen years now. Twelve, thirteen. Lot of things happen in thirteen years. You're deployed, you shoot into the trees, you beget one or two little yellow-brown kids to replace the ones you wasted.

And thereafter I got some education that let me string words together in compound sentences. The better to curse with, my dear.

And it's not that bad to die. I've done it a number of times.

I see the car bouncing rut to rut, approaching the mighty altar reflected in their eyes—Shiprock reflected fourfold. Both have green eyes, the pale green of an avocado. Softer, those of the boy, more feminine, more acute.

They stop a hundred yards away, a respectful distance from the great monadnock sacred to the Navajo. The car door opens and the father steps out, shading his eyes though the sun is behind him, awed by the rock's blinding height. He wouldn't know the term *monadnock* even as he's facing one.

The passenger door swings open and the son appears. He moves with a slow formality so as not to rouse the colossus. He too is silent before the vast volcanic breccia to which they make obeisance. I watch them from shadow: steel fists, tight ass, grimy eyes, dry mouth. They bring me with them. I'm part of the deal.

The father sits on a sandstone ledge, an altar aslant, and swigs from a water canteen. He offers it, the son declines, no wetness desired. The man screws the cap on the vessel, re-screws it to mesh the delicate threads. Both have arrived. Both are stark nuts.

A cloud drifts over the sun, and a thunderhead far to the east. The small black canvas suitcase lies on the sandstone ledge at the foot of the monument stone. The suitcase doesn't fit here. *I placed a jar in Tennessee*, some poet wrote about the oddity of man-made objects in midst of wilderness. *I tossed a beer can in the ditch*, a less poetic soul might brag. The son's voice floats to me, quiet as the cloud.

—So we're at Shiprock now. So finish it, Dad.

—What?

—Open the suitcase.

The father lays his face in his hands and draws a heavy breath as if puffing a big cigar. He seems to be wanting to weep but isn't sure how. The cloud slides away from the sun, but the thunderhead is closer. He straightens up, feels the heat on his face. The slab of stone gleams white. A voice drifts over—

—Does Mom know?

—She's fine.

—She knows what's going on?

—Nothing going on.

—Stop lying, Dad.

—She loves you.

The father sits there, stuck to the rock, bewildered, waiting for the great wing to flex and lift him up to another world, some valley of promise and they the first to claim it. He glances down at the suitcase, the wind comes up, and his eyes narrow to slits. A whistle trills through a cleft in the stone, then withers away. Voices blend—

—I forgot about lunch.

—Corn chips in the car.

History is full of delays. In the countdown to the missile launch, a commander forgets the password. At the cue to spring the trapdoor, a flea bites the hangman. On the cusp of the Apocalypse, archangel Gabriel needs to pee. The father might rise, fetch a bag of chips from the car, and they'd both sit munching, awaiting the top of the hour. But no one moves. A crow shadow flickers between them. The yearning wind rises again.

—You oughta change your shirt. You had that shirt on for two days now. Your mom would be upset. She tries to keep us presentable.

—Just keep talking, Dad. That's good. Talk about clothes.

—I don't know what we're doing here. Some kind of joke.

The father's lips are moving, but his words are smeared. His face shows no sign of what he might be saying. His pupils dilate the moment the sun goes dark. The boy chuckles. Both are standing face to face. And slowly my father Vernon McGurren curls forward and clenches his belly as if in a labor pang. My little brother Zachary zips open the suitcase, gropes in the laundry, produces a hunk of steel and lifts it out like lifting a newborn kitten. His face bears a smirk as if to say *April Fool!* but he only wants to make his father laugh. Then his eyes go dull. He presses the thumb safety upward. The safety is off. He reaches out, grasps his father's hands and places the pistol between the two palms, folding stiff fingers around it. His lips form unspoken words—

Okay, Dad, so the safety is off, but that's okay, you don't want it safe, it's a gun, after all. People have accidents, terrible senseless accidents, but accidents make the world go round. Now we'll have our accident. They'll write us up in the Bible. We need to get ready now.

—That's not what I'm doing, goddammit, that's not what we're here for. I'd never do something like— It'd tear out her heart, your mother, tear out her heart.

—She's a survivor, Dad.

I see my father's doggy eyes. We took Ladybug to the vet to have her put down. She looked at us like that.

The son reaches into the suitcase and pulls out a brown extension cord that he's swiped from the motel. He twists it around his wrists, tries to pull them apart: it holds. He could easily untwist, but its bite is proof of the binding. He wriggles up onto the rough sand face of the killing stone and crosses his ankles.

The father is still in half a curl. He breathes in gasps. His fingers are limp on the pistol grip. A gust and his eyes are red with tears. The white sky is crazed. Minutes or hours, neither has moved. The son nods awake from a stuporous nap, his father a pillar of salt.

—Dad?

No response.

—Please?

The father gapes, inhales the sky. His fingers tighten around the grip as if to squeeze water from it. His words burst out in a volley—

—I need to find the phone book. Where's the damn phone book, Zach? Always a Bible, these places, I don't need the Bible, I need the phone book—

—What number?

That stops him dead. He waves the pistol, carving a question mark in the air.

—Bastard, he's making a joke, he thinks it's funny. I don't think it's funny, we're gonna get in the car and forget we ever—

—Dad—

—I need to load this thing. How do you load—

—It's loaded, so just lay it alongside the head so it doesn't jerk—

—First I gotta load—

A shot explodes. The bullet kicks up sand a hundred feet away. Their eyes are full of the next minutes and years. Their voices are flat, all color bleached out.

—Dad, it's loaded. Do it.

—It just jerked. It just—

—Raise up. More. Okay. Now.

—Turn it up so nobody hears.

—No, Dad, we're out here, there's no TV, nobody hears—

—Turn it up—

—Nothing worth watching—

—Weather report—

—Sunny. Scattered showers.

Their words go to a whisper. All to be heard from where I stand in the shadow is *Count of three.* Several times the legitimate son says *Count of three.* He sounds like he's ready to defecate. People do, they can't help it, even movie stars do, the moment it says *The End* and the credits roll and they run for the can. His dad wants to say it's a test of faith, that it's just pretend, that there's always a sheep or a goat, but he starts counting *One—*

The pistol fires. The shot rings, echoes, same as before. Father and son look puzzled. They never imagined the clumsiness of death, yet the thought of it slips so smoothly into the mind, the way the chiropractor cracks the spindly grandma's spine with one soft push. Eight rounds to go.

The time is come. I step out of the shadow. I'm twenty feet away and my presence is inexplicable. The thunderhead enfolds the tip of the rock.

Both see me without a twitch of recognition. I might be the raven or the crow if they could tell which was which. They hadn't known me at the desks or counters or when I brought the towels. I have too many faces, and all those dark-skinned guys, they blur into Texas chili. Right now I could make a chatty joke about family reunions. I could denounce their racist whiteness. I could ask to share the corn chips. I could adjure tell them to ask and it shall be given, seek and ye shall find, knock and it shall be opened unto you—but they've already heard that stuff. They know that killing is wrong, that blasting the head off anyone made in the Maker's image will stir up the blowflies of guilt. But it's hard to refuse that exclusive birthright, that opportunity, that extra slice of the cherry pie. Plus the enormous relief of getting it over and done.

The father holds the pistol two-handed like a prayer, but the gun sags away and the dad sinks down to his jelly knees. He starts to pray. It's a babble of tongues that only the rock could understand. Sometimes *Please*, sometimes *No*, sometimes *Almighty God!* or *Name of Jesus!* or *Shit!* The son pries the stiff fingers off the pistol, but the father pulls it away. There's something he has to do if he could only remember, but the son grabs his wrists in both hands and jerks it to point in the face—the barrel, the nozzle, the bore, the snout—but no telling whose face it is, his or his dad's, they're so much alike. The prayer muddles on, nothing but *Please please please!* Their actions are not proceeding in any meaningful way.

Zach McGurren stands up sharp, both hands clutching steel. He's forgotten who's to be killed. Too many to choose from—himself or those others out here, all the same. He's only seventeen, he's two-thirds a virgin, he's never killed. I raise my hand to wave hello goodbye, and he points it at me, more or less in my direction, though I can't be easy to see, standing against a sun that burns a red scar in the thunderhead. His eyes are shut tight. I call out to my brother. He hears the ram caught in the thicket. It's the very last question for history class, and his fingers do the squeeze.

—28—

Stubblefield

Gunshots are one sure way to jazz our erectile tissues but after the bloodshed our attention wanders. God sends a sheep to be butchered instead of a son but we don't get all fired up about mutton chops. We need blood—the promise of blood the shedding of blood the reek of blood. Whether a voodoo chicken or your soldier hero it's that flow of bold red sewage that makes it real. We remember every nosebleed every slow welling up from the paring knife slice every stain that won't wash out of the underpants. We're only human: we take our entertainment where we find it.

Of course we want foul deeds—jaywalking or genocide—to be punished. We need Judas to spill out his guts or Pharaoh swamped by the sea or Hitler reduced to sucking off lepers behind a dumpster. Even assholes such as myself feel the need for reciprocity. Therefore I do keep promises. It's only practical to align yourself with the freeway traffic lest you leave a smear of grease that the taxpayers have to wipe up. Granted the Lottery is a scam to wring bucks out of indigent fools but it does pay off a winner. As do I.

God says, *Here's my business card, come talk.* Real estate casinos cable TV the Promised Land—incredible opportunity. Who among us wouldn't say, *Where's your butthole, Lord of Hosts, lemme pucker up?* We dream of putting ourselves in his big pudgy hands to wait for the blessings to flow. But I'm not God. I am simply the Law of Gravity. You jump off the cliff and I do the rest.

But it's good I'm not God because the odds are I wouldn't exist. And it's only a story. A billion stories are born each day but they most all resist the twist into beginning middle and end. Few make the bestseller list and even fewer qualify as Holy Writ.

After their outing to Shiprock our boys were pretty much off their feed. They got in the car and jostled up to the county road. South to Gallup to catch I-40 West and then up to eighty-five mph. I got regular updates from my secretary Wendall whom I call my archangel. He has the flat bloodless affect of a soft-handed serial killer but he's reliable as dry rot. I gave instructions to Wendall and he did the follow-ups.

Vern worried he lacked credentials for a place among the elite but in fact he was on the edge of being over-qualified. He had stuff you won't find on a job application. Internal wasteland. Magical thinking. Cognitive dissonance. Rationalizing the irrational. A Browning .22 among the laundry. Belief in Tinkerbell. You could only detect those talents in the smell of a guy and Vern had the smell and I had a nose for the smell. So Wendall contacted Vern and made arrangements that once he got back to Chico he would fly to Las Vegas to look for housing and start at the ground floor of operations. He reported that when he told him his first check was in the mail our boy was stupefied. I do pay off on my little jokes.

Vern drove all day and all night—I-40 to Barstow then the 395 picking up I-5 North just past Bakersfield—stopping for car naps but fearing motels where lurked the shadowy men with towels. When they stopped at diners he avoided looking at waitresses. She was always the same whether young and busty or old and shriveled. Her eyes were always the same.

And then on the third day having lunch outside Fresno—Wendall told me of Vern telling him in a tone of wonder—he felt the waitress

smile. She was a young redhead with a sharp wide mouth and slant-
ing eyes. In a breath he knew that his life had changed. From now
on the waitress would smile and he would feel it. He would order
whatever he wanted whether on or off the menu. He deserved it. He
had passed the test. It was only his just desserts. And a new kitchen
stove for Merna.

The son apparently didn't say a word the whole trip home.

After calling multiple times but never getting past voicemail
our boy finally got the picture: I had other fish to fry. But Wendall
reported that he sounded wan and might welcome a few last words
from his patron saint. So at last on the final leg of his victory lap I
gave him a call.

—Hello?

I had not the least desire to hear his little whines of gratitude so
I spoke in Kalashnikov rhythm so as not to let a word in sidewise.

—So Vern, just keep your cell phone tilted to where I can hear
you say *Yes* because I love the sound of a voice saying *Yes*.

—Sure. Yes.

—So your outing: not bad. Call it B-minus which is in fact pretty
good. But my instinct is that you have the gift.

I could hear the fireworks in his head.

—Point being we'd like you to start at ground level—call it the
tip of the iceberg—and work your way down.

—Huh?

—Joke, Vern.

—Oh. Okay.

But the specifics were irrelevant as long as blood had been spilled.
Whose blood it didn't matter: blood was blood. Even the blood of
hallucination was fine as long as it splatted the rock. Granted the
human race was setting world records in mortuary science but every
now and then you had to toss raw meat into the maw of Moloch. I
was just having fun with the guy.

—So what do you think, Vern? Does God create us or do we create
whatever God we need? Do we want a God that croons *Rockabye-
baby* or do we need the studded whip of the Old Omnipotent Coot?

They say God will provide but you could say that God will be provided as you desire him whether sold off the rack or tailor-made.

—Are you saying that—

—For example Original Sin: the real sin was creating a couple of dumb adolescents and expecting they'd stay as zippered up as the Pope. And then killing your kid to redeem the sins that you set them up to commit.

He heard me going on like a recorded message double-time. Which was my intent. I knew he yearned for human connection the way a dog whines for a head-scratch. At some point the rattle of words becomes the silence over the face of the deep that's as close as we get to peace.

—But I wanted to ask—

Vern wandered the wilderness hefting an empty bushel basket otherwise known as his head. He was dreaming the American Dream—that big fat joke that nobody even chuckles at any more—seeing the radiant city with green lawns sprouting money. But he knew the fundamental law of survival: if about to wake up stay asleep. Blind faith works wonders if you just stay blind.

—Mr. Stubblefield—

I knew he was driving while stammering on his phone and might go skidding off the road but I was curious to see where I'd go with my random observations. It's hard to talk without these little machine-gun farts of madness sputtering out.

—You're talking so fast I can't understand—

—So what does it mean to you Vern? The death of the past can't help but have meaning. It means cauterizing a wound. It means transcending cause and effect. It means the sad machinery of evolution. It means a second chance for your second chance. It means weird shit happens.

—This connection is kind of—

Or else it just has the meaning that something's dead. Your shame your remorse your chagrin your guilt—it lies there twitching a bit and then it deflates and you go on from there. All the best-loved stories are where somebody has to die. It's the villain or hero or dragon or troll or old yeller dog—somewhere there has to be blood and no matter whose. It's the way things work. Some of us live and some are spat out the revolving door. Too bad for the losers.

—If you— Could I—

—So I make of thee a great nation, Vernon McGurren. Bless them that blesseth thee and curse them that curseth thee. And multiply thee as the stars of heaven and as sand upon the seashore, and thy seed shall possess the gate of thine enemies. Assuming things work out.

—I'm trying to hear what—

—You ever notice, Vern? Check it out. In the whole entire Bible God does not laugh once.

—29—

Vernon

Coming back, it took time to focus. Travel changes things. You're in a new time zone. People seem too real. They've been a blur in the mind, and now they have a smell. We were non-stop in the car and now we sat at dinner—an occasion to celebrate. Merna made beef stew with mushrooms, my favorite.

—Sorry for the mushrooms being canned.

—It's great, hon.

She always talked about wanting to have our own garden, and I always said it wouldn't be long till we did. Now we would have it, I swore, even though people didn't grow mushrooms in their gardens.

—More?

—Sure. Great. Thanks.

She gave me a helping, then scraped the last of it onto Zach's plate. The dependable dumpster, she called him. She watched him, and finally she asked if he'd kept up with his history.

—Hey, lay off, Merna, we're going to move. In Las Vegas he can finish the year and do summer school to graduate, so right now he should take it easy.

She was about to object, I could tell, but she thought better of it. She mumbled something about always liking history, thinking how

other people lived, the dates things happened, and all the kings and
queens who thought they were so big until they found out otherwise.
Then she ran down, and I had to fill the silence.

—Good stew.

I kept watching her. Her eyes were different than before, and I
wondered what she'd seen. She watched Zach when she didn't think
I was watching, but I wondered if she saw it in my eyes—a movie
that played over and over, and then over and over and over, and after
that it played over again.

—No point him dealing with history. It's a whole new life. History
is over and done with. Wipe it out. Forget it. We've got the future.

—I guess.

It wasn't what I wanted to hear. We were supposed to be celebrating. The first check had come, and that was real. The guy had all but
admitted—or his assistant Wendall had—that it was one big practical
joke, but with a purpose. Could you take it? Be a good sport? Not ask
questions? Follow through? Come out the better for it?

—Well, so they'll pay for the movers, and I'll just rent a place we
can land till we find what we really want. And I know you're not crazy
about making another move and neither am I, but at least there's a
future there. If it wasn't us it'd be somebody else. They talk about
equal opportunity, but nobody wants equal opportunity. You want a
deal where you're one up on the other guy, and that's true whatever
your race or religion. That's one thing you learn from history.

I could hear myself playing the same old tune, like the ten billion
songs that boil down to *Oh baby, baby* but don't say a damned thing
about how to get along with Baby across the kitchen table. I said the
same thing a dozen times, but the silence had to be filled and Zach
wasn't helping much with the babble. I took my last swig of the beer.
Merna never liked me to drink at dinner, but this was a celebration.

—But it should be pretty good. I don't know the specifics, just
salary, and that's all I need to know. We're not gonna turn down
money like that. Funny, the guy was all chummy to start with, private
number, all that, and then all of a sudden it's his secretary, his flunky,
whatever. But it's no bullshit. We cashed the check. The money's real.

—And you don't know what the job is?

—I told you, that's not how it works. It's a team, you're part of the team, they work out where you fit.

—So you do what you're told.

—Is there some other kind of job I don't know about?

I went on answering questions that Merna wasn't asking. Las Vegas, casinos, the desert, Stubblefield this, Stubblefield that—it all got said a dozen times, maybe just to hear it myself. I apologized for not taking snapshots but promised we'd go on a real vacation—

—And I'd love for you to have a garden with fresh tomatoes that taste like tomatoes, not those wooden things from Safeway. We'll have a garden, I guarantee, and a new table at least.

I meant it. I was never more sincere. I stared at the spot on the table where the cup made a ring. Now we'd get a new one. I'd miss that ring, I could stare at it forever, but Merna deserved a new table. She started to stack the dishes, and Zach should be doing that, but I started to get up and she motioned me, *No, we're celebrating,* so I sat back down as she took my empty plate.

—I was telling Zach. I was ten or eleven, I'd stand out in the back yard playing baseball by myself. I'd pitch with one hand and bat with the other and strike out everybody. Then I'd come up to bat and hit home runs. Way into the dark.

—What, you threw up the ball and hit it?

—If I was being me. If I was being the other side I'd strike myself out, but I hit it if I was me.

—What was the point of that?

—The point being that was pretend, this is real. We cashed the check, dammit!

I didn't mean to get mad, but sometimes it just came up like a burp. This was supposed to be a celebration. I held up my empty beer can. Merna looked at me, then opened the fridge and handed me another. I popped it. I felt like the cheerleader squad when we were losing by twenty points. Just keep yelling, *Go team go!*

—Course, history, I guess it's mostly wars, but there's always going to be wars. Wars we never even heard about, countries you

can't pronounce, people that aren't even human. Maybe you have to
have wars to keep the population down. Not that it's good, it's crazy,
it's crap. But I liked history too. Till I got out of school. Then, wow,
I was in it up to my neck.

I was making a joke, but they didn't see it. I gave a chuckle to let
them know. Merna dried her hands and looked at Zach. He was staring at the table ring. She spoke to him in a whisper, but I could hear.

—You're not talking much. How'd you like the trip?

He let it lie there. He didn't want to hurt her, I could tell. She
looked so much older now—the pinch of the brow, lines down from
the eyes, loose skin at the neck, tight mouth. I looked at her hands.
She'd always had blue veins on the back of her hands, but it never
occurred to me that her veins carried blood, that they could bleed.

She waited for Zach to talk. There were times her silence was like
a hammerlock twisted up. At last he forced a mumble.

—I killed my brother.

—30—

Zach

They should ask me to explain what I said. We should all break down wailing. They should kneel and embrace me and tell me that I deserve the birthright and life is sweet and I won't have to do book reports. But better that Dad doesn't hear me and Mom just stacks the dishes. I promise to do them later.

—Rice pudding for dessert!

So I live. I carry the promise. I eat my beef stew, take an extra helping, love my mom and try not to piss off my dad. It's just the Law of Gravity, a ram in the brambles. Life is mostly hallucination, so why should I expect otherwise? I'll pass the seed to the seventh generation, assuming all goes well.

Rebecca stopped over to say hello, and under her jasmine perfume I smelled a saltiness. I said my dad had a job, we were moving. She asked what, where, when. I shrugged. She said Miss Plankett would miss arguing with me, and I grinned at that. One of us said be sure to write, but we both sensed it was over between us. We stood on the steps of the trailer, but I didn't invite her in: too much to be said, no words to say it. I leaned against the door, hoping she might come to me, embrace me, sob, and then we'd sneak back to my little cubbyhole and make memories. Why couldn't my imaginings reach the level of tangible illusion, given how fantasy runs rampant in the world? But she only smiled, murmured, *Well, so have fun*, and walked down the walkway out of my life.

And Mom asked if I'd caught up on my history. I might have told her that blood was shed on the history book, which made it hard to read but a lot more truthful. They say that if you don't learn from history you're doomed to repeat it, but I wonder if you really want a psychotic butcher as a teacher. I didn't say that. I knew how she'd look at me.

In the final months of my senior year at Las Vegas High, I marked time. I had no book reports. Dad and I never had that father-son talk that he wanted so badly—wrong father, wrong son—though we had already shared a long wordless communion. And he never really talked about his work except to say it felt great being part of a team and making decent money. He and Mom found a house, cut back on the drink and the fights as far as I could tell, and Mom planted a garden with lots of tomatoes.

Off to college, UCSF, weird but fun. Freed of parental miasma, I could in fact enjoy the occasional weekends at home, the casino shows, the newest extravaganza from Cirque du Soleil. The world opened outward, revealed itself. The memory of the trailer, the coffee ring on the table, the wood-grain linoleum—those were like some old Depression-era novel I'd had to read for American Lit.

Though of course the journey—the glare, the safety catch, glass glitter, gunshot, my despondent wail—was burnt into me, and I could feel the dead tissue of the scars. For a time my silence lingered, but the black dog snarling in the shadows lay more calmly now and rarely showed its teeth. Nightmares lurked, but distant, like the old classic movies in black and white. My jokes weren't as compulsive or as cruel.

I read about the underground coal fire in Pennsylvania that will burn for another two hundred years. My scars felt an empathy. Second year college, something I needed to touch, and I signed up for Creative Writing. For the first assignment I wrote:

There are fires gonna burn. Fires in the mountains, fires in the city, fires on the moon. Your kids crouch behind plastic shields but the fires reflect in their eyes, they're burnt alive and offered to God on a platter. Here's dinner, God, here's proof how much I love you. Eat me and big brother and all the kids in my loins. Gobble us all. We need more salt cause we left our souls at home.

I got a C+, to my chagrin and great good fortune. I dropped Creative Writing and enrolled in Postwar European History, where across the aisle I met Janey. We coupled with great enthusiasm, the first time in the back of her Prius in a double sleeping bag. History was kind to me at last.

The scars are still there—how could they not be?—but I have no need to spew the details. We all have our botched suicides, our idiot frenzies, our murdered hallucinations. These are wounds common to the species, but I need not bear the mark of Cain on my forehead, I can stash it deep in my heart, where hopefully it fades with age. My dark suppressed traumas mostly stay suppressed.

Some part of me, I know, was killed at Shiprock. There are times, late afternoon mostly, when I sit wherever, emptied out, when I feel the sun burning through a thunderhead and my tears welling up. But I'm not unique. We all have a brother or sister whom, in a fit of confusion, we've killed. On occasion, Janey grieves for her long-lost cat, and her grief is as true as mine.

It's perhaps nothing more than what happens to everyone born into the pages of history, where stories swarm like blowflies over the battleground and settle in our eyes—Miss Plankett would cringe at that one. But it's all a story. We construct it, we tell it, believe it, live it, and it serves a purpose in keeping the illusional entity known as *Me* alive.

True, I've been trying to start my story over, haven't quite got past *It was a dark and stormy night* . . . The rest of my life is unknowable, of course, and as subject to weather as all the cavorting toads. But I will have a life of some sort. We're engaged, we're hopeful, we're not afraid of the dark. We might take a trip to Yosemite.

—*The Makings*—

Akedah: the Binding began as an unproduced play that sat on the shelf several years in search of a foster home.

Its initial inspiration was probably hearing the mythic tale in pre-adolescent Presbyterian Sunday School, and despite understanding that it was intended as a parable of faith, feeling appalled. And much later, encountering the Wilfred Owen poem quoted in the dedication.

The impetus for doing more? During the course of our very heavy touring in 1977, we presented a workshop at a Lutheran seminary in Dayton OH—one of many workshops at the time for community groups creating collective performance pieces. The students were all future Lutheran clergy, so we gave them the *Genesis* text of the Abram/Isaac story, asked them in small groups to discuss and find a way of staging what they felt struck them as the heart of the story. Only proviso: try to read it as if you've never known it before, have no pre-established interpretation, simply responding to it personally.

The diversity was vast. Some were conventional, simply changing a detail: Abram brings a pistol, not a knife. God orders the son to kill his father, not the other way around. Others, more radical: everything told from the standpoint of Sarah, clueless and fearful, back in the tent. Or God's order coming through on a CB radio with bad reception, Abram struggling to interpret, in disbelief at what he thinks he's hearing. And it brought to mind a medieval mystery play, replete with angel, ram in thicket, etc., but with a very shaken Isaac on the homeward journey.

One further cross-pollination: in 1982, we produced a bizarre little play *Action News*, alternating the happenings in a doomed radio studio with surreal interludes involving the duo mannng the mikes. One of these interludes—all fairly disgusting—introduced the character of Stubblefield, who has hung around ever since, awaiting another role. For us he represents less the Yahweh of Biblical fame, more the sociopathic con-men of our day who aspire to the singularity of Yahweh.

Apart from the difficulty of finding a stage or an audience for such a story—not a play to sell a lot of season subscriptions—we felt that we had chosen the wrong medium. It's an extremely claustrophobic story—all contained in motel rooms, a car, a bar, a trailer, a gas station waiting room—until it opens out at the end. Ideal for the stage, one would think. But one can feel that entrapment only by contrast with the sweep of the mountains and forest and desert they're driving through. Even the claustrophbia of Beckett's *Endgame* depends on Clov looking out the windows to a barren landscape or Nagg and Nell, confined to trash cans, attempting to bridge the gap between them. So we felt that a prose narrative might better capture that unbridgeable distance between the cup and the lip.

It's not a pleasant story, nor does it represent some philosophic view of what life is like. Life is like life: a rich, beautiful, hideous, huge menagerie. The power of myth is that it invites—demands—reinterpretation but utterly resists definitive meaning. Our work resists "branding"—at the cost of being very difficult to market—but we thrive on the surprise of what springs from the keyboard each day, just as we live for what comes into view with every dawn.

—Bishop & Fuller

—The Makers—

Conrad Bishop & Elizabeth Fuller have been collaborative mates since 1960, having met as undergraduates. Intending an academic career, Bishop completed a Ph.D. at Stanford and taught for five years. In 1969, they co-founded an independent ensemble, Milwaukee's Theatre X, then hived off to form The Independent Eye, resident first in Chicago, then Lancaster PA, then Philadelphia, but devoted mainly to touring throughout the USA. They have performed in 38 states, in Israel and Canada.

They began writing sketches for Theatre X, then for the Eye. In the 1980s they began to write plays for other theatres, including Actors Theatre of Louisville, New York's Circle Repertory, Denver Center Theatre and many others: the full story is readable at www.IndependentEye.org. They have produced four series for public radio, including *Family Snapshots* and *Hitchhiking off the Map*, have done extensive work in adult puppetry, and conducted hundreds of workshops with schools and colleges, community groups and professional theatres cross-country.

Their venture into writing prose came in 2011 with their memoir *Co-Creation: Fifty Years in the Making*. It was followed by three novels—*Realists, Galahad's Fool*, and *Blind Walls*—as well as short stories and two anthologies of their plays.

They now live in Northern California, with visits to a son in San Francisco and a daughter in Tuscany.

Other Books by Bishop & Fuller

REALISTS

In the near future, insane politicos reign and dreams are taboo. A motley band of innocents, targeted as terrorists, plunge to certain death, but by a stroke of lunatic physics plop onto Smoky's ramshackle westbound tour bus, pursued by an empire gone loco.

Amid ghost buffalo and disappearing cities, improbable lovers split and rejoin, children find magic, and a ragtag bunch of loners and seekers bond into a tribe of survivors, weaving a new reality.

GALAHAD'S FOOL

A year after the death of his co-creator and soul mate Lainie, a grizzled, acerbic puppeteer struggles to build a solo show. What Albert Fisher intends as a lightweight spoof turns sharply personal, and he labors to birth a raw myth of love and loss. His aging Galahad, no longer a glittering hero, launches a second mad quest for the Grail. To follow him, his wife secretly changes guises with their frail androgynous Fool. As the work evolves, Albert finds kinship with Galahad's despair and dogged vision, and opens to the risk of new love.

BLIND WALLS

It's a monstrous maze, built by a grief-ridden heiress. A tour guide has given his spiel for so many years that he's gone blind. On his final tour, he's slammed with second sight. The bedeviled heiress is there, but the story is of a young carpenter who lands his dream job only to become a lifelong slave to her obsesson.

CO-CREATION: FIFTY YEARS IN THE MAKING

In the course of the first fifty years of marriage, Bishop & Fuller have collaborated as performers and playwrights, bringing hundreds of stories to thousands of audiences nationwide. Now they tackle their own story—a chronicle of parenting, uprootings, successes and failures, spiritual quests, dancing naked around bonfires, strict accounting practices, and perpetual improvisation.

RASH ACTS: THIRTY-FIVE SNAPSHOTS FOR THE STAGE

A new, expanded edition of unique comedies, nightmares, and quirky dramatic portraits drawn from 45 years of touring by two of America's landmark theatre ensembles. They have also been produced by numerous schools, colleges, and theatres throughout the US.

www.DamnedFool.com